HEART OF TORMENT

LEONA WELCH

To the ones who refuse to surrender to fate.

WARNING

Heart of Torment includes elements of hand-to-hand combat, perilous situations, blood, violence, injuries, death, graphic language, and sexual activities. Readers who may be sensitive to these elements, please take note.

Author's Note

You may notice a change in spelling within this edition. The word Sidhe has been updated to Siddhe.

After publication, I became more aware of the cultural and mythological significance of the term Sidhe in Irish folklore. I adjusted the spelling for my fictional setting in order to respect the origins and folklore associated with the Sidhe.

This change does not alter the characters or story, only the spelling used within this fictional world. Thank you for reading and sharing this adventure with me.

– Leona Welch

1

ERIK

It had been a torturous few days since the small Bavadrin party left for the Siddhe territory. Kole and I grew restless and bored waiting for Ariana's return. Most of her Bavadrins wished to keep their distance, avoiding us as much as possible. Only Willis and Kiora, two of Ariana's closest friends, did not outright ignore us. Willis allowed us to help with repairing certain parts of their town's wall. It brought Kole great joy to see me doing manual labor, something he assumed was beneath me.

"If only your brothers could see their great King now," he had said with a full smile on his face.

Still, what little we could do to assist around the town was not enough to fill my mind with anything but her. Ariana had gone to see the Siddhe King, a man foretold of his cruelty and extraordinary power. She was not defenseless, but she was likely no match for someone like him. I feared that no one was, at least not alone. If I could, I would have tied her to a post and kept her from ever going over there.

Worrying did not suit me well. I had grown accustomed to having a certain amount of control, yet Ariana continuously tested those boundaries. She somehow always found the edge and nudged me towards it. It was extraordinarily infuriating, yet it was also something that drew me to her. Life gained a bit of intrigue by meeting her challenges. She was one of the most exquisite people I had ever met, her heart full of compassion despite the conditions she came from. Love was not a weakness for her but instead a fuel. She did whatever was necessary to protect those she cared for. Even willing to strike a dark deal without hesitation, as she had when she gave her father over to me to protect someone she cared for. She was cunning. In some ways, she was incredibly dangerous, yet that only further drew me towards her, curious to know those dark corners of her mind.

Shaking my head as if that could have loosened some of the thoughts, I continued walking alongside the dirt road. It was my seventh time going down the path. I was long distance pacing while waiting, for it was the day she was expected to finally return from her trip to the Siddhe. I hadn't allowed myself to think of what would happen if she did not return as expected. Though with the sun moving across the sky, my mind began leaning in that direction.

The sound of horse hooves against the dry dirt pulled me from my thoughts.

I smelled Ariana's fear before seeing her, and my stomach turned. Something happened on their trip.

The sight of her struck me still. Her dark hair was wind-blown, eyes hooded, lips set in a tight line. Even Rain appeared oddly subdued, as if the cloud hovering around Ariana was thick enough to shroud the horse as well.

Still, with the strange air around her, relief washed over me at seeing her alive and whole. The rest of the group must have separated, for Ariana rode alone with only Edda in tow. The old one caught sight of me and changed her direction. Dismounting, the Seer walked over to where I stood across the road while Ariana continued to a small nearby townhome. If she noticed my presence, then she did not make it known.

Ariana remained sitting atop her horse in silence, her pulse steadily rising. Nervousness surrounded her, intermingled with the fear already there. The atmosphere felt off. It was like nothing I ever sensed coming from her before. Though she was home and unharmed, she drew no comfort from that. If anything, she seemed to get more tense with every beat of her heart.

I wanted to go to her, but the Seer crossed in front of me. "Erik, better you give her some space and not intervene in this." Never had Edda before used my name to address me. I always assumed she was too senile to remember it.

"What happened?"

Ariana still sat on top of her horse, seeming to stare at the door to a building.

"It should be for her to tell, but seeing as your sight and hearing are so strong, you will soon understand that Landin is no longer with us. As part of Ariana's duty, she is now informing his next of kin." Edda frowned before adding, "Unfortunately, I don't think this is the last time she will have to bear this burden."

Ariana finally dismounted. Taking a large breath, she marched up to the door and knocked.

The door flung open as if expecting the knock. A man stood tall for a Bavadrin with broad shoulders and a muscular build. Realization hit me that it was Willis who stood before her. His golden eyes beheld his Leader Superior. Ariana said not a single thing before he fell to his knees and burst into tears before her. She placed a hand on his shoulder.

Surprised, I turned to Edda, "But he's-"

"Male?" Edda peered at me knowingly.

Bavadrins were always said to have been rigid when it came to sexuality. "I didn't think this was acceptable for your kind."

"Many would probably still frown upon it. But that is a tradition that Ariana will not keep. After all, in the speech she gave after her Ascension, she said something along the lines of love knowing no bounds and that the Bavarians will no longer try to bind it." She arched a dark silver brow.

I then understood why Landin and Ariana never were anything romantic. I also understood that she protected their secret, though it never should have even been one. Suddenly everything Edda had shared when I first asked about Ariana's relationship with Landin made sense.

"How?" Willis asked, his face buried in his hands.

Ariana took another deep breath before answering. "The Siddhe King. Landin was trying to protect me... he pulled his sword."

Golden eyes looked up at her. "Were you injured?"

She shook her head no, though she was only talking about her physical body. The hurt she felt within was likely extraordinary, for she had given up her father to save Landin's life. Her love for him was clear from the very beginning.

Landin likely lost his life while still in the Siddhe territory. It meant that for days now, Ariana traveled with his corpse. I could not imagine the agony she went through during that time.

"Did he suffer?" Willis asked.

She swallowed. "It was instant. There was no pain."

Willis nodded, gaze dropping. Several seconds passed, and he regained some of his strength, rising to his feet.

"We will have the departure ceremony for him tomorrow. You will need to choose a second to help you with the release." Ariana's gaze remained lowered, looking at the ground.

"It is you. You are the second," Willis stated without hesitation, and her attention moved to his face.

She shook her head no. "I don't deserve it. It is my fault he-" Her voice quivered, and it took everything for me to keep my feet rooted to the ground and not go to her side. Even as Edda held out her arm before me as if to bar me from moving.

Willis's strong hands gripped her by her shoulders. "You are his family, my family. His life would have ended long ago were it not for you being in it. You gave him a chance to love and be loved. No one but you deserves to stand with me for his release and departure. He would have wanted it to be you at my side."

A sob escaped Ariana's wavering control, and she would have crumbled to the ground if Willis wasn't there. His arms circled her as leaned her forehead into his chest as she wept.

Together, they mourned the loss.

"Let's go," Edda's said. Her dark eyes turned from them. "After she finishes here, we will have a small meeting to discuss what occurred in the Siddhe territory. Against my advice, Ariana wishes for you and the other Lysian to be present for it."

"Kole?" I lifted a brow at her, pretending to not know his name.

I did not care for Edda's opinions of me or the Lysians, not when Ariana stood trembling in Willis's arms. Whatever happened that caused Landin to lose his life was not good. The fact that she now wished for a meeting, the day she returned, and right after having to go through the challenge of telling

Willis that Landin was gone, meant that whatever she had to share was pressing.

Edda's response to me was a grumble before she turned. I followed her through the streets. Looking back, I could still make out Ariana and Willis holding one another, supporting each other so that they both could remain on their feet.

WILLIS ARRIVED JUST a minute before Ariana. She was the last to enter the small chamber, closing the door behind her. Her gaze avoided everyone as she made her way to the only open seat left. An unease moved through the small space. Everyone except Willis watched her with anticipation. The entire room was silent as if holding its breath. We were made up of Edda, Willis, Kiora, Kole, and me. I was surprised to see such a small group joining the gathering. There were no elders present other than Edda. Outside of the Lysians, it appeared only those closest to Ariana were privy to whatever it was she wished to discuss.

"For those of you who may not yet know, we lost Landin during this trip," Ariana stated, and Kiora's gaze slid to Willis, whose face remained unreadable. It seemed as though both he and Ariana regained their composure in the little time they had before the meeting began. "Clause has requested that I come to stay with him for some time and learn of the Siddhe ways."

My blood went ice cold. She couldn't have been entertaining that invitation. To willingly spend time with the one responsible for the death of her friend.

Somehow, I kept the growl from my throat when I asked, "Requested or demanded?"

"If I do not accept, then he will see it as a threat and attack." Her gaze lifted, finding mine across the table. Having her attention momentarily immobilized me, the flicker of sadness within those green eyes tore at me. Though she tried her best to conceal it, she could not hide it. Not when my focus was intently on her. Every trace of emotion that slipped through the cracks in her calm demeanor may as well have been shouted. It stirred a ripple of anger from within. If I ever got my hands on the Siddhe King, then he would know what pain felt like. I would make sure of it, and I would take my time with it.

"You are accepting." The way Willis said it, it was as if to confirm what he suspected. It was not a question. A completely ridiculous assumption that she was going.

"Yes," she answered, still keeping her gaze locked with mine.

I stiffened. "No. You are not going to live in some mountain with a madman. You are the Leader Superior to your people. You cannot abandon them." It was absurd.

"I would do this *for* them." She clarified, remaining outwardly calm while my control was slipping with every breath.

I shook my head. "Ariana. I will stand with you. My Lysians will stand with the Bavadrins. We can take the Siddhe together. There is no need for this." Sitting beside me, Kole nodded his head in agreement.

The young Sparrow archer turned to Ariana. "I am afraid that I agree with the Lysian. We just got you back, Ariana. I do not wish to let you go so easily."

Thank the Spirit, one of her friends had a decent head on their shoulders.

Ariana's gaze finally broke from mine as she looked at the table before her. "We would lose," she said as if it were a fact, no question about it. "Between the two of us, we may pull together a few talented conjurors while he has who knows how many powerful ones." She then turned to the other Bavadrins in the room. "He has the Dunes Clan. They did not disappear years ago. They live under his command."

Ariana turned to me as she explained who they were. "The Dunes Clan lived in our lands but not under our rule, at least not directly. They were granted freedoms partially because they lived in the desert and hardly interacted with us. But they were incredibly skilled fighters, gifted, their skin enhanced by conjuring abilities. They were rumored capable of standing their ground in hand-to-hand combat with Lysians."

"So, we will find some other way." I was desperate.

Ariana had always been out of reach, even when she had been living in my home. I only recently began to think of her as more than I previously allowed for. And now, she was slipping away before I ever even got to—

"He has Iona," Ariana spoke my sister's name, and my heart nearly stopped in my chest. My train of thought stolen.

"You saw her?" Kole's voice was ghostly.

Her attention slid to his with a frown. "No. But he confirmed it."

"Then we do not know for certain." Though I said those words, I knew I believed the same as her: my sister lived in the Siddhe lands. My hands balled into fists as I worked at keeping them close to my body so as not to break anything with my growing frustration.

"Erik. My mind has been made up. This is not for discussion. It is not your choice but mine to make." Despite everything weighing on her, she kept her head held high. Pain flickered in her eyes, but fear did not. She did not waiver on her decision. The fear I smelled coming from her earlier was for what she had to tell Willis, nothing more. How was it possible for her to face such a decision without terror?

"You are not going to be his prisoner." A growl vibrated my throat as I bared my teeth.

Edda's dark gaze cut to me. "What's the matter Lysian, you only like her being *your* prisoner?" Every Bavadrin in the room looked at me with a spark of anger, except for Ariana.

"I never harmed her." I seethed.

Edda's lip curved up. "Sure, not physically. But what of the mental pain you caused?"

"Edda," Ariana said in warning, but it did not stop the old bat.

"You tore her away from everything she knew, leaving her to wonder whether her people lived or if they were burned to ash. Whether she would meet the same fate as those who had given life to her. Despite that, she found it in herself to forgive you. And when she finally tried to break free of your hold, you attacked her." Her already black eyes seemed to further darken. "Tell me, Lysian, how long did it take you to decide to let her go instead of to burn her out of existence?"

"You know nothing." I hissed through clenched teeth.

"No?" Her brows rose in mock surprise.

"Edda, that's enough." Ariana's voice was flat.

Edda turned to her. "You should hear this too, so you know how close to death you could have been." Her eyes then sliced back to mine. "You know what I can do, Lysian?"

"You're a Seer," I stated.

"More like an out-of-control wrinkled onion, if you ask me," Kole mumbled under his breath.

Kiora chortled, somehow unbothered by the growing tension.

Edda smiled viciously. "I can see things, some clear, others not so much. I knew this entire mess was heading Ariana's way, and in it, I saw you, Erik, and the threat you posed. I am the one who taught Ariana to use her conjuring. So, do you think I simply forgot to teach her to not use her hands as a crutch?" She scoffed. "That was done on purpose because, with a crutch, you would see her as weak. Thus, in that moment of heightened anger and before you had enough time to truly think things through, you would be more inclined to set her free. If she conjured properly, chances were higher that it would have ended in one of your deaths. I spared both of you from that pain."

My throat went dry.

Edda laughed. "Don't look so pale. You would have mourned her death if that had been the outcome. I know for certain that she would have mourned you if things ended in her favor. But it left too much to chance. So, she had a crutch, one that would save her life when she found herself at your mercy. Placed in that position, just because she desired to trust you instead of dropping you to your knees and taking the breath from your lungs as she should have."

Ariana closed her eyes. "I will not ask you again, Edda. One more word of this, and I will have you removed from this room."

Edda shrugged, brows raised, as if she had no idea the discomfort she was causing. "I just thought to remind you that some of those who you place your trust in so eagerly may not be deserving."

"You are one to talk." Ariana leveled her stare at the old woman.

"Pardon?" Edda's tone turned sour, her lips thinning. The entire room stilled.

"You knew more of the Siddhe than you had ever let on. You never told me of the threat there, that our own kind was being stolen away. You expect me to believe this is the first you know of any of this?" Ariana shook her head before continuing. "You had supported the outrageous belief that conjurors were taken by the Spirit to a better place. That they were gifted something special. It sounds ridiculous now, but everyone believed it partially because that is the story you supported. When in reality, who knows what type of horrors they have endured under that monster's command." There was a sharp edge to Ariana's words. She placed responsibility on Edda, and she had a point to do so. If the old woman was a Seer and knew of the truth, why did she keep it hidden for all these years?

Edda's eyes narrowed. "When should I have informed you of this? When your father was alive? When you were imprisoned by the Lysians? When you hardly had a chance to start your new life here as the Bavadrin Superior?" She challenged Ariana with questions; however, they only revolved around informing Ariana.

As an advisor to the previous Bavadrin Leader Superior, she could have told him of the dangers. Perhaps he wouldn't have cared. Though the way Fraser behaved when he decided to punish me for a crimeless act, he did not believe me. There was no hesitation which likely would have been present if he knew the truth. Edda never shared the reality of the Siddhe with Fraser.

Ariana took a deep breath. "I do not have the will to argue, but do not pretend to be innocent." She viewed all who were in the room. "I am going to go to the Siddhe lands, and I do not know for how long. Clause has spies here, for he knew things he shouldn't have. Therefore, what we share here in this room is to stay between us and those paramount to the plans to come."

She turned to Willis. "We will need to prepare for a war, for I do not see this ending in any other way. I will also want to train before I leave in several days. All of you at this table are invited to develop a training strategy for me. Ideally, it will involve all of your skills together. We will meet in the morning the day after tomorrow to go over whatever you may come up with and go from there. However, tomorrow morning we will have the departure ceremony for Landin, and the rest of the day will be yours to do with as you all see fit."

"When do you think the forces will need to be ready by?" Willis asked, as if the mention of Landin did not carve at his heart.

She shifted in her seat. "I don't know for sure, but I hope I will be able to learn as much as I can while I am with the Siddhe and pass that information to you as you all prepare."

"How would you get the information out?" I asked, even though this plan was ridiculous. How much training could she get in several days? It was not enough time.

Ariana turned to Willis once more. "Clause said I could bring no one with me, but he meant Bavadrin or Lysian. A wolf, on the other hand-" By her demeanor, it was evident that she saw this as a long shot and a hope. Though how would taking an animal be helpful?

"Of course. You will take Shay." Willis agreed at once.

Ariana shook her head. "She is your alpha I could not-"

"She is the smartest and strongest. Plus, she has bonded with you more than any of the others. She will go with you." His words were final, and Ariana responded with a small smile that never reached her eyes.

"The wolf?" I asked to ensure I was following the conversation correctly.

"Yes." Willis turned to me. "I can communicate with the wolves. I will need to spread the pack out across the land, but whatever Ariana learns, she can share with Shay, who will pass it along to the others and ultimately to me."

So, from the first trip bringing Ariana back to her home, when the wolf joined us, she communicated with Ariana's now second-in-command. Apparently, the Bavadrins always had more up their sleeve than I ever imagined. The stories always told of their conjuring gifts and how they often differed from the Lysians. Never had I heard of someone communicating with animals.

"How far of a distance can you communicate?" I thought back to when that wolf greeted us the first time.

Willis sighed. "Far enough, and with some more practice, perhaps even farther." He looked drained, as if sleep eluded him completely even before Ariana's return. Though he attempted to put on a solid and stern front, it was clear that sadness wrapped itself around him, likely squeezing the energy from him with every passing moment. Yet, he appeared determined to not allow it to hold him back from his duties. I had to give it to him, for losing someone so close and being able to sit in a meeting such as this. He had more grit than I gave him credit for.

"How did Landin die?" Kiora's attention shifted between Willis and Ariana.

Silence spilled through the room before Ariana answered, turning to her friend. "The Siddhe King touched him, and his heart stopped."

Kiora released a hiss of a breath, leaning back in her seat as though Ariana's words had blown her back. "One touch, that is all it took." Her attention cut to Ariana. "And I do not doubt that you lashed out. What did that do to the great Siddhe King? You hurt him?" Kiora pressed, despite knowing the pain such questions were causing.

"No conjuring can touch him," Ariana answered.

Kiora scoffed. "And you expect us to just fall in line and watch you walk into that monster's home? Would you let me just go off on my own doing the same thing if the roles were reversed?"

"Careful child, you should not be questioning your Leader Superior in such a manner." Edda's raspy voice only added to the growing tension in the room.

"I am not questioning the Leader Superior," Kiora snapped. Her attention shifted to Edda before returning to Ariana. "I am talking to my friend right now. You would never let me act so recklessly with my life. Please, let me fight for you." The Bavadrin's words resonated with me, for they echoed the thoughts in my mind. I wished for the same thing.

Ariana shook her head, her gaze dipping to the table. Licking her lips, she looked up once more, a fire in her eyes. "Don't you see? You are fighting for me. Clause is terrifyingly powerful, unlike anything I have ever seen. Yet I do not think he invited me there to hurt me. I need all of you to be safe while I am gone and to prepare for what is to come. All that I am doing is buying us time. I plan to return, but I need something to return to. Which is why we cannot act rashly." No one responded to her words. "I cannot lose anyone else by my irresponsibility."

She blamed herself for Landin's death.

"I do not support this plan and do not care for your words." Though Kiora's tone was harsh, tears lined her eyes. "You care to protect your heart, but what of ours?"

"Kiora," Willis stated her name in warning, like a whip smacking the air.

She turned to him with fury. "Of everyone in this room, you should agree with me. You just lost your partner, and now you want to have Ariana walk into the arms of the monster who took his life? You truly think she will be safe there?"

Willis did not flinch at her words, did not raise his voice or show any sign of anger when he said, "I feel the same concerns as you. But she is our Superior. This decision is hers."

"Unbelievable." Kiora looked around the small room before turning to Ariana. "If you do not survive this, then I will kill you. I will find you in the Spirit realm, and I swear that I will make you regret this decision."

"I know you will," Ariana said, and it felt as though the tension finally broke in the room.

Kiora deflated and leaned back in her chair once more.

Ariana then addressed the room. "Thank you all for coming today. If you wish, you can stay to share thoughts on my training now." She turned to her second. "Willis, you do not have to be here for this." She tried to spare him, to give him time to begin healing from his wounded heart.

"I would rather stay and help." There was a glimmer of desperation in his golden eyes. He needed to remain. Needed a distraction, and what better one than to prepare for war?

Ariana nodded, rising to her feet. "I will see you all again tomorrow morning for Landin's departure." Her gaze briefly met with mine before she left.

I was torn, partially wishing to follow her, to talk to her alone. However, she did not want it. I knew that much. At that point, it was best to remain in the room and discuss the plans for her training, though I did not know how much could be crammed into such a short time.

Everyone seemed eager for the same distraction. The room busied itself with plans as soon as Ariana stepped out. Not all of us agreed on the strategy to train her, causing several arguments to break out but ultimately, we found our way to a somewhat cohesive plan. Until Willis and Kiora began arguing where it would be best for the archers to be in the training.

Edda sat silently beside me, observing the room. I felt her gaze wander over to me.

"If she wasn't hindered in her conjuring, what were the chances that I would have killed her?" I asked the old witch. Kole was the only other who heard. His attention drifted towards us before refocusing on the disagreement moving amongst the Bavadrins.

She cackled. "You should know yourself better. To not need to ask such a question."

My jaw clenched, and I did not respond. Though the thought swirled around in my mind. Unyieldingly it refused to settle, and I found myself disinterested in whatever the disagreement was in the room. Edda struck a chord, for I had considered taking Ariana's life. Despite her saving mine just days before, I contemplated ending hers.

"Listen." Edda leaned towards me after a moment. "Ariana is on a difficult path that needs to be taken. There is no other route for her now. You making it more difficult for her is of no use. Do not break her down in an effort to keep her here where you imagine it to be safe. This place is not safe. No place is. Instead, help prop her up, give her your strength. I am afraid she may need you in what's to come." For someone who always wished to place space between Ariana and the Lysians, she surprised me for her stance unexpectedly felt softer.

"I will help her in whatever way I can," I assured her.

Edda smiled, her small hand reaching out, grabbing hold of my chin. For her tiny size and age-worn body, she had quite a powerful grip. "I know, Lysian." She then pulled away and frowned. "I want you to know that everything I have ever done since her birth was to protect her from that monster." Her voice was low, words noticed only due to my Lysian hearing.

She was protecting Ariana from the Siddhe King since her birth? Why would she ever assume to have needed to do something like that, unless it was because of Ariana's conjuring? Edda must have known the Siddhe collected conjurors, so she did her best to keep Ariana hidden. Was that all?

Edda stood without waiting for a reply and left.

2

ERIK

We stood near the edge of a great lake not far outside the Bavadrin city gates. The area was hidden in their forest. Incredibly tall trees reached towards the clouds, greedy for warmth and light. The sun was still low in the sky, causing the foliage to cast long shadows. Natural mist curled around the bases of the trees and over the lake. The world felt gray and dreary. It was as if that place was made for mourning the dead.

Four Bavadrin men carried a pallet with Landin's body wrapped in fabric. The mist appeared to part for them, and I couldn't help but wonder whether it was Ariana's doing. They lowered the pallet onto the lake's edge, partially in the water.

The sound of a single violin moved through the forest and over the lake. It surrounded us as if it were a living thing. The tune whispered of loneliness. A song, deeply sorrowful, set the tone of the entire space. The otherworldly music paired with the shadows and mist created a heavy atmosphere.

Ariana approached from behind us with Willis at her side.

He wore a thin cotton shirt and pants, though it covered most of his skin. On the other hand, Ariana wore a simple white dress, shoulders bare. She must have been freezing, for the morning was kissed by winter, which lurked just around the corner. Everyone around wore cloaks with all buttons fastened to protect from the chill in the air. To her credit, she did not show how completely freezing she must have felt. When Ariana and Willis reached the pallet, they bent down, pushing it further into the lake.

They then continued, moving into the water, and that was when I noticed that both of them were barefoot.

"How is she not painfully cold?" Kole asked from beside me.

Kiora, who stood to Kole's other side, answered. "She is, but I am afraid it is greatly overshadowed by another pain."

My attention drifted to my right, where Edda stood silently, sorrow evident in her eyes.

"I never knew you cared for him," I whispered to her, for she never seemed to favor anyone except for Ariana.

"He was a decent boy and a good friend to Ariana," Edda stated. There was a long pause before she continued. "But my heart does not mourn for him. It is for her I mourn. She will continue to feel pain like this. It will not end here. I wonder if I have made the right choices."

"What do you mean?"

"You will soon understand, Lysian." Edda ended the conversation.

Ariana and Willis continued into the lake, undoubtedly bitterly cold. Yet there was no hesitation in their steps as they continued moving with the pallet till the water reached Ariana's upper thigh. Only then did they finally stop. The pallet floated out into the water with a gentle push, drifting further and further away.

The two of them stood there in that horrid lake. Her toes were going to freeze off if they remained out there much longer.

A thick mist curled around them, surrounding the pallet Landin's body rested on. The moisture moved over the water and on to the shore. Fog shrouded us as it blended into the thinner haze already there. This was Ariana's conjuring. Surroundings became more obscured until I could poorly make her and Willis out, and the pallet was lost entirely in a gray fog.

Ariana raised a hand, and Kiora, along with dozens of archers standing on the shore, lit flame to arrow, poised to strike.

"What are you doing? You can't see." I looked from the water, the fog, Ariana, to the young sparrow standing beside Kole.

Her breath slowed along with her heart as she prepared to fire that burning bolt into the gray air. Ariana's arm fell to her side, and dozens of flaming arrows were released at once, soaring over her head. They landed on something in the water, and fire covered the pallet, finally showing its location.

"You may be a Lysian King." The Sparrow addressed me, her sharp gaze meeting mine. "You may have better sight and hearing, but you are no Sparrow." Bright hazel eyes challenged me. "Let this be a lesson to never underestimate me again."

"How did you do it?" Kole turned to her.

Her lip curled. "You will likely only learn that if you ever find yourself on the other end of one of my arrows."

"I guess I will need to learn to go on with never knowing," he mumbled, and she then smiled fully.

"Boy!" Edda called for the attention of a Bavadrin child. He scurried over to the old witch at once. Large warm brown eyes looked up at her. "Run ahead and make sure a warm bath is prepared for the Leader Superior." The boy nodded and ran off into the forest towards the town. Ariana was going to need that bath to bring her back to life after freezing out in that lake.

Everyone endured the cold, watching the fire consuming the pallet. Ariana remained in that water, her back to all. I wondered what emotions her face portrayed at that moment and then regretted even thinking about it. I did not wish to see her tortured and sad. Yet, I could not look away. While everyone watched the distant fire, I watched her. A breeze gently pulled at her hair yet did not touch the mist that she controlled. There was a distant sound of a liquid droplet falling into the water, and I wondered if it was the sound of a tear that had escaped from her.

Still, we had not spoken since her return, not really. I told myself that I would allow her some time once she returned, but it was challenging to stay away. I walked past her room last night just to make sure she was safe. The rhythmic beating of her heart let me know that she was in there. The heavy sigh let me know that she was awake even deep into the night. Neither of us slept well that night.

Ariana and Willis finally turned, making their way out of the lake. Though she stood straight with her shoulders back and enveloped in fog, I could tell she was shivering. Shaking, wet, and hardly dressed for such weather, she made her way past some of her people, and everyone seemed to come alive as if awoken from a sorrow-filled trance. They began gathering what belongings they may have brought, turning to start the track home.

Ariana appeared drained, each of her steps incredibly slow as she walked. What energy she had was zapped by the freezing cold. A tremble worked its way down her body, yet she did not fold her hands across her chest to warm herself. She might not have minded the torture of the cold, but I could not bear seeing her this way.

Fire was not the only thing my conjuring allowed me to do. I called on my strength, pulling it to my skin, releasing heat before a fire ever sparked. Never had I needed for cloaks or anything for warmth. I only wore them to fit in with everyone else when the seasons changed. In seconds, my cloak warmed enough that wisps of heat curled from it.

Weaving through the slow-moving Bavadrins, I made my way to Ariana.

"Better let her be right now." Kiora appeared at my side. A trace of worry passed over her as she looked in Ariana's direction. I moved past the Sparrow, carefully stepping around others.

"Hey." It was all I could think of to say.

Ariana slowed, turning her green eyes to me. She looked a shell of who she typically was, haunted by pain. I hated it.

Slipping off my cloak, I wrapped it around her while she simply stood there, viewing me without so much as a word. Her lack of protest was taken as acceptance, and I began fastening the buttons to keep the heat in. Her gaze weighed heavily on me, observing.

When I finished, her hand lifted, touching mine, and I halted, looking at her once more. There was such a mixture of emotions swirling in those eyes, and I found myself wishing that I could have done more for her.

"Thank you, Erik," she whispered before her hand dropped from mine. Turning, she continued the journey home with my cloak around her. I would have given her my shoes if she hadn't been likely to fall in them.

"I'm surprised." The Sparrow came up beside me once

more. "I imagined you trying to swoop her up and carry her home."

The thought had crossed my mind, but Ariana would likely not have approved.

The Sparrow viewed me with narrowed eyes. "Are you not now cold yourself? Or do you think you're a big strong Lysian, and so the cold won't touch you the way it would her?"

"It won't," I answered her, holding up my hand. In an instant, a fire began dancing across my fingertips.

"Neat trick." She smirked. "How do you do it?" Her question did not make sense, for surely she knew what I was. Though Kole had recently asked the same question of her, I just realized that she was subtly providing an answer.

"Find yourself at the end of one of my flames, and then you will know," I said, and her smile widened. That was how the Sparrows did it. How each of their arrows found their proper marks in such conditions. They were conjurors, all of them.

3

ARIANA

The departure had been perfect. Obscure shadows painted the morning, reflecting the feelings of my soul, cold and dark. It provided a seamless atmosphere to dive into the depths of mourning.

My life had been forever changed by a cruel twist of fate. The worst was that I had been warned. The Spirit told me of the difficult path ahead, and I had not heeded the prophecy appropriately. Had I listened, then perhaps Landin would still have been living amongst us, making us laugh at his foolish jokes.

His laugh. I would never hear it again.

My shattered heart managed to crack further.

I numbly walked to the hot bath drawn for me, steam still rising from the water. Gently, I removed Erik's cloak, hanging it on a chair. It smelled so much like him. The scent brought a sliver of life back into my broken and mangled soul. The smell of him probably gave me more comfort than even the warmth the cloak provided. Peeling off my dress, I dropped it on the floor before going to the tub.

Sore muscles contracted as the bathwater touched my cold skin, burning as I sank into the tub. I sat there, too tired to clean myself. After a while, my bones began finally warming.

A strange numbness enveloped me, holding me incredibly tightly. I felt detached. Like I was not actually living my life but viewing it while moving amongst the world. I was not myself and instead just a shell of who I had always been. Some foreign version of a girl I never got the chance to be. I loathed it.

I wanted to feel something other than that numbness. Yet, no amount of thought, meditation, or attempt at escape allowed me to get past it. A deep dark wall imprisoned me with my pain. I feared losing myself to the cruelness of the world.

Death was not the end. Landin lived with the Spirit now in a land of light. Even though I told myself that, it did nothing to help me feel better. He was gone, torn away from my life and from Willis. My chest hurt thinking of Willis.

Moving a hand through the water, I felt the weightlessness of its pressure. What I would do to drown out the noise inside of me. Holding my breath, I dipped my head under, keeping it there until my lungs burned for air, forcing me to come up. Rubbing the water from my face, my gaze landed on the cloak. Erik.

The anger of my decision had been written all over the Lysian King's face when I informed everyone that I would soon leave for the Siddhe. Did they genuinely think I wanted any of this? I wanted nothing more than to remain with them. To feel safe, surrounded by those I trusted and cared for. But that was not what fate had planned for me.

What was fate but the sister to death? Fate wrapped the rope of life around every living being, weaving knots of trials, twists of fortune, and turns of heartbreak. Over time the ropes grow heavier, dragging their bearers down, threatening to crush them beneath their weight. And when the burden becomes too great, fate passes the soul to her brother, and death has his way. Every destined path ultimately led to the same ending. Death.

Even Clause, with all his grandeur and control, would eventually find that his fate, in the end, did not differ from any other. His vast power was not indefinite. I refused to believe he was an exception to this rule of fate and death. If he wished to keep me close, then I would become his tether. I would tighten the threads, weigh him down, and edge him closer to his own ending.

The water surrounding my body cooled, and I forced myself out of the tub. I moved with heavy limbs, feeling as though nearly all the energy leached from me. After struggling to put on clean clothing, I made my way to the bed, but rest never came.

No matter the exhaustion, my mind would not give me peace. Instead, it trapped me in a barless prison of thoughts. Ideas went in circles that never led anywhere. Around and around, in never-ending loops. I was going to drive myself mad.

A knock came from the door, startling me from one of those looping thoughts. Whoever it was did not wait for my response. They jiggled the handle, finding it unlocked, and strolled right in.

"Kiora." I forced myself to smile. It was good to see a familiar face, giving me something else to focus on.

"Ariana," she stated, no smile in sight. Closing the door behind her with a kick of her foot, she made her way towards me, carrying a tray of food. Wisps of heated moisture rose from the warm tea she was careful not to spill. Setting the tray down on the table next to the bed, Kiora plopped down beside me. "How are you doing?" She asked.

"I have been better," I admitted, looking at the tray before turning my attention to her. "You aren't mad at me?" The last time we spoke, she had been livid.

"I am furious with you. But I can hold a grudge while still caring about a friend." She brought her legs up onto the bed, crossing them at the ankles as she leaned back against the wall.

I mimicked her, leaning against the wall. "After all these years. I'm happy I got to see you again before..." My voice trailed off, for I was unsure how to end the sentence. *Before I left for the Siddhe for who knows how long?* It didn't seem like a good topic to bring up with her.

"Just remember what I said. If you die, I will find you in the Spirit realm and kill you all over again." Hazel eyes cut to me, and it was clear that she meant every word.

Despite her anger, a warmth in my chest spread at her presence. "I'm glad you're here with me."

She nodded, looking down at the tray between us. "You know, I came here one time after the Sparrows were told to leave by your father. You were still young, as was I. I saw you with him, with Landin. The two of you were laughing about something, and I remember feeling such jealousy. It sounds silly now, but back then, it felt as though I had been replaced."

Her words stunned me, for I never knew any of this. She returned? "Kiora, no one could ever replace you."

She smiled sadly. "I know. Your heart is large enough to love more than one person. But like I said, I was young and didn't know any better. So, I left without you ever knowing that I even snuck into the city to see you. Though I did not know Landin and spent most of my life secretly hating him, I also am thankful for him. He was there for you when I was unable to be. And I am so sorry, Ariana."

I reached for her hand, taking it in mine. "You have nothing to feel sorry for. *Nothing.*"

She smiled sadly. "Neither do you." Her gaze settled on the tray of food and she nodded towards it. "Eat something. Tomorrow, you begin training, and you will need your strength to survive what we have in store for you."

I moaned in mock protest, yet took a piece of bread and cheese and scarfed it down.

Kiora shifted lower in the bed and lay down beside me. After finishing the bread, I joined her, and we both stared at the ceiling. She said nothing, but her presence alone was a welcomed one. Kiora felt like home to me, even though we had been apart for such a long time. She was still my Kiora, and I was hers in return. It was as though no time had passed since we parted years ago, even though we were now older. Fate brought us together once more, and I feared where it would take us next.

I did not know how much time passed before Kiora finally turned onto her side and looked at me. "You know, that Lysian King is smitten with you," she stated, a crooked smile finding its way to her lips.

I snorted. "Yeah, sure." Yet, my face warmed at her comment.

Kiora bit her lip, a devious look in her eyes. "Have you two... you know." Her smile morphed into a mischievous grin.

"What? No!" Not quite a lie. I never slept with him, which was what she was insinuating.

Her gaze narrowed even further. "Oh, please. I may not be a Lysian, but I am not blind. He is an attractive specimen, but more than that, I see the way you both look at one another.

There is definitely something there. There's no point in trying to hide it from me."

I shifted onto my side, facing her. "And what way do we look at one another?"

"You both just respond to each other, like you orbit each other, drawn together. If I can tell, then Edda certainly knows it too. Do you deny you like him?"

"He is a Lysian King." I sighed and turned, looking back at the ceiling. The memory of that early morning when he tried to sway my mind from ever going to the Siddhe territory sent a shiver skittering down my spine. I should have listened.

Kiora poked my side as if to try to get my attention. "So?"

"I am leaving soon." I shared another reason why pursuing anything with him was unwise.

"And you will return." She pointed out. For a moment, neither of us said anything. "Have you two kissed?"

"Kiora!"

"So, you have?" She sat straight up, staring at me while I continued avoiding meeting her eye. "Look. He cares for you. I wanted to hate him. I did. For taking you from us, placing your life in danger. But everything he does, it's like he is trying to protect you, to shield you from the world. I know you are powerful in your own right, but something has Edda on edge. *Edda*. I always thought there was nothing in the world that could startle that woman. Yet, she is startled. I worry about what you still must face ahead. If the Lysian King wishes to be your shield, to protect you from some of what heads your way, then you should let him. Do not make things harder for yourself than they need to be. You no longer need to stand alone."

"I don't need a shield," I stated, glancing at her.

"Don't be stupid. I am your shield, and you are mine. We all need people around us who will fight for us, especially when things are so uncertain. You are my friend and my Leader Superior. I would give my life for you if it came down to it." There was a certainty in her voice that left no room for doubt.

"And I would give mine for you," I said to her.

She smiled a sad smile. "Deep down in your soul, I know that to be true. But, ultimately, you would not be able to because of the duty you have for your people." Kiora laid back down. "If Erik offers help, then you should accept it. That is my official advice."

"Noted."

"And if he offers you his *body*..." She smiled suggestively.

Heat rushed to my face. "Kiora!" I snapped.

She shrugged. "Lysian or not, like I already stated, he is attractive. If he offered *me* his body... oh, the things I would do to him."

My vision darkened, and Kiora barked a laugh. "So, you do care."

Groaning, I brought my hands up to my face, rubbing my eyes.

"I don't get it. You have no problem giving yourself over to the Siddhe, but this is something you are having such trouble with? What are you afraid of?" Her brows were drawn, and she looked at me as though she truly could not understand.

"This just isn't the time to be concerned with such things."

"There is no time like the present." Her hand found mine. "Where you are going, I have no idea how difficult it may be there. If it is anything that I fear, then you will need some powerful memories and moments to hold on to in order to survive. I say let the Lysian become your escape. It is not using him if you both care for one another." A mischievous smile found her lips a new. "I am certain he would be more than happy to distract you."

I sighed. "I don't know." My thoughts went to Erik anyway.

"Well, you know my opinion on the matter," she said, rising to her feet. "I need to get going. I should get some target practice in. Skills need to be kept sharp and the arrows true, especially when come tomorrow they will be aimed at you." She winked before pivoting and walking to the door.

"Good luck." I offered her a smile.

"Never needed it." She smirked, pausing at the door. "If you need anything, you know where to find me."

Kiora then left, and I found myself alone with only my thoughts for company.

They did not make for good company.

I only thought of Landin for a long while, of the hole in my chest left by his absence. It had been more than five days since his death, and still, I could not escape the thoughts of him. It was not that I wanted to forget him. I would never forget him. I just did not want to feel this way anymore.

My heart was broken.

A piece of me was gone and would never be returned. His absence left a void.

The sun moved across the sky while I remained in my room, consumed by everything that seemed to have been occurring around me. I wondered what Clause would do with me once I came to him. Would he genuinely teach me things to make me stronger, as he had said? Would he try to use me in some way? Why did he even gather conjurors? What was the point of taking our people? There were so many things still unknown. In the weeks to come, I'd do my best to answer as many questions as possible.

My thoughts shifted towards the Lysian, who continued to surprise me with his gentleness. Kiora had been right. Something did pull me towards him, and I did not seem able to help it.

Erik was predatory the way Lysains were always told to be, yet he was also kind and capable of compassion. He drew me in until suddenly, he seemed to become a light in the darkness that surrounded me. As much as I tried not to rely on that light, it was constantly there, warming my cold skin, and trying to melt my frozen heart. Though it brought me warmth, it also brought danger.

A flame of light was helpful when managed and kept at a safe distance, yet he was not one to be controlled. Getting too close to a flame risked being burned. Was it worth it to brave that fire?

I lay on my bed staring at the ceiling while my mind continued its whirlwind of confusion. Concentration eluded me, for I couldn't think of one thing long enough to form a coherent thought or opinion. My thoughts were made of shattered glass, and ideas bounced around like reflected light from a flickering flame.

A knock at the door pulled my attention, giving me something concrete to focus on.

"Come in." I sat up.

The door opened, and Erik's sapphire eyes found mine.

4

ARIANA

"I'm not disturbing you, am I?" Erik asked, standing on the threshold.

Warmth spread through the room at his presence.

"Only disturbing the tumultuous thoughts of a Bavadrin who seems to continuously find herself in precarious situations," I said.

Erik looked as though he did not know how to reply to that statement.

I offered him a small smile. "It's fine. I welcome the distraction of your presence." I patted the open space on my bed, inviting him to have a seat.

Gently, he shut the door behind him and looked over towards a chair in the room before returning his attention to the bed. Finally, he walked over, taking a seat beside me.

It was the first time we had been alone together since my return home.

His proximity sent my pulse climbing. Dark eyes turned to me, holding me captive. I was freed from the prison of his home, yet his nearness caged me, and I couldn't escape the pull he had. I never could.

"How are you doing?" he asked, concern gracing his features. His brown hair was brushed back, highlighting the strong angles of his face. Strikingly handsome, that's what he was.

How to answer such a question? I shrugged. "I'm as well as can be expected, I suppose."

His gaze remained on me, heavy and intense. "I'm sorry about Landin," he murmured, and suddenly my heart hurt once again. I found myself jumping to my feet and walking across the room to look out a window. Wrapping my arms around myself for warmth, I tried to keep from spiraling back into that darkness which I just managed to partially crawl out of.

"I appreciate your concern Erik, but that is not something I wish to talk about right now." Not when I finally began thinking about other things besides Landin's death. Even though my mind remained fragmented, it was better than being entirely swallowed by the pain of losing him.

Silence spread through the room. Though I faced the window, I could sense Erik's attention on me. "Are you certain that you want to go through with giving yourself up to the Siddhe?"

I sighed and turned to face him, leaning on the windowsill. "It is not something I want to do, but yes, I will go through with it. This is also another matter I do not wish to discuss any further. If you have come here just to sway me from my decision, then I would prefer you leave."

Erik's gaze darkened, the air around him thickening. "Ariana, I'm not trying to control you. I know you are free to decide what you think is right for your people." He stood from the bed. "Will you accept help from the Lysians if this ends in war?"

"Of course, I will, but you will need to flush that out with Willis. There may be spies here, and I don't doubt there may be some in your lands too. It makes sense. How else would the Siddhe know how to target conjurors and know so much about me? Because of that, I don't want your forces moved to my lands, not yet, anyway. We need to keep the Siddhe in the dark for as long as possible."

He chewed on his lip as though in thought. "Would you approve of Iver coming here?"

Surprised, I searched Erik's face for any hint of a reason. "Your brother? Why?"

There was a moment of hesitation. "I think he is a conjuror."

Think? He did not know such a thing? "What kind?" I asked.

Erik sighed, running a hand through his hair. "I actually am not sure. He has kept that part of himself hidden from me and everyone we know. But there are things he can do that make no sense if he did not have gifts."

I was surprised that Erik did not seem to have ever asked his brother of this. Or perhaps he had, and Iver just denied it. How would this be any different if that was the case? "And you think he may emerge willing to help now?"

Erik shrugged. "I don't know, but call it a gut feeling. I believe he will be useful in what is coming if he can remain serious enough to focus. Iver has always been a bit of a wild card. He does whatever he wishes. When I was only his brother, it was entertaining, now as his King, it's only ever aggravating."

I looked at the floor in thought. A conjuror. If he was anything like Erik, then he would be powerful enough to truly help with the looming threats ahead. I would accept any help I could get. "Yes, you can invite him."

A mischievous smile found its way to his lips. "Good because I already sent Kole to the border to call for him."

My gaze shifted up, holding his, "and what if I had said no?"

"Then Kole would be highly annoyed, but he would have to travel again and rescind the invitation," Erik answered with a playful smile.

"You put me in a difficult situation there. Either agree with you or risk Kole's anger," I replied teasingly.

Erik's smile momentarily grew, but then retreated. He turned, taking a seat on the bed again. Placing his elbows on his knees, he lowered his head into his hands. Running his fingers through his hair, he shuddered. There was something else troubling him outside of the request for Iver to join.

"What's the matter?" I closed some of the distance between us, alarmed by the sudden deflation of his mood.

Deep blue eyes looked up, meeting mine. "This is my fault. Clause wants you because he knows what you can do, and he wouldn't know a thing if I had never taken you in the first place. I want to protect you, but I don't know how. You are going to leave in several days, and if something happens..." His voice trailed off as if he couldn't bring himself to clearly voice his concern.

I had no suitable reply, for he was right. There was a chance that we may not see each other again after I left. The cold truth sent an icy shiver crawling up my spine. Erik was torn, just as I found myself to be. We had no time together to explore what seemed to draw us to one another. We may never even get that time.

What was it that Kiora had said? *There is no time like the present.*

So instead of saying anything, I began slowly closing the distance between us. Dark blue eyes tracked my movements. When I stepped in between his legs, he pushed himself off his elbows, sitting straight up.

His handsome face looked tortured as he skimmed my body before ending on my gaze.

I hesitated, teetering on an edge, heart thundering in my chest.

Throwing caution to the wind, I bent down, kissing him.

My lips gently collided with his, and his arms circled me as if they had always meant to be there. His entire body tightened with tension. A soft growl reverberated through him when his tongue met with mine.

Instantly, I found myself drowning in his presence. The scent of him encircled me, touching me where his hands had yet to wander. His lips fueled the fire previously ignited by him. All the heaviness keeping my mind and soul imprisoned began burning away. I wanted him to incinerate me till there was nothing left. For him to make me into ash, something light and capable of being blown away by a breeze.

My fingers threaded into his thick silken hair, and I pushed my knees onto the bed, straddling him.

If only Kiora could have seen me then. The thought left me as soon as it entered, for Erik was taking every inch of my mind, claiming it as his own.

His hands gripped me harder, holding me to him. His lips moved with mine, diligently working to consume my unspoken fears. His breath became ragged, matching my own.

It was as if a band had been pulling us together until it snapped.

He stood, lifting me off the bed with him. My pulse further spiked until Erik broke the kiss. He turned around and lowered me onto the bed before taking three large steps away. I shivered with the sudden cold that surrounded me now that his body no longer did.

"You're making it nearly impossible for me to control myself." The way he said it, it nearly sounded like a threat with that low and rough voice. My already racing heart began beating harder.

"Then stop controlling yourself," I challenged.

His eyes darkened at the invitation to take me, uninhibited. Tension coiled around him.

However, he remained where he stood.

"You are drunk with sorrow," he replied, not moving a single muscle. "I don't wish to be something you live to regret."

His kindness of not wanting to have me while I was drenched in sadness was both thoughtful and incredibly maddening. I was no child to be protected, someone not knowing what she asked for. It was true that sorrow made a home in my heart, and it felt as if it would stay there for the rest of my life. However, that was not the only emotion I was capable of feeling, and it was certainly not something I wanted to experience in this moment.

"I'd rather be drunk with you," I answered boldly.

Erik looked at me with surprise, as if he did not know who this person was before him. He made no move to close the distance he placed between us. The cold of his absence crept up my arms.

"Do you not want this?" I asked, wondering if I had perhaps made an awful mistake. Was it possible I entirely misread him and his desires?

His jaw clenched. "I think the answer is obvious, but under the conditions we find ourselves, this would be born of desperation."

Nothing was heard outside of his admission.

"Then we both want each other, right here, at this moment. We want the one we see before us. I do not know who I will become in the future. Whoever it is, you may not recognize her. May not want her." My gaze dropped, and a shiver ran down my spine as I voiced a fear that clung to me. Laying it bare for him to see.

A dark blood lust was born in me the moment Landin's body hit the dirt. I felt it alive in my soul as it slowly paced back and forth like a trapped animal. Its claws cut into my chest with every silent step, digging away at the person I had always been. Inside, I was a bloody mess. It chipped away at me, demanding retribution for the damage to my heart. The sensation was so incredibly dark, and I was confident that it would only grow as time passed. I could not contain it. In the end, I was going to destroy Clause, even if I had to destroy myself in the process. I felt that unbreakable thread of fate as it wove around me, tying me to the monster.

"I am afraid I may not recognize myself," I murmured.

"I will always recognize you." The determination in Erik's voice was absolute.

My gaze lifted. "But will you want a monster? I am afraid I will need to become one to truly stand against the one I am about to face." I let Erik see my fears. My head was always held up high as I pretended to walk the path before me void of hesitation, yet that was not the truth.

I was terrified.

Not of death, but of what I would become if I survived.

Erik held my gaze before finally breaking it. Pivoting, he moved to stand at the window. Resting his arm on the framework, he leaned his head on his forearm, peering out at the darkness beyond. "I do not believe you to be capable of becoming someone who no longer draws me in. Even if you spoke lies, cast webs of deceit, and had the blood of others pooling at your feet. I would still desire to be near you. Still want you."

I observed him as he faced away from me. His powerful frame, propped up against the window, focused intently on something outside. Even with his attention elsewhere, I could feel him everywhere in the room, for his presence had such a heavy weight to it.

"How can you know that?" I asked, greedy to know what made him so confident in believing such things. To that point, he only ever knew me as a stubborn woman who cared for those around her. However, that was not all I would become. Clause was not the first to draw on feelings of vengeance from me.

My mother's death had been painful, but I was still a child, and Edda had been there to guide me as I grew. She shielded me from the world the best she could, and she protected me from myself. Still, Fraser lit a slow-burning flame of revenge. The path of vengeance was already well-traveled for me, and once Landin was taken, that path was exceptionally easy to rush down and push beyond. Every ounce of pain fueled my hatred. No one could shield me any longer, not from the world or from myself.

Erik answered with his back still to me. "Because if you want me at all, then you already want the person you are afraid of becoming. Lies and deceit were used against you and your people when I came here to break the treaty. Taking someone's life is not something that bothers me. Your father, I would have killed him myself if I was not concerned with how that may turn you against me, making you more difficult to control. And my hands, they are stained with so much blood. I no longer know the number of lives I have taken, Lysian lives, belonging to those who rebelled so long ago." He released a cruel laugh. "And you think I would desire you any less for doing what you can to protect those you care for?"

The mood in the room dimmed.

Finally, he leaned away from the window and turned to me. His jaw was tight as his eyes met mine and held. The deep blue of his irises was significantly chilled. "This is who I am, Ariana. I am not some gentle King. I am the predator your Bavadrin stories warned the Lysians to be." He spoke as if he were admitting to something, as if unveiling a secret I would not have known otherwise.

Anger bubbled within me. He thought I was such a fool? I watched him fight and kill five Lysians before my eyes. It quickly became abundantly clear that those were not the first lives he took, and I was confident they would not be the last. I knew he attempted to use me for his own agenda when he hoped I would be easy to control so that he could direct the Bavadrins. Nothing that he said came as a surprise.

"You insult me, for I am neither dumb nor blind," I stated flatly. "I already know all those things about you, and I also have seen that those are not the things that define who you are. There are other sides to you, Erik, for I would never have tried to save your life if that was all you were." I stood from the bed. "I know what I want and what I don't. I don't want your pity or concern where there needn't be any. I am not some sheltered girl for you to protect. I am the Leader Superior of the Bavadrin people. I'm completely capable of making decisions for myself." Pivoting, I walked to the door, opening it. "Sleep well, Erik." I turned to him, gaze colliding with his, waiting for him to leave. If he wished to only anger me, then I wanted him gone.

He looked from me to the hallway beyond and paced

towards it. Each step was purposeful and precise, moving with silent grace. Approaching the exit, his hand reached out for the door, grabbing hold of it while I moved away, giving him room to leave. Sapphire eyes stared at a spot in the hall, and he stilled just shy of reaching the threshold.

I braced myself for whatever he thought of saying next. The way things were progressing, chances were he would bring up Clause, Landin, or insult my ability to understand the situations I found myself in. None of those were things I planned on discussing any further with him.

Erik went perfectly still for a heartbeat that felt like an eternity. He then gently shut the door, remaining inside with me.

My heart stammered, afraid to hope that perhaps he had given up all those things that held him back, at least for the night.

The air trapped within the room became electric.

When he turned to me, it was as if all that had been restraining him evaporated entirely. His gaze pinned me where I stood, and the intensity in those eyes were incredible. I couldn't move a muscle even if I wanted to. The unyielding desire burning in him was evident and potent. He looked upon me as if I were entirely his for the taking.

A tremor skipped through me.

Confidence came off him in waves. Any trace of uncertainty drowned in it. Slowly and with intent, he moved, closing the space between us until he towered me.

Raising his hand to my face, his thumb brushed along my jaw and his fingers slid around the back of my neck, holding the base of my skull. My breath hitched. The overwhelming feeling of his complete attention caused my stomach to flutter. He looked at me as though he were a wolf and I his prey. The power coming off him was completely crushing. Yet, I did not shy away. Any fear of him I possibly clung to had been replaced with desire. His power was a safety net to catch me.

My breathing turned shallow.

A smile pulled at his lips, clearly knowing the effect he was having. And when he finally leaned down, there was no hesitation. His lips crashed with mine, powerful and demanding. He was neither restrained nor gentle as he picked me up and carried me to the bed.

I was set on fire with every touch. Every graze of fingertips over sensitive skin. Every kiss. Every lingering breath. It was too much, and yet I needed more.

Somewhere along the way, we lost our clothing. Discarded somewhere in the room. Thrown out of existence. Because nothing existed other than him.

His hands explored my body. Running across my ribs, over my breasts, between my legs. Fingers traced delightful patterns over me before plunging into me. My toes curled.

Spirit, help me. I was going to burst into flame.

A moan slipped past my lips, back arching.

Erik chuckled darkly, enjoying the way my body responded to his *everything*. His mouth brushed against my ear. "I'm going to make you mine, Ariana."

Those words nearly unraveled me completely.

His hands moved over me as if he owned me. My flesh, his to command. Every lingering touch, every purposeful stroke, had me coming apart. He took me to an edge and held me there. I wanted to jump. Needed to jump. Erik withdrew his hand from between my legs and I growled in protest.

The hard length of him brushed against me. My body tensed, nearly going out of my mind with anticipation. He eased himself into me, releasing a throaty groan as I stretched around him. Nothing was slow after that. He pulled out only to slam back into me without warning. My hand flew to my mouth to stifle a scream. The last thing I needed was guards flooding into the room, thinking I was being attacked. Maybe I was.

Another predatory chuckle came from Erik as he pushed into me. He grabbed my wrist, removing my hand from my mouth and pinning it to the bed. His lips found mine, stifling my reckless moans with his mouth. The feel of him was stunning. I drowned in the fire of him. Drunk off everything *him*.

Tension in my body built till it had nowhere to go and I shattered into a million pieces.

I came undone.

"I would recognize you anywhere." Erik's voice filled the void of my mind, bringing me back to life. "Always."

5

ARIANA

A steady rhythmic beat welcomed me from a blissfully
dreamless night. Glorious warmth surrounded me.
As I opened my eyes, I was startled by the sapphire
gaze watching me. The sound was that of his beating heart,
easily heard while my head rested on Erik's bare chest. His arm
circled me, hand sliding up my spine and back down, holding
me close. The small of my back warmed by his touch.

A smirk worked its way onto his face. "Surprised?" The
gravelly tone caused my pulse to spike.

I shifted to better view him. "Uh, no. I just– I suppose– I
wasn't sure whether you would still be here in the morning."

"You rather I had left?" He arched an eyebrow, eyes
gleaming.

Heat prickled the nape of my neck. "No. I'm glad you're
here." That was when I noticed nothing separated any part of
me from touching him. In fact, nothing separated me from
anything. My body lay utterly bare under the sheet. And his...

"Are you blushing?" Erik asked with a growing smile.

"What? No." I quickly gathered more of the sheets around myself. "What time is it?" I asked, suddenly desperate to change the subject.

"It's about half an hour before your scheduled meeting with everyone." He watched me with an amused glimmer in his eyes.

"What?" I jumped out of bed, taking my sheet with me to cover myself with. "I need to go." I took a step away before twisting back towards him. "*You* need to go."

Erik rose from the bed, wearing absolutely nothing.

Beautiful. His body was mouthwateringly beautiful.

I spun around, facing away from him. "Put something on and go! I need to get dressed." My cheeks instantly burned. I could only imagine how red they were.

"I'm not stopping you from dressing." He answered with a low laugh, his enjoyment of the situation clear. I remained tense, my heart pounding in my chest, chiseling away at bone. Following a brief shuffling behind me, he came around into my line of sight. Erik remained shirtless; however, at least he had pants on. I tried not to look at him.

He paced towards me. "Today, you're shy? After what we did last night?"

"Stop it," I said and couldn't help my gaze from wandering over his skin. Last night was remarkable. The taste of him, the feel. Desire stirred, and I forced my eyes to look anywhere but his body. "Where is your shirt?"

"No idea." He replied without even looking for it. His focus remained entirely on me. *I would recognize you anywhere.* The words he said flooded my thoughts and my heart continued with its antics against my ribs. Like a calling card letting him know, very well, of the effect he was having on me.

"There's no time." I turned and walked towards the wall. He needed to take the passage to his room, so no one saw him leaving half-naked. With Erik staying in the compound, I doubted that the passage would remain hidden for long from the Lysians anyway.

I opened the false door and turned to Erik, "follow the narrow hall till it ends. That's your room."

"There's a secret passage connecting our rooms?" His eyes brightened in surprise. "It did sound like some of the walls were strangely hollow."

"Yes, now out you go." I angled my head towards the dark opening. I usually needed a candle or light of some sort to see by, but I figured a Lysian with all their superior hearing and eyesight could make do in the dark.

I wasn't sure what I felt at that moment. Emotions surged, still all over the place. Thoughts threatened to rip me apart and drown me in worries. For days, my mind imprisoned me in painful torment. Except for last night. Erik became an oasis, a drug to drown out the sound in my head. And in the night, in the Lysian King's arms, I finally found rest.

He strode towards me with silent steps.

The Lysian King reached out, taking my hand in his larger one. Bringing it to his lips, he placed a fleeting kiss on my knuckle, and my heart skipped an entire heartbeat.

"I'll see you soon," Erik murmured, eyes bright and promising. He then left. Clearly, there was more that needed to be said, more I wanted to say, but time was not a luxury we had. At least not yet. Perhaps someday, time would slow, and we could spend days doing nothing more than enjoying each other's company.

My focus shifted to the task at hand. I needed to train, to prepare for my departure.

Half an hour later, I was nearly running down the halls to the meeting room. I doubted anyone would be terribly upset by my few minutes of tardiness, but I couldn't help this overwhelming feeling of being late. Punctuality was chiseled into me since childhood, and it was likely something I could never shake.

I entered the room, evidently the last to arrive. "Sorry everyone, I seem to have overslept this morning," I said, making my way to my seat, trying not to let my wet hair drip on anyone as I passed.

"Beauty sleep suits you," Erik commented with a smirk pulling at those devious lips of his. My face instantly warmed. He sat before me, looking so well put together as if he had all the time in the morning to come to the meeting while I was a mess. Next to him sat Kole, his icy gaze moving from me to Erik before narrowing.

"Kole." I was eager to ignore Erik's remark. "Erik told me you went to send word for Iver to join us. I take it that your trip went without trouble?" I hid the surprise of even seeing him at the meeting. He must have traveled half the day and the entire night to deliver the message to the Lysians at the border before returning.

"Yeah," he said, still looking suspiciously between Erik and myself. Those analytical eyes showed no trace of exhaustion.

"Great. We are about to go over a training plan for me for the rest of my time here. Feel free to share any thoughts you may have on it."

"Right," Willis spoke, pulling attention from me. "We have set a path for you to run through the forest to a clearing. Along that path, the sparrows will be waiting and firing their arrows which you will need to block. If one hits you, then you are considered dead and will restart the entire course. Following their assault you will need to fight me to get by. Eventually, you will make it to the clearing with Erik. He will use his conjuring to a certain distance. Once you cross that threshold, both you and he are not to conjure. At that point, Erik is essentially standing in for Clause, and since your conjuring does not affect Clause, your goal is to subdue or eliminate Erik without letting him touch you."

The obstacles created for me were going to be difficult to overcome. "Great. I am to fight a Lysian without being touched by him."

"Not just any Lysian." Kole chimed in. "He is one of the best fighters among us."

"You wanted a training," Willis said. "We are not going easy on you. I'd rather this be unnecessarily difficult than not enough to properly prepare you."

"This is certainly not unnecessarily difficult." Edda finally spoke up. "It may not be hard enough," she mumbled.

"We can adjust the difficulty and reformat things as we go, but this is our starting plan." Willis turned to Kole. "You can fight Ariana on foot with me."

"Is she to use her conjuring against us?" Kole asked.

Willis viewed me. "You are not to touch our lungs, but you can conjure. If you progress quickly, then eventually, we will try you not conjuring at all."

"I brought you something." Kiora stood, picking something off the ground and placing it on the table. A long shirt made of a chain material and a helmet. "We will use flat-tipped wooden arrows, but I am afraid they will still hurt. This will ensure nothing vital gets punctured."

I frowned. "I'll accept the shirt, but not that helmet."

"I insist," Kiora pressed.

"I won't be able to see or move well with that thing on my head blocking my peripheral vision. Plus, you and your archers should be able to avoid firing at my head. Unless you think you are incapable of it?" I raised an eyebrow in challenge.

She rose to my bait, folding her arms over her chest. "We certainly are capable of something as simple as that."

"Even when she is running?" Kole asked, earning a look of disgust from Kiora.

"Do not insult me, Lysian," Kiora said, pursing her lips. "We are Sparrows. You'll see soon enough what that means."

"When will all of this be set up and ready?" I turned to Willis.

"We spent most of yesterday laying out the plan and scouting an area. We are ready now if you are."

"Well." I stood from the table. "No time to waste."

They led me out of the city to where training would take place. Kole and Willis alternated how far up the trail they waited for me to help keep an element of surprise. Everyone took their positions, and then we began. It took me several attempts before I could finally get a decent distance before being hit by one of the Sparrow's arrows. My sides and back hurt from the previous blows while I ran forward. A thick wall of mist surrounded me, forming a barrier. Unfortunately, it also obscured my vision. I tripped, the dense fog fracturing enough for an arrow to cut through the cracks, hitting my lower back.

"UGH!" I fell, rolling onto my side and panting.

Erik appeared out of nowhere, holding his hand out to help me up.

I flinched, startled by his sudden presence.

"What are you doing here?" I asked while still on the ground, trying to catch my breath.

"It seems like you will never make it to me at this rate," he commented.

I grunted, rolling over and getting to my feet without his help.

A smile tugged at those talented lips, and the thought of it warmed me from within. "You disagree with my assessment?"

"Get lost," I said through clenched teeth. I needed to maintain my focus, and he wasn't helping.

Kiora's voice came from somewhere amongst the trees as she yelled out. "Hey, loverboy, we are in the middle of training!"

"Loverboy?" Erik's eyes sparkled as he turned from the forest to me.

Exhaustion and irritation protected me from feeling an ounce of embarrassment.

I turned to leave and go back to the start of the course. Staying too long in one place without a distraction, and my mind wandered back to thoughts of Landin. The pain would again encase me in its stiff embrace.

"I can help you," Erik said from where I left him standing, his tone losing all its amusement. Something about his voice drew me, the finality of that statement.

"How?" I turned.

"Your conjuring. You can use it to sense the arrows while not hindering your sight so much as creating a solid wall around yourself." His eyes harbored such certainty that I didn't even question whether it was possible.

"Show me."

He smiled, closing the space between us. "The archers, how do they land their marks without having to see them with their eyes?"

"Their conjuring."

"They use the breeze to help carry their arrows, but that also allows them to see through feeling. I can do the same with my flames, and so can you. At the ceremony for Landin, you used your gifts to clear the mist path for the Bavadrins carrying the pallet without even looking at them. You did that by feeling. You need to sense the world and not think so hard."

I shook my head in disappointment. "I don't know if I have time for this, to learn this."

His eyes sparkled with the way the sun hit them. "You are already doing it. You just haven't realized it. Close your eyes."

I stared at him.

His lip twitched. "Go on, I won't bite." Something about how he said it caused my heartbeat to pick up its pace. He *winked* at me.

I suppressed a smile and obliged.

"Now release your conjuring. Let it spread naturally. Do not form a wall, do not solidify it. Instead, just reach with it."

My chest grew warm with power, and I let it seep through me before falling from me and out into the world.

"That's it. Now feel it, the way your mist moves over the ground, the way it reaches for the trees, climbing ever so slightly. Explore your surroundings." He remained quiet as I pushed myself to move without actually moving, to touch the world as he instructed.

"I'm going to step away now, and I want for you to tell me where I am in relation to you."

"Okay." I agreed, keeping my eyes shut.

If he moved, then I did not know it, for his steps were soundless. I searched down the thread, tethering my powers to me, and stretched through it. I nearly gave up before noticing the smallest of disturbances. As if I built a spider web around me and could feel the movement in the distance.

"To my left," I said.

"Good." I heard the smile in his voice. "Again."

Silence settled once more before I sensed that tug on the web of mist. I felt the disturbance shift. "Behind me." He did not answer, but I discerned the transition, him changing direction until he stood somewhere ahead. "In front of me."

Something else entered the web of mist. Where Erik's movements were gentle, a soft tug on my conjuring, this was different. It flew incredibly fast. It did not tug but cut, momentarily severing my ties to the mist wherever it passed. Its trajectory angled towards my ribs. The mist solidified into a thin edge and sliced like a blade, cutting off the object. I opened my eyes in time to see the arrow fall at my feet before ever reaching me.

Kiora yelled out, "WOOOOOOHOOOO! That's my girl!"

Erik stood before me, a proud smile on his handsome face. "You did well."

"Thank you." A smile matching his found its way to my lips.

"Atta boy loverboy! I knew there was a reason I liked you!" Kiora added from her position amongst the trees.

I was going to kill her.

Erik's smile grew, laughter touching his eyes.

"Get back to your position." My cheeks grew hot.

"Loverboy will do as you command." He dipped his head, turned and left. A soft chuckle escaped him as he went.

On the next attempt at the course, I finally made it past the Sparrows, only to be taken down by Kole and Willis. Several attempts later, the sun was setting, and the day's training was at its end. Still, I could not get past the two of them.

I likely could not have gone much longer that day, anyway.

My body nearly broke, muscle and bone thoroughly abused. Near the end, my pace slowed, legs wobbling with the strain to keep me up and moving. The entire day took a toll, and I was still so far from the goal.

6

ARIANA

Enormously powerful flames surrounded me. Fierce fire surged, pressing against the mist I shrouded myself with. My senses overwhelmed by it. A loud hissing formed from where flame met fog.

My body grew weary and tired with every moment that I funneled all my strength into my conjuring. This was the first time I got past Willis and Kole, only to be stopped cold by Erik's flames. As the fire climbed higher, it fueled the raging storm within. Anger melded with pain before condensing with disappointment for not getting past this point.

I screamed in frustration, throwing every bit of energy I could at breaking through the relentless blaze. The sound of my voice lost itself amongst the hissing.

Fire converged above, closing the last bit of blue sky that there was.

I couldn't breathe in enough oxygen.

The world spun as my head pounded angrily against my temple.

Mist evaporated as the well I pulled my conjuring from ran dry. Instantly the flames vanished, Erik noting the weakening on my end. Cool, delicious air made its way into my lungs once more.

Panting, I folded over, placing my hands on my knees for support as I gulped down breath after breath.

Despite the cold of the day, sweat wet my brow, dripping down the side of my face. The heat of the inferno Erik controlled was severe enough that I had no idea how my skin had not melted off the bone.

"You okay?" Erik asked from beside me.

"Fine." I straightened, only for the world to tilt as my head stubbornly continued to spin. I was so weak. How could I even hope of standing against the Siddhe?

An arm came around my waist, pulling me towards him, his body supporting mine. A few breaths later, the world stilled, and I pushed him away.

"Stop it," I snapped.

Confusion touched Erik's features, softening them. "Stop what?"

"The hovering."

"This is basically the first I have seen you all day," he stated, observing my face as if looking for a hint as to what thoughts were running around in my brain.

I released a sharp breath. "If I fall, I can get up on my own. I don't need your help."

He scanned my face. "What's with you?"

"Nothing." I turned, marching away.

"We should take a break," Erik said from behind me.

"No." I continued forward.

A hand caught my wrist, halting me. "You are exhausted. We all are tired and can use a break to eat and rest."

"I need to keep going." My gaze dropped to his hold on my arm. "Unhand me." Suddenly desperation came over me, pushing me to go, to keep moving. I couldn't break. Not when I needed to improve. Not when resting threatened my mind from crumbling in on itself again.

I could hardly manage the mess I had become.

My life had turned into a nightmare I could not wake from. Landin was gone. There was no recovery from that. The cold within settled deep into my bones, one that could smother even the hottest of flames. I did not know whether this was something I could ever heal from. Even in the daylight, with my eyes wide open, I found myself too deep in the nightmare. My only hope was to keep moving, to never stop. To not think.

Erik's gaze searched mine. "Pushing yourself without rest will only worsen the quality of your performance and growth. You will push yourself into the ground right where you stand if you keep going like this. Not moving forward in any way."

His words were sound, but I was not in a place to hear him. I tried to turn and leave, but his hold remained. "Let. Go. Now." I demanded.

Erik's jaw clenched, yet he released me.

Spinning around, I didn't even get to make a single step before a wall of fire formed, barring me from going anywhere.

"You are hurting, and you are using this training as a desperate escape from that pain. It is not constructive, nor is it helpful," he said from behind me while I stared at the flames.

Pivoting, my glare clashed with his. Determination etched into his handsome face. There was no lenience in his stance on the matter, but this was not his home, not his lands. It was mine. I did not follow his orders.

My muscles tensed, my body growing rigid. "You seem to

forget where you are. I will drop you to your knees if you do not drop the flames."

Erik's gaze narrowed, and he took a single deliberate step towards me. "If that is what you need to do. Then go ahead." There was not an ounce of uncertainty in his tone.

"You think I won't?"

Midnight blue eyes scanned my face. "I am certain you would if I were an actual threat."

He was wrong.

I smirked just before shoving all my strength into the mist that filled his lungs in the blink of an eye.

Erik's hands flew to his throat moments before the Lysian King dropped to his knees before me. The flames keeping me cornered dissipated.

I withdrew my power, allowing him to catch his breath as he coughed while still kneeling in the dirt.

Slow clapping pulled my attention to the side, where Iver came into view. "My, my, that was certainly fun to watch." He casually approached, eyes dancing with mischief before landing on me and hardening. "But incredibly foolish of you."

I couldn't hide my surprise at seeing him. How was it he arrived so quickly? He would have only recently gotten the request to come to the Bavadrin lands, and the trip would have taken days.

"It's fine," Erik rose to his feet, face red, expression completely unreadable.

Iver tisked softly before turning to me. "When attacked, is it not the instinct to fight back? When one cannot draw a breath, does the body not respond of its own accord in an effort to overcome the threat? You are lucky he didn't burn you out of existence. Lucky that he has that amount of control over himself."

"I said it's fine," Erik snapped at his brother.

"What the hell is going on?" Kiora's voice shook the forest.

"We are done for the day!" I yelled back. There were still a few hours till sunset, but with the way tensions were running, it was not going to end well if we continued. And I had a new distraction. There was a conversation I needed to have with Iver.

The Sparrows came out of their hiding and the forest was briefly alive with hungry archers making their way back to the city.

Iver turned to his brother. "You mind if I have a private chat with our Bavadrin Leader Superior?"

Erik's gaze leveled at me. "Fine by me," he said to Iver without breaking eye contact. A ripple of tension moved between us, thick and strangely uncomfortable. A pang of guilt rushed through my stomach for the way I had just acted towards him. "I'll see you later," he said before leaving us.

I watched him as he strode away, not once looking back before disappearing into the forest.

Iver and I walked to the edge where forest met with grassland and sat underneath a tree.

"You impress me," Iver stated simply.

"For some reason, I do not think you often give such high compliments." I viewed him, wondering what specifically he might have found impressive.

He smiled. "I do not."

"Is it because I took back my freedom from the Lysians?"

Leaning against the tree, he angled his face towards me. "It's that you managed to take it back with zero bloodshed. And then still offered us a hand in standing against the Siddhe."

I shrugged, watching the breeze push the blades of dry

grass like living art. "I had little choice, for I do not plan to live out my life under the command of another."

"You did have a choice. You did not have to tell us that Clause reached out to you. You owed us nothing. Yet you shared the information because you wished to help us even after we took you from your home and threatened your people. You also helped before you even took your freedom back."

I turned to find him already looking at me, his gray eyes glimmering. "Helped how?"

"Kole and Eislyn. Whatever you said to him has changed his life." Whatever expression he saw on my face caused him to chuckle. "Kole didn't tell you, did he?"

"What happened?" A nervous tendril wrapped around me. That night, after talking to Kole, when he destroyed the sitting room, my heart ached for him. I was afraid to have done more damage than good.

"He apologized to her. She apparently briefly fell apart in Erik's arms. Which is significant, for she never lets others see her cry or exhibit anything that may be portrayed as a weakness. And now the two of them can exist in the same room without hostility." His gaze remained entirely focused on me, and there was a weight to it. Something about Iver's presence was heavier than normal. Troubled. Though not about what we were currently discussing.

"I didn't do anything, only talked to him a little."

He tilted his head. "You used your Bavadrin mind magic for good. And for that, I thank you."

I nearly laughed. "There is no magic there. Only a friend."

He squinted at me. "It was magic."

I shook my head, accepting the fact that it was an argument I didn't even want to try and have with him. "Well, perhaps you can repay me then."

"What do you have in mind?" His tone grew serious.

I licked my lips. "Are you a conjuror?"

He was not quick to reply. "Why do you ask?"

"Erik thought you may have abilities that could be helpful with what's to come." He held my gaze without responding. "I have been to the Siddhe city for a single dinner, and I already know just how over our heads all this is. I am asking for your help, Iver. If you are willing to give it."

He viewed me, studying my face. "Are you certain you wish for my help in this?"

"Do you not want to save your sister?" I didn't understand his question, his hesitance.

"Perhaps she may be saved without my need to conjure."

"Perhaps. But I do not think we will ever win without everyone giving it their all. Clause has armies of conjurors at his disposal. Even *alone,* he is incredibly powerful."

Iver nodded before looking out at the grasslands. His gaze moved towards the horizon. "How much do you trust Erik? Do you trust him with your life?" Those cunning eyes returned to me. "True unflinching trust."

What did that have to do with anything? I was thrown off, prepared to ask him why that was important in the situation, but instead found myself saying, "I think so."

He shook his head, the movement barely there yet somehow loud at the same time. "You need to be certain." The warning, which I realized this was, caused something to tighten within.

"Why?"

"Because he is my King, and my conjuring exceeds his," Iver stated simply. "Once he knows what I am capable of, then I will be at his disposal. He could use me against anyone he wishes. And if I ever truly oppose him, then it will be seen as a challenge. If I fight him, it would end in someone's death, and I do not wish to kill my brother. Despite how it may seem, I am relatively fond of him." He paused, letting the gravity of his words sink in before he continued. "So, Ariana. I will ask you again, how much do you place your trust in my brother?"

"Do you not trust him?" I asked, in shock at what he was divulging.

Iver shrugged a single shoulder. "He has always been somewhat power-hungry. I did not want for him to use mine for his own goals. To more easily control the world around him."

"Your goals do not align with his?" For all I knew, they had the same intentions of freeing the abducted conjurors.

"Sometimes they do, and sometimes they don't." His head moved side to side before stilling with a sigh. As if this conversation was burdensome.

"And you are willing to bring your powers to the light now?" I stared at him in disbelief.

"Depending on your decision."

"Why me?"

A small smile tugged at his lips. "My brother seems to have grown more than I had ever given him credit for. If you trust him not to abuse the power I have, then I trust your judgment."

I shook my head, hardly believing what I heard. "But you know him so much better than I do. And you don't even truly know me that well to place such weight on my opinion."

"I never knew him as his prisoner," he stated simply. Iver was right. A lot could be said about how a person treated their prisoners. Erik had been kind to me then. He still was. Whatever this power Iver had, I trusted Erik with it. And suddenly a new wave of guilt settled over me for what I had just done to him. Erik was trying to help me, and I lashed out. Iver then added, "Perhaps I have already made my decision, and am only curious as to what you would choose, given the option."

I forced the thought of my remorse out of my mind and focused on the prince before me. "I trust him. Show me what you can do."

Iver nodded, rising to his feet. "Very well."

7

ERIK

Iver and Ariana stepped inside my room. Her eyes met mine before she looked away, a blush spreading across her cheeks. She seemed uncomfortable holding my gaze for the first time I could ever recall.

"How was your talk?" I asked, looking from Ariana to Iver before returning my attention to her.

There was a pause of hesitation. Her gaze drifted briefly to Iver, who made no sign of answering the question. "It was good. Iver has agreed to help."

"All of my Lysians are at your disposal. We will all help," I stated, knowing that was not exactly what she meant by it. So, my assumptions of him, perhaps being a conjuror, proved correct.

Ariana's gaze flickered to my brother once more, and she inclined her head towards me. As if inviting him to elaborate.

Iver sighed, drawing my attention. "She means I will help with my conjuring."

I always suspected he harbored a gift. Yet hearing his admission still stirred something uncomfortable within my chest.

My gaze narrowed. "And why now?" He had years to step up, to help. However, he never did.

"Ariana says she trusts you with her life," he stated.

I release an irritated breath. "So, you place so much weight on her opinion of me? A woman you hardly know. Over me, your brother." I was trying to keep my growing anger from escalating.

"If your prisoner trusts you that much then, yes." Iver shrugged as if it were that simple.

"She was..." The words died on my lips. Ariana had been my prisoner. That fact weighed on me.

"Iver's conjuring is impressive," Ariana said, breaking the tense stare between my brother and me. "He is more of a threat to my people than even you are." She took a single small step towards me before stilling. "And you will have that power under your command now."

I snorted, gaze slicing to Iver. "I always had that power. I *let* you keep everything a secret."

He nodded, accepting the truth of my words. "You did. You've never known the extent of my conjuring, however, and still don't. I am not so sure you would have had the same restraint if you'd known sooner. In fact, you likely would have used me here when you went on your mission to break the treaty. A lot more Bavadrin lives would have been taken."

My jaw clenched.

Ariana took another step towards us. "Even if you would have conjured, Erik would have still heard me call out his name when he was about to... take a life." Ariana's attention settled on me, her face softening. Hurt swam in her eyes as she remembered the day I broke free and captured her. The significance of those emotions only compounded with the torment Landin's death brought her. "I do not doubt that Iver's conjuring wouldn't have changed how things progressed between us after that." She then turned to Iver. "This is useless to discuss. Just show him what you can do."

"Very well." Iver took two steps towards me. However, before his second step, there was a brief disorientation before him, and it was as if he had walked through something. He vanished, only to reappear in another corner of the room.

That was not the end of his tricks.

He then held up his hand, *fire* burning from his fingertips.

It was remarkable.

"How is that possible? You have more than one conjuring ability?" I could hardly grasp it.

Iver shrugged. "Conjuring intrigued me, and so I learned."

Surely, I misheard. "You simply *learned* all of this?"

"Yes."

"If Ariana was to show you what she can do, how long would it take you to learn it?"

"It depends on the complexity. It's always different."

Ariana's head tilted as if in thought. "Then who taught you to reappear in another location?"

"No one teaches me, but I suppose that is beside the point. I used to have a friend who vanished long ago. She couldn't move her body the way I could, but she could multiply and move objects. I found her gift so fascinating."

Ariana frowned, intently watching Iver. "Show me."

Iver casually looked around the room, leisurely walking through it. He stopped at a desk and picked up a feather quill. There was a brief glimmering distortion next to his hand, and when he moved the feather through it, several feathers surrounded him, suspended in the air.

"Malavika." The name was barely a whisper on her lips, yet it drew our attention like lightning. We knew that name.

"Where have you heard that?" Iver pulled the feather back, his hand dropping at his side.

"She was there. A Lysian, working for Clause." For a moment, we all stood silent until Ariana asked, "But she can't disappear and reappear like you?"

"No," Iver shook his head, placing the feather on the desk. Though he answered her question, he looked distracted. As if his mind was elsewhere. "She can only use objects. I mimicked her conjuring and pushed myself to develop it into my ability to move through it myself."

My gaze lingered on that feather, discarded on the desk. Something harmless, but what if it weren't a feather? What if he held a blade? "I still don't understand. All this time, you've been hiding such a unique ability. Such power. Why?"

Iver smiled, though it did not touch his eyes. "I don't wish to be anyone's puppet or attack dog. I also don't want to be placed in a position where I am forced to fight you because of a fundamental disagreement."

Disgust coiled in my stomach at the insinuation. "You thought I would force you to use your conjuring in ways you didn't want to?"

"You have always had a bit of an aggressive streak. Yes, you have a heart and love those important to you. But you also do not hesitate to destroy what is in your way. Father sharpened your quick brutality on the Lysian rebels, ensuring you would always be swift to act and merciless."

Anger surged through me as I twisted away, taking a few small steps before turning back. "I would never have forced you to do something like that."

Iver shrugged. "Easy to say now."

"Stop it." Ariana stepped between us. She faced Iver. "What are you trying to prove? Why are you trying to push him?"

He snorted. "You haven't learned a thing, have you? Still stepping between two Lysians when you shouldn't."

She let out a breath. "You are in my home. I asked for your help and am grateful for it, but please stop trying to get everyone riled up. Everything is stressful enough. I cannot handle more problems coming from my friends and allies." Tension tightened around her, seeping through her and into the room.

Something shifted in Iver then. His brows furrowing. "What's the matter?" His gaze then lifted to mine. "What do I not know?"

Ariana looked up at me over her shoulder. "He doesn't know what's going on?"

"Not completely." The Lysians and my brothers knew nothing other than Ariana returned, and that we were discussing plans moving forward.

She turned back to Iver. "Clause killed Landin. He invited me to come to stay in the Siddhe lands for some time. If I refuse, then he said he would destroy us. In efforts of stalling and trying to give us more time to prepare for this war, I am going to go back there again."

"I'm sorry for your loss," Iver stated, brows knitted in concern. To his credit, it sounded as though he truly meant it.

"Thank you." Ariana's voice was soft, sadness clouding her eyes.

Iver shifted his attention to me. "Why did you not tell us? All we were told was that Ariana returned, that we were going to continue preparing for war, and that the Bavadrins will stand with us."

"I needed time to figure things out."

"Time to come up with a different plan?" He smirked, looking at Ariana. "Erik wants to stop you."

"No one can stop me," she said at once.

His lips curled. "From what I witnessed earlier, you using your mist to make him cough. It doesn't look like you have much of a choice if Erik truly tried to."

She took a step towards him, head tilting as if she wasn't sure if she heard correctly. "I'm sorry. Were you not there at the end of this last practice?"

I could still practically feel her mist in my lungs, stealing the air. The sensation of it burned and lingered. None of it was comfortable.

"Oh, you think you were in control?" Iver shook his head with a laugh. "That was an illusion. My brother gave you control. He could have reclaimed that power at any moment and burned you to ash."

A growl rumbled through my throat. "Ashes, Iver. Stop trying to rile up trouble. There's enough of it already."

Rolling his eyes, he turned towards me. "Oh, please, Erik. Don't tell me you haven't considered just tying her to a bed and going to war without more of a plan."

Ariana's heart skipped a beat.

Iver's gray eyes fastened on her. A slow smile spread across his face. "Well, well, well. Perhaps she would enjoy being tied to a bed."

"Iver," I snapped.

He, of course, ignored me.

"What a lovely rose color on your face." Iver stepped towards her. "Tell me ar-" His voice cut off, and his hands went to his throat. Ariana's abilities stripped oxygen from his lungs.

A shimmer appeared around him, and Iver vanished, reappearing in another part of the room. Still choking.

"That won't work," Ariana said before releasing her conjuring.

Iver coughed violently as his lungs burned for air. "Not–" he gasped between breaths. "Nice–"

"You know what isn't nice?" Ariana addressed him with a bitter tone. "You putting your dirty little fingers where they don't belong."

Iver straightened after gulping down a few more breaths. Though by the gleam in his eyes, he was far from finished. "My fingers are not dirty. Though if you would like for me to place them somewhere more pleasant, all you need to do is ask." He smirked suggestively.

I snapped.

The distance between us shrank in the blink of an eye. I threw him up against a wall. My hand gripped his throat, and I nearly crushed it while keeping him pressed against the stone at his back.

"Erik." There was a flicker of alarm in Ariana's voice.

Iver's gaze fastened to mine, and for once, he did not speak. His hand wrapped around my wrist reflexively before he froze. The pulse in his neck warmed my palm with every beat of his aggravating little heart. The blood barely squeezed through where I applied enough pressure to finally render my brother silent.

"Your games end now," I said between clenched teeth. "I do not have patience for this. Is that understood?"

"Yes." The word was hardly audible.

I released him, and he braced himself against the wall, hand at his throat for the second time in the last few minutes.

His attention found Ariana. "I'm sorry. I didn't mean to disrespect you."

Her gaze narrowed. "Then what was your intent?"

"Partially to see how you both react under a little pressure."

Ariana shook her head as though she couldn't believe him.

"To test me," I stated. "Your tests and games end here, or I will see it as a sign that you wish to be King yourself."

"You know that isn't what I want," Iver stated, looking at me.

Ariana pivoted, walking towards the door. For how exhausted I knew she was, she carried herself with her head held high and a powerful stride. "I'm tired. I'm grabbing food and going to bed." She stated before leaving without waiting for a reply.

"You're lucky I don't incinerate you," I growled at my brother. I didn't know if I even could, for he had fire-conjuring abilities himself. That realization angered me even more.

His gray eyes settled on me. "You are awfully protective of our new Bavadrin friend."

"Your point?"

"No point, just an observation."

"Go to bed, Iver." My dismissal of him was crystal clear.

He pouted. "I just got here and so was not yet given one."

I opened the door and angled my head towards the hall. "Not my problem. Now, get out."

Iver pretended like a full-body shiver ran through him. "Oooh, Icy," he said before finally taking his leave.

8

ARIANA

With a sigh, I rolled over, glaring at the moonlight seeping in through the window. It reached across the floor, not quite touching the far wall. All I could do was stare at it. My thoughts were trapped by the walls in my mind.

The night claimed the sky a long while ago, yet every minute that passed, I only got more and more lost in the darkness of my thoughts. There was no way out, no escape. Worries loomed, spanning the concerns of the future to events of the past. Round and round the fears went, slowly closing in until the pressure of them constricted my chest.

I could not avoid Landin's death. Could not change the outcome, for it already occurred. So then, why did my mind always lead me down a path of *what if's* that may have led to more favorable outcomes? The thoughts were pointless. Yet they consumed me as if they were the most significant thing.

It was torture, all of it.

I released another countless sigh, turning onto my back.

Torture came in many forms, and my brain was doing a splendid job of it.

A slight knock tugged at my attention. The sound came not from the main door but from the secret one.

I sat up, head-turning to where the passage hid behind a large tapestry. *Erik.*

The wooden floor pressed cold against my feet as I stood. Grabbing a robe, I put it on over my silky mid-thigh nightgown before padding over to the door. It creaked, slightly opening.

I could hardly make out the dark figure in the shadows before me, but I didn't need to see well to know who stood there. The air buzzed with his strength. I *felt* his presence.

Taking a step back, my head angled towards my room in silent invitation.

With a predatory grace, Erik entered, finding his way to the moonlight, which highlighted the strong features of his face. There was a faint glow around the fabric of his shirt, drawing the eye to the physical strength hidden beneath. He was breathtakingly masculine and clearly favored by the moon.

My gaze locked with his. "Couldn't sleep?" I asked.

His lips pulled to the side. "It appears neither of us could."

I nodded, glancing at my bed and the mess of sheets. Evidence of the wreckage also within my mind. With a deep breath, I forced my attention back to him. "Look, I'm sorry about earlier. I shouldn't have used my conjuring on you in that way."

He shrugged a single shoulder. "It isn't like I left you much choice to do otherwise. I cornered you."

"You were trying to help me see reason. Everything you said was correct. I just didn't want to hear it."

Erik stepped out of the moonlight, closing the space between us. Raising his hand, the backs of his fingers grazed my cheek. Warmth spread through me. My eyes involuntarily slid shut, face leaning towards the comforting touch. "You have been through so much. Still going through so much. Anyone in such a position would find it difficult."

I moved out of his touch. Though his sentiment was kind, it did not help. "I am the Leader Superior. I do not have the luxury of letting struggles affect my judgment."

He shook his head. "You're-"

I held up my hand as if to stop his words while interrupting. "No. I do not wish to discuss me. Not tonight."

A silence spilled between us, and I wondered whether he would ignore my request.

He didn't.

"Do you wish to talk about anything else?" The Lysian King asked, his voice gentle.

"Actually, yes." I hesitated, wondering what he would make of what I was about to share with him. "When I saw the Spirit at my ascension, it told me that I would meet a conjuror of illumination who would be helpful to me. At the time, I thought the Spirit meant you. Illumination meaning a conjuror of fire, something to see by. But now, I think it may mean a conjuror who can explain and understand. Someone who can illuminate."

His head tilted in thought. "You think it could be Iver?"

"I have never seen or heard of anyone having his gifts before."

His gaze cooled. "I'd have to say that I agree. He is certainly unique."

My attention turned to the window, and I made my way across the room towards it. "I suppose in the end, it doesn't truly matter. We would benefit from his help either way. Whether he is the one the Spirit meant or not."

Dark eyes followed my movement. "That is certainly true."

I stared out at the tree line beyond the city wall. Even in the night, I never feared what was out there. All of it was home. However, now, I didn't even trust all the people within the city's walls. My false sense of safety crumbled, showing the illusion I lived in. A mirage that evaporated the moment Clause entered my life.

"You are remarkable, you know that?" Erik said with such certainty that it stilled my thoughts. His using such a word to describe me sent warmth through me.

My lips parted, and a trembling breath slipped past them before I replied, "I am ordinary. I just find myself in complicated situations." I kept my attention on the forest beyond.

He walked soundlessly through the room until standing behind me. I caught a glimpse of those intense blue eyes in the faint reflection of him in the window's glass. Even with the space between us, my skin heated with his proximity.

"You are anything but ordinary." His voice sent another shiver down my spine. Eyes remained fixed on me through the glass. He took another step, entering my space without actually touching me. "Do you wish for me to leave?" His voice was deceptively soft.

I stared at him in the reflection, captured by all of him, unable to look away. My heart hammered against my ribs. "I'd rather you stay."

When those words left my lips, thick tension connected us, and the Lysian king standing behind me moved even closer.

My body burned when his hand reached for my hip just before he stepped into me. His breath tickled my neck when he craned his to look over at me.

I turned my head, finding that heavy stare. I could lose myself in those eyes for eternity and would never tire of exploring. The corners of his mouth curved as if he knew the effect he was having on me. My gaze dropped to his lips, which he took as an invitation.

He closed more of the space until his mouth met mine. Slowly, I lost myself in him, with the way his arms tightened around me, the way his tongue collided with mine. He tasted divine.

I wished him to never let go. To stay trapped in that moment, consumed by him.

Our lips parted only for him to leave tender kisses running down my jaw and over my neck. Fire addictively burned through my skin wherever he touched. Devouring me. The knot in my stomach began melting away until I felt lighter. As if his touch pulled the toxins from my mind.

A small moan escaped from me while he kissed my throat, igniting the skin there.

He began speaking in between kisses, and it did something to me. "Would you...prefer...I be... gentle... or rough?"

Never had anyone asked me what I wanted before. The question stunned me speechless.

The only thing I recognized was my need for him as it burned through me, desperation clawing within me.

Teeth scraped against the column of my throat, followed by a tongue, and then his mouth. I tilted my head, giving him unrestricted access. "Ariana. Tell me." He pressed the words into my skin. "What you prefer."

One of Erik's hands moved up my side, lazily making its way over the swell of my breast before taking hold of my throat. His touch was firm yet gentle as his fingers forced me to turn my face towards him. His mouth found mine once more, and with every breath, he seemed to deepen the kiss as if there was no limit to the depth.

Gentle or rough? I enjoyed both. However, I needed one over the other. I needed my mind thoroughly silenced.

Even with his firm hold, he allowed me to pull away slightly, breaking the kiss.

Hungry eyes found mine, and his entire stance tightened as though it was a struggle to refrain from closing that tiny bit of space where our breaths mingled.

"I can't think as clearly when you are rough," I said, letting him know what I needed. For my mind to be wiped clean.

Erik's lip curved at the side, and his eyes took on a dark gleam. His hold on me tightened, growing a commanding edge. The hand at my throat immobilized me as he craned his neck, kissing me once more, pressing a smile into my mouth as I softly moaned into his.

He released my throat, hand traveling to my shoulder. The space around us eclipsed as if the moon's light could no longer cut through the tension connecting the two of us. Nothing existed but me and him. And that was enough.

I was forced to break the kiss when he pushed me forward. Not expecting it, my cheek nearly met with the cold glass in front of me, my hands gripping the windowsill for support.

Erik grunted in approval as his fingers dug into my hips, possessive and unyielding. His grip was bruising, a claim against my skin. He moved behind me, freeing the length of him before his hand slipped beneath my robe and between my legs. A sharp gasp left my lips as he thrust a finger into me without warning—one, then two, stretching me with ruthless intent. My body clenched around the intrusion, heat surging through my veins at the sheer dominance in his touch.

His other hand found my breast, kneading roughly as he pulled me back against his chest. My head lolled against him, breath hitching, lost in the firestorm of sensation. But he did not take his time. He did not grant me the luxury of easing into his hunger.

Without warning, he bent me forward, hiking my robe and nightgown up in one swift motion.

A strangled cry tore from my throat as he drove into me, burying himself in a single, unforgiving thrust. The stretch was overwhelming, almost too much, yet I craved it, needed it. Erik set a brutal rhythm, his hips slamming into mine, filling me again and again.

His hand slid up my back, wrapping around my throat as he wrenched me upright, forcing my spine to arch against him. The pressure of his grip, the relentless way he took me, sent my mind spiraling. Pain and pleasure tangled like twin flames, consuming me from within, reducing me to nothing but raw sensation. Every nerve burned, every flicker of pain only sharpening the pleasure.

Nothing existed except for me and the Lysian King, whose mercy I was at.

Pressing my hands into the cool glass in front of me for support, I tried to gulp down breaths between the wild sounds torn from me.

"You are mine," Erik growled in my ear.

I moaned in response.

His hand tightened on my hip, his other at my throat. "Say it." He demanded and released his hold enough so I could respond. Except I couldn't. The pressure inside of me, the feel of him entering me over and over, I could not formulate words.

He growled and entirely pulled out of me. *No.* The fire inside of me burned for release. Flame licking my nerve endings, raging for the loss of the feel of him between my legs. The hand at my throat pulled me till my back fell flush against his chest. His other hand moved lazily over me in desperately teasing, torturous strokes.

"Say it." He commanded, breath hot against the shell of my ear.

"Erik," I whined, *trembling* in his hold.

"Mmmh, I can't say I don't enjoy the sound of that." I was rewarded with a finger entering me, moving in and out, while his thumb traced precise patterns over me. My legs nearly gave out. "But. It is not what I asked." His voice was deliciously coarse. He removed his hand and pushed himself into me again. Slowly. So slowly.

The groan that escaped him nearly had me coming apart.

How? How did he have such control?

"Say it." He growled, as if angry that it was taking so long.

"I-" A moan cut me off as it ripped through me with the way he slowly pulled out and slammed into me.

A dark chuckle. "You what?"

"I- I am-" Another yell burst out as he did it *again*. *Bastard*.

"You are what, Ariana?" His voice gained a dangerous edge, and it had me dying with need.

"Yours." I nearly growled myself, desperate for him to stop this torture. He brought me to the edge and toyed with me there. "I am yours," I finally managed.

"You are mine," he replied in agreement before finally giving me exactly what I had asked for.

9

ERIK

Ariana lay beside me, her head on my chest, arm draped over me. Sunlight seeping through the window touched her hair, giving it a golden glow around the edges. She looked ethereal. The most beautiful woman I ever had the privilege of knowing, of touching, of sharing time with.

My fingers moved idly over her skin, grazing her back and shoulder. She looked so serene, untouched by worries, her face relaxed. It would all be stolen as soon as her eyes opened to start this dreadful day.

She was leaving in a few hours.

The past several days blew by so quickly. Ariana improved in her training the entire time. However, she could never complete the course. Trying to subdue me without letting me touch her skin was nearly impossible. I didn't need to physically take her down, for one touch meant I won, and she then started the whole thing over.

"I can feel you staring at me," Ariana mumbled, keeping her eyes closed.

My hand pauses over her shoulder at the sound of her voice before continuing its journey over her skin once more. "Can you blame me?"

"You know what I look like." She opened a single eye, finding me while keeping her cheek pressed to my chest. What I would have done to keep us in the moment longer.

"And you know what a sunset looks like. Doesn't mean you don't take the time to marvel at its beauty whenever you can." I comment, earning a snort from her.

"What time is it?" She asked.

"You have about an hour until you need to get up and get ready to go."

A shudder moved through her, and she rolled over, pulling sheets to cover up with.

She brought her hands to her face and kept them there. Though she put on a brave face, I knew fear circled her like a hungry wild cat stalking its prey. It was all too much for one person to bear. Even though she had the help of Lysians, she tried to shoulder as much of the burden on her own. The girl did not even have time to fully mourn the loss of her friend because of the Siddhe looming over her.

"What are you thinking?" I asked, hoping she would let me in.

Her hands fell away from her face, and she turned to me. Her gaze traveled over my chest and stomach before returning to my eyes. "Just about how delicious you look." She offered a smile that did not quite make it to her eyes.

My arm snaked around her, and I tugged her close, resting my chin on her head as she curled into me. "You will get through this and return to your people, to me."

She took a deep breath. "I'm scared." Her words were hardly a whisper.

"You would be crazy not to be. But, you are one of the bravest and most powerful people I know. If anyone can get through this, then it is you." I said the words for her as much as for myself. They needed to be true.

"What if- What if I can't find a way out of there? I will do my best to learn as much I can of the Siddhe and their lands. I know I will help win this looming war because of this decision. But if I cannot sneak away before the war breaks out–"

"I will find you," I said.

She shifted, looking up at me, and began shaking her head. "No. I mean to say that if I am trapped, then so be it. Countless lives shouldn't be risked for one person."

My hand found her cheek. "I will come for you," I said again. She began trying to shake her head once more, but my hand stilled her. "Ariana, I won't stop searching until I find you. I will find you and bring you back."

Her eyes swirled with so much emotion, a small glimpse into what was going on in that head of hers. Even as she lay in my arms, she offered me a peek into the pain experienced by her, but no more. Her gut reaction had always been to hide those things from others. To put up a strong front.

Desperation to protect her ate at me. It ripped into my heart, leaving a bloody mess I could hardly conceal. Letting her go to do this was one of the hardest things I ever did.

And now, with her staring at me with those large eyes. They crippled me.

My lips found hers.

In her kiss, I tasted the same desperation I felt. The two of us hopelessly tried to forget the weight of the world pressing on us. Instead, we sought to lose ourselves in each other. A fleeting bliss encased us in a warm cocoon of safety and we thoroughly enjoyed those moments.

In each other, we found an escape and safety.

In her, I found my world.

WE STOOD at the back gate of the Bavadrin city. One hardly ever used, making it the perfect place for Ariana to leave unnoticed by most. She had already briefly addressed her people, letting them know she would be gone for a while and that Willis would lead in her absence. When some pressed for more information, she remained vague on her answers.

Ariana patted her horse, the one I had given her what felt like so long ago. Rain was packed with supplies and looked eager to get going on a trip. Two guards flanked the horse, on their own mounts. They were going to accompany Ariana to the border, after which she would continue alone with the wolf, Shay.

"Iver is going to be actively involved in our plans moving forward," Ariana said to her small parting party.

"Why is the little brother of the King now joining us? Can't Erik just fill his Lysians in?" Kiora asked.

"You know of me?" Iver smirked, cocking a brow.

"I know you're trouble." She leveled her gaze at him.

"He is a conjuror, a strong one. We will need his help." Ariana informed them.

"Perhaps we should have had a private meeting before deciding such things?" Edda asked.

Ariana's green eyes snapped to the Seer. "No. I want this to be as transparent as possible. We need each other."

Edda's lips thinned. "Perhaps we do. But we are still separate races and people. It is not abnormal to have some level of division."

"I disagree." She then turned to Willis. "However, regardless, what happens after I leave will largely be in your hands."

"I will follow your example," Willis stated. "The Lysians will have a part in planning how to get you and the others trapped by the Siddhe back."

It pleased me to hear not all Bavadrins were so adamantly against this union.

Ariana viewed us, gaze moving among our faces. "When I saw the Spirit at my ascension, I was told that a conjuror of illumination would help me. I think that person might be Iver."

"What?" Iver glanced at her, eyes rounded in a look of surprise.

"The Spirit told me that the conjuror of illumination would be of help. I thought it meant Erik at first, but now, I think it may be you."

Iver turned to Edda. "I definitely need to try that magical juice."

I sighed. "Why can you not stay on topic?"

My brother smirked. "I am. That magic juice helped Ariana see the Spirit. Maybe we all should drink some and see what happens."

Edda snorted. "That's not how it works, little one." Her use of the term *little one*, when Iver towered over her was nearly comical. Though she certainly had all of us beat in age.

"You're just old and grumpy," Iver mumbled at her with a fake pout before turning to Ariana. When he viewed the Leader Superior of the Bavadrins, the look on his face lost all of its mischievousness. "I will do what I can to help you and both of our homes."

Ariana moved towards him. "Thank you." She then hugged him.

Surprise touched Iver's features before he draped a single arm around her. "You are stronger than you know," he said to her by way of farewell.

Ariana stepped back, and her gaze landed on Willis. She closed the distance between them and hugged him. "Good luck with everything."

"We will be ready. If anything ever happens, and you need us to get you out of there, tell Shay. We will prepare for war until that moment."

She nodded before moving on to the next person, Edda. Ariana hugged the old woman without hesitations. "Stay safe," she said to her.

Edda scoffed as if the words were unnecessary. "Try to not push Clause too much for answers. He can have a short temper." She gave her a bit of parting advice. "And, remember who you are, where you come from." The last bit was said with an air of warning. It sent a chill down my spine.

"I'll be sure to keep that in mind." Ariana moved to step away, but Edda grabbed onto her arm, halting her.

"You will return to your people," Edda said to her. "I know it in my bones to be true."

Ariana released a breath. "I do not typically ask you of the future, for you never give straightforward answers. I have always waited for you to choose to share things with me. And yet, I find myself overwhelmed with the desire to ask you this. If you have seen my return, can you tell me whether we will win against the Siddhe?"

Edda frowned, her hand remaining on Ariana's forearm. "That is unclear."

She swallowed, hesitating. "What about me? Will I even recognize myself after this is over?"

Edda's response was a second embrace. "I have loved you for your entire life. And I will love you until the day I die." Not an encouraging answer. What was the Seer getting at? What did she know?

Ariana visibly shuddered, her eyes shutting, yet a single tear still managed to slip through. "I have always loved you too," she whispered, her voice breaking.

When Edda released her that time, she did not stop Ariana from finally moving away.

The next goodbye was with Kiora. The Sparrow looked like she was both angry yet on the verge of tears. They embraced. "May the Spirit give you strength and shelter from the storm you are about to enter," Kiora said.

"I'll miss you," Ariana whispered to her before turning to Kole.

As she approached, Kole stiffened as though uncertain about how to take the hug that would be thrown his way. Ariana tried to wrap her arms around his massive body, and a heartbeat later, he wrapped his around her in return. "I have no doubt you will have that Siddhe King wrapped around your finger just like you had us," Kole grumbled to her.

Ariana pulled away from him, a look of surprise on her face. "And here I thought no one could ever get one over on you and your King."

Kole chortled. "Only you."

Ariana's eyes softened, lips wanting to tug into a small smile. "Thanks." She then looked to me.

As soon as she stepped towards me, my arms accepted her. Warmth accompanied the feel of her body. I welcomed the scent of her, breathing her in.

My lips found hers, and she did not shy away from the kiss. Instead, she rose onto her toes and deepened it. Her fingers tangled in my hair, keeping me close as our mouths moved in sync.

It was as if the world evaporated. Briefly, it was just the two of us sharing a moment outside. Until the weight of everything tinged everything with heartache.

Ariana broke the kiss first, but she did not move away. Instead, her eyes remained shut while she inhaled deeply, as if trying to memorize my scent too. And when her eyes finally slid open, her gaze drifted over my face as if making an effort to commit it to memory.

"I'll see you soon," I said to her, my voice like gravel.

Her eyes swirled with something I couldn't quite place. It was like pain and hope melded into something entirely different.

"You will," she said firmly.

I kissed her once more, desperate to prolong the moment. Overcome with the desire to not let her slip through my fingers.

And yet, slip away she did, into the home of a murderous crazed King.

I swore to the Spirit then and there that I would do whatever was necessary to bring Ariana safely home. To bring her back to me.

10

ARIANA

A couple days of travel did not seem long when the thing waiting for me at the end was a monster. I felt *him* in the room just beyond the threshold of his mountain castle.

Sorin of the Duns Clan stood at my side, lingering at the entry with me. Like before, he came to the border to escort me through the Siddhe land. However, this time I was alone, apart from Willis's wolf. She was my tether to everything I knew and loved.

Sorin's gaze shifted to me while I stared at the massive open door. An inviting warmth seeped out of the castle, yet it offered no oasis. Instead, it threatened to smother me, taking my freedom. For on the other side stood my enemy.

The air around Clause remained as stagnant as I remembered the last time I had the displeasure of interacting with him. Its dark control seeped out of him, making its way towards me before I even saw him. Suffocating.

My entire body stiffened, and I could not bring myself to

cross that threshold into his domain. Desperation clawed at my chest, wanting nothing more than the Siddhe King dead at my feet, or at least to have a healthy distance between us. The pressure of his presence intensified, and I knew that the space between us shrank even though I did not move.

Clause eventually came into view. His silver-white hair combed back, not a single piece out of place. He stood dressed in black from head to toe, immaculate and form-fitting. Gray, cold eyes met with mine and held. There is no warmth there, only a simmering edge, a danger. Yet I refused to back away. Instead, I squared my shoulders, keeping my head up.

"It's so good to see you again, Ariana," he said with a curve of his lips. The smile was void of any surprise. As if he always knew I would come to him. His gaze then dropped to the wolf at my side. "And you brought a friend."

I forced out a steady breath. "Since I could not bring a Bavadrin, I figured perhaps an animal. A companion from home." I tried to force my voice to come off warmer than I felt. Attempting to sound as though I desired his favor in this small matter. "It would mean a lot to me if you were to allow her to stay with me."

"Would it now?" That heavy gaze returned to me. The darkness in his eyes sparkled, clearly enjoying that he harbored the power when I asked something of him. That I allowed him to grant me something, to show me some type of favor.

I did what I could to keep from clenching my teeth. "Her name is Shay, and I have known her since she was just a pup. As long as she is allowed out, she can hunt for herself," I added trying to clarify that she wouldn't be a burden.

The King's head tilted. "If having a pet is what you desire, then I see no issue with it."

"Thank you." I dipped my head in thanks. The action caused my jaw to tighten.

"Tell me, are you hungry?"

I looked back up at him. "Not quite." Never would I have an appetite around him. Nausea coiled in my stomach like a snake, tightening around the pain I held within.

"Well then, we shall go explore a bit. I can briefly show you around." He held out his arm for me to take. An invitation to further enter his space and that dreadfully stagnant air surrounding him.

"Mind if Shay joins?" I inclined my head towards the wolf.

He shrugged. "Not at all."

Trying not to grit my teeth, I finally crossed the threshold into his home. Shay remained at my side as the door closed behind us. I slid my hand around Clause's arm, and he brought it closer to his body, pulling me towards him. The Siddhe King became a living shackle attached to me.

My skin crawled at his touch, revulsion twisting my stomach, threatening to have me vomit. And if that happened, I doubted I would turn in any direction other than his. That thought alone brought me a tiny speck of pleasure.

Soren trailed us silently, keeping a respectable distance, though never straying.

"You will be free to explore my home and my city. I will make myself available to you whenever you desire. The only thing I require is for you to break your fast with me in the mornings and to accompany me to dinner every evening." He informed me as we walked at a leisurely pace.

We moved through the expansive hallways, and I could not even focus on the artistry of the walls, ceiling, and floors. Not when Clause's touch nearly had me stumbling over myself. His free hand slid over mine while I held onto his arm. His thumb found my wrist and pressed into it.

"Why does your heart race so?" He turned towards me as we strode down the hall. "There is no need to fear me. You will not be harmed here."

I released a breath. "It is the possibility of *my* control slipping that I fear." I gave him a partial truth. A healthy dose of dread indeed ran through me when it came to the Siddhe King, but I refused to announce that.

"You do not have good control of your conjuring?" He inquired, not quite grasping precisely what I meant.

"No. I fear that my sanity may slip, and I may find myself with my hands around your neck. If my conjuring cannot take your breath, I would find another way to do it. But you can see how with your *gifts,* touching you like that would not be suitable." We would soon learn just how gracious a King he was, whether he was truthful when stating that I had nothing to fear. My comment tested boundaries. It also served to remind him that I did not welcome his touch or his control.

A smile curled his lips once more, not at all offended. His feet stilled, halting me beside him. "You harbor such passions for me."

Disgusted, I released his arm, pulling my hand free. He allowed it, and suddenly I could finally gain a bit of space between us.

"You killed my best friend," I hissed between clenched teeth. I never planned to bring it up, at least not so soon. But life seemed to have other plans.

His smile faltered then. "You are upset that I freed you from someone who was holding you back?"

Heat burned through my chest at his unapologetic reply. At the indifference in the way Clause spoke of him. "You do not get to make that decision. Landin never held me back. He helped me in every aspect of my life."

Clause shook his head as though he didn't believe me. "No. Your love has blinded you, shadowed what that man was to you. He did not help you up. He held you down."

My body stiffened. "You do not get to make that decision."

"That boy made his own decisions, which landed him with consequences. I will not be threatened." Gray eyes held mine, unwavering.

"Didn't I just threaten you?" I bit out.

He took a deliberate step towards me and paused. "You wish for me to punish you?" The slight upward pull of his lips did nothing to soften the edge of his voice.

I think I stopped breathing.

For whatever reason, the Siddhe King found interest in me. Even though I hated having his eye, the use of holding it shouldn't be something overlooked. I needed to find the Siddhe's weaknesses, Clause's weaknesses, if we were ever going to have hope of freeing the stolen Bavadrins and Lysians. I needed to use him, not push him away, not nudge him towards forcing his hand against me.

Clause reached out, fingertips brushing a strand of my hair. "Your words may threaten, but they will soften with time when you finally see that I am not your enemy here. You have yet to stand against me physically, but I suppose a warning would serve you well. If you ever draw a weapon against me, you will regret it. I did not bring you here to hurt you, Ariana. I wish for us to learn from one another."

Learn from one another? He came off as though he believed himself to be the Spirit's gift to the world. As though there was nothing left for him to possibly learn.

"What can someone like you hope to learn from me?" I

asked, for I did not believe he truly expected anything like that. Instead, they were words used to likely try and appease me. But I wouldn't be so easily controlled or manipulated.

Clause withdrew his hand, hiding it within his pocket. And suddenly, my lungs moved more freely, drawing breath.

"I think there is quite a lot for the both of us to learn. As for your friend, I apologize if the consequences of his actions hurt you. That was not my intent." He viewed me with a casualness that made the hairs on the back of my neck stand. "I hope that we can be friends."

My breath nearly left me. Friends? The King was truly mad. "I would caution you of your desires. For it appears my friends have a risk of winding up dead." My words were meant as another threat, though he simply found amusement in them.

He chuckled. "You have a fearlessly sharp mind."

"Should I not speak freely?"

"No. By all means, continue. I love hearing what you are thinking. It has been too long since I have had access to such wonderfully unfiltered thoughts." He then inclined his head towards the hall. "Shall we continue?" He did not try to retake my arm. Instead, he kept his hands in his pockets.

That minor act caused the tension in my shoulders to relax a bit.

We made our way through more of the building before stepping out onto a massive balcony.

The view stole my breath from me.

Mountains surrounded the city. Sharp, gray, snow-covered peaks glistened in the sunlight. In the center of it stood short stone buildings. Some looked like shops, others homes. Dirt roads curved around the city, filled with people, young and old, who made their way through the space. Off to the side was a forest and what looked like possible farmland. All of it, nestled within the mountain range, out of sight from the rest of the world.

I leaned against the balcony railing as if the view pulled me towards it. The entire thing looked magical. It even felt enchanted.

"This is the capital of the Siddhe territory," Clause stated, though his gaze remained fastened to me as if gauging my reactions.

"It's remarkable. Do people live outside of these mountains too?" I asked, turning to the King.

"Some. But you will remain within these mountain walls while you are here, where it is safe." His tone and face gave nothing away. Though my interest spiked.

"Is it not safe past the walls?"

His attention finally left me, turning towards the mountains surrounding us. "They are not places for someone like you."

"Someone like me?"

"Gifted."

Why? It was clear he did not wish to dive into the topic, so I pocketed it for the time being. I had more than enough to start with when collecting information. My attention drifted back over the city below. "May I freely explore down there?"

"Of course." He turned to me once more. His gaze drifted over my face while I kept my focus on the people far below. "This city is my home, and my home is yours."

"Great. Can I go now?" I turned to him.

It looked as though he suppressed a smile. Though why I hadn't the slightest. "Do you prefer me or Soren accompany you? Or you wish to go on your own?"

Ideally, on my own, however, that would come later.

"I'll take Soren," I stated, figuring having a guide would prove helpful. My gaze slid to the Dunes Clan member standing a few meters behind us. His eyes met with mine but showed nothing.

"I look forward to hearing about your exploration at dinner," Clause said, reminding me of his expectation to share meals. Though I could explore, I remained chained to him.

"Can hardly wait." I didn't even try to sound pleased as I pushed off the railing and walked towards Soren, leaving the King on his balcony with his pretty view.

Soren turned, falling in step with me. Together, we moved down the hall. I didn't slow until the Siddhe King was finally out of sight. Only then did I turn to Soren. "I'll need you to show me the way out of this castle. I have no idea where I am going."

His response was a grunt, but he picked up his pace, staying a step ahead and leading me into the city.

11

ARIANA

Soren and I weaved through the streets for hours. Nothing looked quite the same. Houses made of stone lined every road, yet none were identical, just like the people. A vast majority harbored the pointed ears of the Siddhe nationality. However, there were others, some with the half-points of crossbreeds. Some with the sharp teeth of the Lysians and some with the dull teeth and ears of the Bavadrins.

"Do all the races get along?" I asked Soren under my breath after catching a glimpse of children playing with a ball. They kicked it around a small courtyard. Dirt caked their skin and stained their clothing, clearly marking them as coming from less fortunate families. However, their smiles appeared genuine. Their laughter and spirit spread through the surrounding streets, bringing a certain charm to the area. But most remarkably, all races made up the group of children.

"They do," Soren stated, glancing at the kids before turning back to the street. "Here, we do not separate based on race."

The way he said it was as if an underlying meaning was hidden amongst the words.

"And how are you separated?"

"We keep apart the gifted from those without conjuring abilities."

I turned to him. "So, everyone within these mountain walls..." I couldn't finish the sentence, for it scared me.

"Is a conjuror," he confirmed.

So many. Thousands of people, all conjurors, all under the Siddhe King's command.

As we weaved through the streets, we eventually made it to where the roads and buildings ended and trees began. A forest took up a chunk of the valley surrounded by mountains. Dark, green, and lush, it breathed a sense of freedom into the city perimeter. Offering an escape, even while within the mountain-made walls.

Shay released a soft whine, looking from the forest at me. Her tail rhythmically swayed side to side.

"Is it safe in there?" I asked.

Soren glanced at Shay before turning to me. "Your wolf will be fine."

I looked at Shay's wide, awaiting eyes. "Would you be able to find your way back to me?"

She released a soft snort and dipped her head.

"Then you may go."

The wolf shot forward, rushing into the woods.

"I take it I can also explore if I ever felt the desire?" I asked, shifting my attention to Soren.

He folded his arms across his chest, skin marred by intricate cuts from blades. His gaze held mine, though I could not read him. "You too can explore whenever you would like. But I would advise you not to go alone or risk getting lost. The forest is quite extensive. And if you wish to go on your own hoping to find a secret way into this city, then allow me to save you the trouble and tell you that you will not find one."

My gaze narrowed. "What makes you think I would want to find a way into the city and not out of it?"

Soren's dark eyes scanned my face. "The Siddhe King is many things, one of them being a man of his word. If you wished to leave, he would let you."

A low laugh slipped through my lips, tinged with anything but happiness. "Yeah, with the promise of war if I was to do so."

"Still, the choice is yours."

"And what kind of choice did you make that led you to stand at his side?"

Soren's jaw clenched. He offered no answer. Instead, he tilted his head to the side. "We should continue. So that we get you back in time for dinner with the King."

I turned and began walking in the direction he gestured towards, dropping the subject for now. He clearly harbored no fondness for me, and that was something I needed to work on if I ever wanted to get answers from him.

We were nearly back to the main castle when a long rectangular-looking compound grabbed my attention. The building itself was nothing interesting, but the surrounding people caught my eye. There were several of them, spanning from old to young age, made up of all the various races. An elderly Lysian looking man hopped on one foot, supported by a younger Siddhe under one arm and a Bavadrin under the other. None of them noted me while I stood in the street, watching as they helped the injured man. They disappeared into the building, leaving the front door wide open.

"What's in there?" I asked.

"It is a building that houses some servants."

I turned to him. "May I have a look?"

Soren shrugged. "Yes, though I doubt there will be much to look at," he mumbled, following me as I crossed the street.

I passed over the threshold and paused, taking everything in. The compound was essentially a single room with a couple dozen beds throughout the space. My eye drew to the two boys lowering the older man onto one bed.

Someone sitting in one of the other beds, leaning against the wall, coughed, gaze settled on me. Suddenly, the entire room froze. Noticing my presence, all eyes turned to me.

"Sorry, I don't mean to interrupt," I said, uncertain of the best way to introduce myself.

"You lost, highborn?" The one leaning against the wall asked. Piercing green eyes cut into me with thick judgment behind them. His ears came to slight points, and his mouth was void of elongated canines. Mixed blood likely ran through his veins, part Siddhe and part Bavadrin.

"Watch your mouth." Soren stepped up beside me. "She is a guest of your King. You will show her your respect."

The man looked to the Dunes Clan leader, completely unbothered as he whistled lowly. "A guest with Soren as her guide?" His gaze cut to me. "Interesting."

I glanced around the room. It was filthy. Tracked in dirt left a film on the wooden floors, cobwebs dusted the corners and ceilings, and the beds looked like no one ever washed the sheets.

"You all live here?" I asked.

"These beds aren't here for decoration." The man who had addressed me already stated flippantly.

Soren tensed, attention flickering to me as though suddenly waiting to follow my lead. He looked poised to strike if I requested. Did he expect me to attack a man for not being friendly?

"It's okay," I said under my breath, and Soren's muscles loosened.

I turned to the older Lysian sitting on one of the beds. The middle of the mattress sank under his weight. Such a bed offered no comfort, used as only a barrier to separate a body from the floor. The two younger boys who had helped him moved towards the back, each took to their own mattresses.

"I saw you limping outside," I began, taking a step deeper into the room.

The old man laughed lowly, a hand scratching the back of his gray wiry head of hair. "Ah, yes. I am afraid I irritated an old injury. I assure you, I am still up to perform my tasks." His gaze slid to Soren's briefly before returning to me. Caution tinged his blue eyes, throat bobbing as he swallowed. Was he afraid?

"Mind if I see your foot?" I took another step towards him.

He looked at his leg, a brief look of mortification passing over his features. "I uh... It's really alright. I assure you." He moved his foot onto his thigh and gripped it roughly, as if to show that it was not bad. However, I caught the slight jerk when pain shot through him at the touch.

I stepped even closer to him. "Maybe I can help you," I offered.

His gray bushy brows pulled together. "Are you a conjuring healer?"

I shook my head no. "Not the conjuring kind, but I know other ways to help. Herbs, ointments, using the gifts of the natural world."

"Maybe you should let her help, Gorm," one of the younger boys said. Concern shined in his eyes when he looked at the elderly man.

Gorm sighed, glancing at the boy sharply before turning back to me. "Well, you now know my name. Everyone calls me Gorm. I suppose I would like to know the name of the woman I am about to assault with the view of my disgusting smelly old foot."

Rumbles of laughs simmered around the space from the boys, breaking some of the tension. Even the grumpy man with the piercing green eyes released a rough chuckle.

I smiled, closing more of the space until I stood at the side of Gorm's bed. "My name is Ariana."

He began untying his leather boot. When he looked at me, his blue gaze warmed yet remained tinged with uncertainty. "Well, Ariana. I am sorry for what you are about to experience." It took him a minute to finally remove his shoe and sock.

A hideous wound on the heel greeted me. Yellow, red, inflamed, and the surrounding skin looked hot to the touch.

"How did this happen?" I knelt beside his foot. He wasn't wrong. It smelled like rotten flesh, and yet I could not deny that being next to it was far more appealing than having dinner with his King. Revulsion twisted in my stomach at the thought of Clause.

Gorm frowned, looking over his toes at me. "I stepped on something, and it cut into my foot. I didn't realize until late that night, and now it's just been slow to heal."

He didn't even realize it? I reach out, gripping the back of his foot.

"Dear Spirit, why are you touching it?" He grumbled, yet allowed it.

I brushed my pinky nail over the underside of his foot, some distance away from the angry wound. "Could you feel that?"

Gorm's cheeks became splotched with red. "I feel a lot of

things right now, the primary thing being mortification. As for your touch, no. I didn't feel a thing."

I released his foot, turning to Soren. "Do you all have a place where I can get some medical supplies?"

"You're serious?" he asked, looking at me as though he didn't understand.

I rose to my full height. "Why wouldn't I be?"

"You're..." He didn't finish the thought as his attention instead moved over the people in the room. Soren then glanced towards the entrance behind him in thought. "We need to head back. It is almost time for your meal with the King, but perhaps after that or if you'll be tired then tomorrow."

"You're eating with the King?" One of the young boys asked, eyes large in wondrous surprise.

"Apparently," I said to him with a small smile, noticing a closed door behind him.

"What is beyond that threshold?" I asked no one in particular.

The boy turned, looking at what drew my eye. "Oh, it's just a small room with some supplies."

Soren did not oppose as I walked over, grabbing the knob. Figuring it safe, I twisted, and the door opened with a creak. It was a small room with a window and even a sink, though broken parts of beds and who knows what else filled most of the space.

"Does any of this stuff get used?" I asked, looking around, and taking a mental inventory of the clutter.

Gorm released a gravelly laugh. "It's used to store stuff. I have been here a good long while and have only seen more things added to the collection, never to be removed."

I closed the door, turning back to the elder. "After my

dinner, I will be back, and we will have your foot healing in no time."

His brows drew together. "Thank you." There was a sincerity to his voice that warmed me just as it saddened me. Had no one shown kindness or compassion to the servants if they injured themselves? If so, then I wanted to help them in the moments when I couldn't collect information to destroy their King. Perhaps I could protect them when the Siddhe kingdom came crumbling down, or perhaps they could even help me bring it down. I would free them of the shadow Clause cast over them.

With a small smile and nod, I left them to go share a meal with their King, hoping that just maybe he would allow for my time within his prison of a city to be meaningful. That with my help, he would place a noose around his own neck without even realizing it. I just needed to find a rope strong enough to withstand him to do it with.

12

ARIANA

I sat at the table in front of the Siddhe King. While his gaze often drifted towards me, mine diligently avoided him. I looked at the intricate detail of the walls, the mosaic patterns decorating them. I observed the food on my plate; the steam rising from the heat of it. When I picked up my fork, I took painstaking interest in observing the cutlery before putting it to use. My attention shifted amongst all things except for the person seated directly in front of me.

"How did you like the walk around the city?" Clause asked, leaning back in his seat after taking a bite of pheasant.

I turned to him, finally giving him the pleasure of my attention. "It is quite the city."

"Do the people look... tortured or abused?" He quirked an eyebrow, a smirk fighting to curl at his lips.

"Just because I didn't find any tortured souls yet, does not mean they are not out there," I replied, reaching for a glass of water, and taking a sip.

A slow smile warmed the King's sharp features. "You are so determined to paint me a monster."

Because you are one. I forced my jaw to unclench. "There is a building where some servants stay outside the main castle. I would like to offer them my aid in helping with injuries and ailments." We would see how *kind* he was willing to be.

Clause viewed me for a moment before responding. "Are they injured?"

"Not in a way that would prevent them from continuing to be of use," I answered carefully.

A smile pulled at the side once more. "Not even here a day, and you already are trying to protect my people from me?"

I licked my lips, drawing his eyes to them, which caused me to shift uncomfortably in my seat. "Listen. You got what you wanted. For me to be here, to learn from this experience. But, while I am here, I would like to help the people if I can. I'd like to get to know some of them."

His head tilted in thought while his gaze continued to hold mine. "You would not prefer to teach children or find a more pleasurable environment to spend your time in?"

"I prefer to work with the people I found."

His brows drew closer together. "How is this helpful?"

"What?"

"How is this helpful to you or to me? As leaders, what would serving a few *servants* do?" Those cold gray eyes held my stare, yet judgment and disdain did not color them. Instead, there was an air of wonder. As though he were truly curious about my motivations.

"You said we are to learn from one another?" I asked.

Clause nodded.

"Well, they may be just servants in your eyes. But we built our civilizations on the work of people in various positions. You remove the servants, and how many of your highborn will even know how to draw themselves a hot bath, let alone build a home? Showing the servants grace and appreciation will help inspire them to work harder and better. Ruling through fear may keep them working, but if they harbor love and respect, then you will feel it in their quality of work. They may even push themselves to do better."

"So, you think you can improve their performance?"

Did he really need me to give him a reason for my desire to help others if I wished to? "Possibly. I can at least improve their lives. But if you are worried about performance, maybe consider feeding them a little better."

"Feeding?" His eyebrows rose in surprise.

"The younger boys there looked thin." I nodded. "Giving them more sustenance may help with productivity. Especially if any of them handle harder labor activities."

"I can assure you they are getting a lot more here than they would otherwise."

I snorted at his response. "Just because something is better than something else does not make it adequate."

Clause reached for his goblet, swirling the red liquid in it. "You are free to do whatever you wish regarding the servants. And if you would like, I will see that their food rations get a boost." He took a sip of his wine.

It momentarily stunned me by how easy that seemed. Mistrust flared to life. "Why?"

He pulled the cup from his lips, head tilting. "Why?"

"Why agree so easily?" I was certain after he asked me for the point of helping them, he was going to be harder to sway.

"Because you wish for it, and it is nothing for me to allow it. If it brings you a sense of pleasure to interact with servants, I do not care to stop you. And perhaps if it improves productivity, then things should change a bit regarding their care."

I nearly wanted to say thank you, though stopped myself. He did not deserve my thanks. This was not something done due to kindness. He could see for himself the kind of condition his people lived in, that the food rations of those boys left something to be desired.

"So, what is your first lesson?" I asked, changing the subject.

"Lesson?"

"You said you would teach me to be stronger if I came here."

A smile curled at his lips. "Eager to strengthen yourself in hopes of taking me out?"

"With conjuring?" That was clearly something that would not be possible as long as conjuring could not touch him.

"With that clever mind of yours."

I nodded towards my fork. "Maybe if you teach me to use my mist in a way where I can use it to send this fork through your heart from a healthy distance."

He *laughed*. The sound rich and unbothered by the threat I threw his way.

I gritted my teeth, waiting for him to stop being so sickeningly entertained by my words.

Clause eyed my food. "Are you finished eating?"

The plate was halfway cleared off, and I had not taken a bite in a while. I ate as much as I could manage with the disgust coiling my stomach because of the company.

"Yes."

"Care to join me for a walk?" I didn't respond immediately. I didn't particularly love the idea of spending more time with him if the meal had ended and I was free to go. When I did not jump at the invitation, he continued, "If you wish to learn, I would like to start with the history of the Spirits. And there is a place I would like to show you if we have this talk." He stood from his seat, waiting for me to follow.

"You mean the Spirit?" I followed his lead, standing from my chair.

"No. I mean spirits. Two to be exact."

"Lead the way," I answered with a frown, uncertain about where this was going. He remained at my side while taking me through the vast hallways.

"Tomorrow morning, I will have a servant come by and get your measurements for a dress. You can tell her what you would like to wear for the party we will have next week to welcome your arrival." He casually told me as we made our way down a stone hall before turning onto a staircase and rising.

"A party?" I eyed him.

"I wanted to give you a week to get settled before having you attend any events."

"And if I refuse?"

"Refuse a chance of being in the same room with my generals and important people to the Siddhe King? I doubt you would want to miss out on such an opportunity." His gaze slid to me in challenge. He knew I wished to see him crumble, yet he had no concern about that possibility coming true.

I did not rise to the bait and remained silent.

He led me up higher until we found ourselves in a long hall. Window archways opened one side to the outside, the city on full display below. Torches lined the other wall, which was solid stone. A beautiful array of rich colors painted the rock with images, drawing the eye stronger than even the city and mountain views on the other side. The pictures told a story.

Clause paused at the first image. The painting was of two beings floating above thousands of people, one swathed in black, the other in white. Both of their faces remained obscured by the shadows of their hoods.

"There were always two Spirits," Clause said. "One, the Spirit of light. The one everyone thinks of and worships. It is the one that brought us the gifts we typically think of with conjuring. The various effects on elements such as mist."

Gray eyes drifted to me before turning to look at the floating figure wrapped in darkness. "The other is the Spirit of darkness. It also gifted conjuring, but a different kind. Its gifts spanned the shadow world, not something you can touch, but something still very real. Conjuring in the form of Seers, Dreamers, Telepathy, and Empathomancy came from this spirit."

Clause took a few steps to the next image, and I followed at his side. The picture portrayed the two Spirits holding blades at each other's throats. "There was a rift that formed between the two gods. The history books and sacred documents are not clear what it was. But their division was the reason the great war broke out."

The next image was of people slaughtering each other. Rich red paint coated the base, as if the earth flowed with blood. "Each Spirit tried to squeeze the other's control out. The Bavadrin's harbored the most people with the gifts of the Spirit of darkness, and they found themselves surrounded by the conjuring of the Spirit of light, the Lysian and Siddhe strongholds."

"But I conjure with mist, the gift from the Spirit of light," I said.

"One does not exclude the other."

"I am Bavadrin."

"Your people harbor both gifts, more so than any other

race," he stated and nodded for me to move further down the hall.

The image painted mothers holding their dead babies. Fathers mourning the loss of their families, children crying. "The spirit did not make the treaty. At least not alone."

I looked at him in shock, yet his attention remained on the painful image before us. "The tears and sacrifices of your people formed the treaty."

"The Bavadrins?"

"Those with the most powerful of conjuring gifts came together. They made a deal with the Spirits for protection. They laid down their lives to put a stop to everything. To protect the lands. Their sacrifice was so profound that the spirits stopped their feud and agreed to a truce."

"They killed themselves?" I looked at him in shock.

Gray eyes flickered in my direction. "No. They did not simply take their lives. They sacrificed themselves. To protect the unborn, to protect the lands from more death. To protect all people of our world."

I shook my head, looking at the images lit by flickering flames before me. "Why is this story not told?"

"The Spirit of the light always searched to be seen in a positive view. It controlled the narrative. And the Spirit of the darkness simply stepped back, heartbroken by the pain brought on by their decisions. It allowed itself to disappear from most of the history told in our lands. However, the sacrifices drew together the spell and the so-called curse which would protect the lands for generations remained."

I turned to him once more. "When I ascended, I saw a Spirit. It wore dark robes."

"It was a Spirit of darkness." He answered my question without my having to fully ask it.

"Why not the one of light?"

"The Spirit of light set loose its narrative for history and then left a long time ago. Darkness still lingers, call it sentimental. It also favors those who still possess its gifts. You may conjure mist, but if you saw that Spirit, then you also have a gift from the dark."

"It doesn't care that I assumed it to have been the wrong Spirit?"

Clause laughed. "Its mind is of another world. The Spirit does not care for things the way you and I may. It likely could not care less about that."

The wind picked up, tugging my hair wildly, causing the torchlight to flicker. Though it was not the breeze that sent a chill down my spine, but a thought triggered by a reminder of that time I shared with the Spirit. "When did the Siddhe cross the border for the first time?" I asked, uncertain whether he would answer.

Clause reached out, brushing my hair back over my shoulder and out of my face with the back of his fingertips. As if he wished to see me clearly.

"The day you were born," he answered.

The words of the Spirit replied in my mind then. *It was your birth that was the curse.*

"And the curse?" I asked, my heart in my throat.

His lip curved, eyes remaining unbothered. "We shall see what the meaning of it is. As you can see, the translation of history got lost, if not changed. What's saying that the Spirit of light did not want the treaty broken? That it is not a curse, but a gift that the breaker will receive?"

The way he viewed me, it was as if we both were considering what I was. One thing I certainly knew, where he was concerned, I was no gift. I was going to be his curse and his downfall. This was the one future I fully accepted.

13

ARIANA

I lay in a luxuriously enormous bed in the room provided for me. My hand absentmindedly found Shay and ran over her fur. Last night she found me just before I fell asleep, pawing at the door. It was a relief having her return without problems, my little tether to home, my little spy.

Light seeped in through the three massive windows in the room, a beam of it hitting Shay's face, causing her to squint as she observed me.

"Did you have fun exploring?" I asked, and she raised her head, allowing me access to scratch under her chin. Shay's eyes closed as she leaned her face into my hand, enjoying the moment.

In those quiet moments, I found glimmers of peace, but it never lasted. My thoughts always drifted to Erik and held, torturing me with fears of the unknown.

I will always recognize you. My heart stopped with the memory of that declaration.

I will find you and bring you back. My heart restarted.

I clung to those promises with desperation that bordered madness. Terrified of the chance that there might be a future where I never saw him again. The thought alone sent a sharp ache through my chest, a hollow pain nothing soothed.

I missed him. All of him. Not just the comfort of his arms, where I felt safest, but the way he ignited something untamable inside me. I missed his voice, the low growl that rumbled in his chest when he was angered or provoked. I even missed his insufferable need for control. The very thing I loved to defy.

And now, without him, I was adrift in the silence, haunted by the echoes of his touch, his voice—and what we still might be. If only given the chance.

Shay's attention shifted abruptly, looking at the door to my room. In an instant, she jumped from the bed, her ears perked and eyes trained. Startled, I stood, looking toward the door just moments before a knock sounded against the wood. Quickly grabbing a robe, I made my way towards the second knock.

I opened the door and found a petite girl with short curly hair and large brown eyes standing on the other side, a tape measure in her hand.

She quickly dipped her head before turning to me once more with an enormous smile on her face. "Hi, I hope I didn't wake you. I'm here to get some measurements. But I can come back later if that would be better?"

Her teeth were not sharp, neither were her ears. Bavadrin?

"No. Now is fine," I said, moving aside to allow her entrance.

She stepped inside without hesitation, even as she glanced at Shay. "Cool wolf!" The girl bent down, holding out her hand for Shay to examine before running it along the wolf's neck.

"You are not afraid?" I asked, surprised by her lack of caution.

"If she was going to harm me, then a magnificent creature

like this one would be something to fear. But the wolf is not giving off any signs that she wants to hurt me." The girl reached out then, brushing her fingers over Shay's cheek. "You're a sweet little alpha, aren't you?"

My body tensed. "How do you know she is an alpha?"

Brown eyes flickered to me, and Shay simply tilted her head while still viewing the stranger.

"The wolf is giving off the emotional signature of an alpha," she answered before rising to her feet. "And you are strangely suddenly giving off a nervous energy."

"Excuse me?" I asked through clenched teeth. Tension shot through me.

This girl is a threat.

Her mouth opened to respond before snapping shut. She held up her hands. "Oh no, you're upset. I am so sorry! I know better than to always read emotions, but I was just so curious about you and couldn't help myself. I'll do better, never again. Not without permission." Suddenly she was the one nervous, shifting from one foot to the other. She stilled, only to bow. Deeply. Casting her eyes to the floor, and holding there even as she said, "Please don't tell Clause."

"What are you?" I asked. One sharp glance at Shay and the wolf moved to stand at my side.

"I can read emotions. It's part of my conjuring. I can also kind of influence emotions, but that can be a bit more tricky... I promise to try to not look into your feelings uninvited again. Sometimes it sort of just happens." The girl was nearly rambling. Still bent at the waste and staring the ground.

"Stand up." I waited for her to right herself before asking, "What's your name?"

"Olive." She lowered her gaze to the floor in submission, waiting for direction. The girl seemed nice, though was that really who she was or a mask she wore? Her gift could certainly be dangerous if we stood on opposite sides.

"It's fine, Olive. You just startled me, and I am afraid I have been a bit on edge since arriving. Much of everything here is new to me. I'm also not used to being around so many who conjure and are so open about their gifts." I walked to the window and further pushed the drapes out of the way to lighten the space more. "Is this an okay area for the measurements?" I asked, pointing to a well-lit open spot in the room.

"It's perfect." The girl came to me, unraveled her tape measure, and got to work moving around me. Her steps were airy and light, her smile warm. She seemed pleased with having something to focus on.

"If you don't mind me asking, where were you born?" I hoped the question sounded casual enough.

"I was born here. The Siddhe lands are my home. But I suppose that is not what you are searching for." She paused, her gaze meeting mine. "My parents are Bavadrin, born and raised in your land." She then turned back to her work.

Heat ran through me. I drew in a deep breath, willing to keep my emotions as neutral as possible. "How did they wind up here?"

"How does anyone wind up here?" She mumbled before saying, "It's not important."

My jaw clenched. "It is to me."

The girl glanced over her shoulder at Shay, who sat in the center of the room watching us. "My parents don't talk about it." She turned back to me. "It's best not to ask certain questions." It sounded a lot like a warning.

"What happens if I ask those questions, anyway?"

Her brown eyes held mine for a moment, as if deliberating

how to answer. "To you? Perhaps nothing. To someone like me, nothing good."

"Are you afraid of Clause?"

She snorted softly. "Is anyone ever not afraid of a King?"

"My people do not fear me," I said.

Olive's lips curved into a smile. "Yes, they do. All fear leaders, even the kind ones. They may not fear you unjustly harming them, but they will then fear disappointing you. Either way, fear is fear. Trust me, I know how people feel." She stood, stepping away from me. "All done. Now, regarding a dress, any likes, or dislikes?"

"Anything but black," I answered with a shrug.

Olive arched a brow. "You don't wish to match the King?"

"Considering I don't even really want to be here... No."

Her face lit up. "You really want to give me creative control, minus a single color?"

"Why not? If I hate it, then I am sure I could just wear one of my dresses from home."

Olive's eyes gleamed. "I swear to you, it will be the finest thing you have ever worn. I am the best of the best around here, with design and garment creation." Her pride was clear with the certainty she spoke with.

"I have no doubts." I offered her a small smile.

The girl dipped her head and moved to exit the room.

My voice stopped her just before she opened the door. "May I ask you something else?"

She turned, smile falling from her lips. Her gaze held mine, and I did not know if she was reading my emotions despite her promise not to. "You are free to ask whatever you wish."

"There is a Lysian here by the name of Iona. Do you know where I can find her?"

Olive glanced around the room as if making sure no one

else was around. "I'm sorry. I do not." There was something she was not telling me.

I closed the distance between us, reaching for her arm. "Please. If you can help me."

"I will help you however I can, but not with this."

I withdrew my hand. "Has Clause harmed her?"

"She..." Olive hesitated before shaking her head. "No. He hasn't." She sighed before swallowing as though her throat was suddenly dry. "Listen, if you came here just for her, then you shouldn't have wasted your time."

"What's that mean?"

"Trust me, she is not suffering as much as you imagine. She is not the polite little princess she once was. Actually, I doubt she was *ever* polite or much of a princess." I could have sworn something like disgust flickered behind her eyes.

"Why will you not tell me where she is?"

"Because if the King wanted you to know, then you already would. And if he chooses to keep that from you, then I do not desire to go against his wishes."

I lowered my voice and asked my last question. "If I granted the people here freedom, would they return to where they came from? Do you people want to be free?"

She shrugged. "What is freedom? I doubt it truly exists. We all live in one form of prison or another. Yet not all prisons are terrible. The Siddhe land is where I grew up. It is all I know." Her gaze flickered to the wolf and back to me. "I would caution you against this kind of talk. Clause favors you, but if you wish to keep the liberties he has granted you, then you should be careful with what you share and ask of people."

I nodded, and with that, our conversation ended. The girl showed herself out and left me standing in my room, staring at the closed door. With a sigh, I turned to Shay. "Well, I guess it's time for me to get ready to share yet another meal with this wretch of a King."

Shay growled lowly, as if agreeing.

AGAIN, I sat before him.

Again, his eyes observed me while I endured it.

The servants filled the table between us with far too much food for two people. Eggs, meat, bread, cheeses, and fruits covered the space. I placed some bread and cheese on my plate, along with berries.

"How was Olive this morning?" Clause asked after swallowing a bite of whatever he had on his plate.

"It was fine." My eyes met his, and I was uncertain how much he knew, whether this was some sort of test. Someone so controlled, like him, likely kept himself well informed. He probably already knew the details. I placed the cheese on top of the bread. "I think I made her uncomfortable." My attention shifted to the bread in my hands as I took a bite.

Clause chuckled. "Usually, it's the other way around. Olive makes others uncomfortable because of her gifts." He studied me a moment. "What did you say to her?" The question could have been a test. The Siddhe King asking regarding something he already knew the answer to, just to see what I would say. The way his subjects seemed to be around him; I would have bet that Olive told him all about our conversation if he had.

I swallowed, choosing to openly show my hand. There was likely no point in hiding it, and if anything maybe honesty would work in my favor. "I asked her that if I freed the people here, would they want to leave?"

"Interesting." He tilted his head, viewing me. Those cold gray eyes portrayed nothing that was going on in his head. "You asked her such a question, without simply assuming the people here would go running at the opportunity of leaving? I thought you viewed me as an abominable leader."

"Just because I do, doesn't mean others do too. I would like to know how your people feel about you. Apparently, that question may make them uncomfortable."

He took a sip of water. "And if I asked you such a thing while you were under the rule of your father. Would the question not make you uncomfortable?"

"Only because he was an abominable leader."

Clause's lips quirked at the side. "And if I ask some of your people this same question today. You do not think it may make them uncomfortable? All of them would simply agree with no concerns?"

I didn't respond, because I didn't know. Such a question would likely make most uneasy. He was unfortunately correct about that. So instead of answering him, I asked him something else. "I doubt you allow most others to talk like this to you or about you. So why are you letting me?"

The pressure of his gaze not once lightened. It remained heavily centered on me. "You're right. Most would never dream of it. But you are a visitor, not a citizen, and so I encourage your curiosity." Though he gave an answer, I felt as though there was more he wasn't sharing.

I leaned back in my seat, viewing him, refusing to shy away from the all-consuming presence he commanded. "What game are you playing here?"

His head tilted. "I assure you. It is no game."

I didn't believe it. "I just, I don't understand. You force my hand into coming here. Why? It is not just to prevent the Bavadrins and Lysians from joining to start a war against you.

You allow me to challenge you when no one else can get away with something like that. Why?"

He leaned forward then, his gaze searching mine as though he could see into my soul. It was an unnerving thought. "I see you as more of an equal than anyone else I have met in my long life."

A smile found its way to my lips at the ridiculousness of his comment. Did he expect this line to work on me? I could have laughed. Clause saw himself as a god, an absolute. It surprised me he didn't pretend he was one of the Spirits himself. "You do not see me as an equal. The first time I came here, you had Malavika put on a show in order to show you my conjuring. You see me as a puppet."

His gaze narrowed ever so slightly, growing a sharp edge. "That was before I fully understood what you are."

"What am I?" I pressed. This entire conversation had taken a turn.

"Remarkable." The word was a compliment and said with such certainty. "You are who you have always been."

My cheeks warmed with the discomfort of how forward he seemed, yet not forward at all. "That isn't an answer. You are dancing around all of my questions."

Clause leaned back in his chair, taking with him a sliver of the pressure surrounding me. He viewed me a moment before finally offering an answer. "When you first came here, and I touched you. I influenced your feelings through your conjuring, and you took back control from me. That does not happen."

"Never?" My mouth grew dry. What did that mean?

He slowly moved his head from side to side, not a single silvery white hair out of place. It was brushed back, as if to harshen the brutal angles of his face. He was the embodiment of a disciplined control. "Only with you. Amazingly, I found this girl who has gone unnoticed and who has the power to with-stand and challenge my sway. She knows herself enough to do so. You are exquisite, Ariana."

"Yet my mist cannot touch you," I stated, for I was not truly immune to him.

"Not unless I desire it to."

My pulse raced at the thought that he somehow considered me powerful just for knowing my mind. Then it spiked even further as another thought entered. "If I actually wanted to leave, would you allow it?" I asked.

His gaze narrowed, and my heart skipped a beat.

I found myself speaking again before he even answered. "If no one has ever withstood whatever you did before, am I viewed as a threat?"

"If you are a threat, then I would like the opportunity to have you understand," he simply said.

"Understand what?"

"Me."

I shook my head, not knowing where this was going. He wanted for me to understand him? Perhaps I would have tried to, if there was an ounce of compassion in his icy heart. Instead, he took life without a second thought, and played games with those who still lived. Understanding was not something he sought. Absolute control was the only thing he accepted.

"I am finished answering questions for this morning," he said, placing his napkin on the table.

My heart was in my throat and I didn't know whether I should back down or push forward. Neither decision was great. Ultimately, the tension inside my mind won. "I only have one more. Where is Iona?"

"She is busy." His jaw tensed for just a moment before his eyes softened.

"Doing what?"

"You are so inquisitive. So curious about things, it's refresh-ing." His gaze moved over my face. "Your servant friends cleaned out the small room in their compound for you. Seems that they welcome your presence there."

"They did?" I looked at him in surprise. It was very clear that he shifted the conversation, and he did it well, for my interest was stolen. However, the other questions, those he did his best to avoid truly answering were not going to be forgotten. I would find the truth.

He nodded. "Soren got some supplies, healing herbs and such, and is probably there now unpacking and trying to figure out where you want things."

"Is breakfast over?" I asked, placing my napkin on the table. A strong desire to go there and see what was being done came over me.

"It is if you want it to be," he answered and I stood at once, the chair scraping across the floor.

"Do you wish for me to take you there?" He joined me in standing.

I shook my head no. "I know the way." I also needed a break from the stagnant air that surrounded him.

Clause smiled just before I turned away and finally left him, determined to someday soon find the answers to my questions.

14

ERIK

The torture of Ariana's absence was all-consuming, to the point of potentially driving me mad if this continued for much longer. She has been in the Siddhe lands for over a week, and every day that passed only made things worse.

It was difficult not to think of her, of what she experienced, what she felt. I constantly had to force her from my mind in order to be of any use to those around me. But my thoughts always circled back to her.

With a sigh, I refocused, looking at Iver, who was teaching some of the front-line Bavadrin soldiers to prepare for Malavika's potential attacks. The soldiers were all given bright yellow ribbons with the goal of tying them around the wooden sword Iver relentlessly jabbed them with from a safe distance. The poor men rubbed their tender chests and bellies in between training attacks. Even with light armor covering their most vulnerable parts, the pressure of the hits still likely added up to the point of a constant gnawing sensation that only intensified with each following blow.

"How hard is it to tie a ribbon to some wood? This is not even a sharp blade, which could cut through ribbon easily!" Iver yelled out before thrusting his hand out once more. Dozens of wooden swords shimmered to life in front of a few dozen men. When he pulled back, a single yellow ribbon clung to his weapon.

"One measly ribbon will not suffice! She would have sliced through Spirit knows how many of you at this point. Her blade would be slick, dripping with blood. It would stain the yellow with ease. We need as many ribbons tied to the weapon as possible, to draw the eye easily!" He lectured before attacking again.

That was Iver's clever little plan. A way to pinpoint where Malavika was, and then he would use his conjuring to go to her and take care of the threat. From what we knew, Mal needed to be close enough to see what she was doing, yet far enough away to remain safe and able to concentrate on her conjuring. She would be at the battle, but not at the front lines. Instead, she was likely going to be tucked away, and incredibly lethal. She was Clause's weapon, nearly matching that of Ariana's Sparrows.

I closed the space between my brother and me. When he pulled the sword back, void of any yellow ribbons, I placed a hand on his shoulder, preventing him from attacking again. "You should give them a break so they can refocus on the task."

Iver sighed, turning to me, his sword hand falling to his side. "Perhaps you are correct. These Bavadrins do tire quicker than our kind." He then looked at the men he had been torturing for the better part of the morning. "Fifteen-minute break! Then I expect you all to do better!"

The men's sighs hissed through the forest, drawing a smile from Iver. He always loved torturing others.

"Willis had given me the go-ahead to bring some of our soldiers and begin joining forces. I sent Kole last night to pass along the message," I filled my brother in on the recent developments.

"I'm sure he is chompin' at the bit to get Eislyn over here," Iver commented as he shifted his weight, leaning back against a tree.

"He certainly is." The thought brought a smile to my lips. It had been a long time since I looked forward to having both Eislyn and Kole at my side together. Their hot-headed anger kept us all fractured, but now, the pain began healing. All of it partially because of the woman who now was a world away.

"Any new information or theories as to why Clause keeps the conjurors within his capital city's walls and the ungifted outside?" Iver asked, his gaze drifting to the men who took their break by huddling together to sit on a few logs in the distance.

I shook my head. "That remains a mystery. But Ariana is working on trying to learn more on the matter."

Iver frowned. "There has to be a reason for it." His gaze dropped to the ground in thought before rising to meet mine once more. "What of our sister?"

I sighed, before leaning against a tree across from him. "Ariana has asked a few people about Iona. She even asked the servants she befriended, but they have refused to tell her. They know something, but seem scared to share information. From what has been gathered, she is at least alive. Some seem to suggest she is not in any need of help."

A breath of a chuckle escaped Iver. He changed the subject from our sister. "That wolf, Shay, is quite useful. Who knew the Bavadrins harbored such gifts?"

"If only the information sharing could go both ways," I grumbled.

Iver released a laugh, knowing gray eyes sparkled as they met with mine. "You have known her for how long and she has you so worried about her you can barely keep from marching over to the Siddhe lands all on your own. Ariana has experience with managing hostile environments and I think she is possibly the best equipped to succeed in the position she finds herself in now. She will survive this. Hell, she may even thrive, despite the arduous task before her."

"I cannot help but worry about her." The words left me in nearly a whisper.

"Because you love her?" Iver's comment drew my eye to him, and he shrugged a single shoulder. "It's obvious. You do not need to admit such a thing to me. I know it is true."

I shook my head, leaning it against the tree, the bark rough against my scalp. That word, love. I did not allow myself to think of it, though how could one describe my reactions towards the Bavadrin Leader Superior? The way she stole my attention, whether or not physically present. How my blood reacted to her. My boundless desire to make her mine. "You are aggravatingly insightful at times."

He flashed a smile. "I am insightful *always*." The smile fell from his lips, brows pulling together as a new thought entered his mind. "What do you make of all that two Spirit stuff Clause told Ariana about?"

"I do not know. Ariana went over what Clause had told her with Shay, and apparently, the wolf thought she was pretty shaken. The wolf thinks Ariana seems to believe it."

His eyes narrowed. "And you don't?"

"I'm not sure what difference any of it would make at this point."

"You do not think if we praise the correct Spirit, that it would not smile upon us and grace us with luck?" Of course, my youngest brother would find this interesting to consider. I, on the other hand, sidestepped the thoughts altogether.

"The Spirits have left us in this world long ago," I answered with a shrug. Ariana and this looming war consumed my thoughts, leaving little room for anything else.

Iver's eyebrows rose towards his hairline. "Do you not believe that Ariana interacted with the Spirit of darkness at her ascension? And if she did, do you not think she has the favor of that Spirit?"

I sighed. "Iver, what do you want from me? I don't know. Did Ariana see something, or was she just delusional from that poison they had her drink? I believe she thinks she saw something, but was it real or something created by imagination and a hallucinogenic? I don't have the answers."

His gaze sharpened. "I wonder what the little old Bavadrin makes of all of this. After all, if we believe Clause's story, then the Seer's gift is definitely from the Spirit of the dark."

"Edda has been keeping to herself a lot this week. I do not know what she makes of any of this mess." That was another irritation. The woman who helped raise Ariana had withdrawn. I expected her involvement in everything, whether or not desired. Instead, she offered little to no input.

Iver pushed off the tree. "And isn't that peculiar of the Seer? To retreat at a time like this." I had to agree with my younger brother there.

Footsteps drew my attention as Willis walked through the forest towards us. Iver's gaze drifted to him as he nodded in greeting before turning to me. "Well, I better get back to training this lot if we are to have any hopes of fighting the

Siddhe." My brother then quickly returned to torturing the Bavadrins with his conjuring jabs.

"How are they doing?" Willis nodded towards Iver and the men.

"Improving, but slowly," I commented, turning toward him. "How is she?"

Willis exhaled heavily. "If there was anything wrong, I would tell you." His gaze met mine, and something softened in his eyes. "But I suppose that doesn't help someone in your position when it comes to her."

He came up next to me, his attention moving to Iver while he gave a brief update. "The Siddhe party went well last night. Ariana has Clause's favor. Somehow, she is maintaining it despite constantly pushing the boundaries." There was a slight disapproval in his tone as if he wished she would soften her approach with the Siddhe King.

"Did she learn anything new?" I asked.

"She learned about Clause's family a bit more. He's had a dark upbringing. I think he feels he can relate to Ariana in that way. It is something that plays to her advantage. She also continues to gain the trust and favor of more of the help." Though he said nothing negative, a frown pulled at his lips. There was something he did not seem to like.

I nodded. "If everyone in that city is a conjuror, then even the servants could be of use if they choose to stand with her when it all comes tumbling down."

Willis turned to me. "Shay continues to search for a way into the city, but walls made of mountain seal it tight. She could not find any openings yet. Other than marching through the front door, there has been no secret entrance."

I frowned. Hoping Shay would have found a weakness by now, but the capitol was a fortress. My frustration deepened as my thoughts shifted back to her, and an unsettling feeling crept through me.

Willis had frowned just moments ago. Why?

"At this party..." My voice came out measured, though my pulse quickened. "Was she forced to dance with him?"

Willis studied me for a heartbeat, his silence thick with hesitation. Then, finally, he spoke. "Several asked her to dance. She denied all but two." His eyes met mine. "One, a servant boy. The other, the Siddhe King."

A slow, controlled breath filled my lungs, but it did nothing to temper the heat rising within me. "I take it he was respectful?" The words were even, but I felt the fire licking at my veins, the burn of something I did not want to name.

If Clause wished to befriend her, he *must* have been respectful. He *must* have kept his distance. But that knowledge did nothing to quell the fury curling inside me at the thought of his hands on her, pulling her close, holding her. *Ashes*. The fire in *my* veins scorched.

Willis's attention drifted over my face, as if considering what to say. "Clause favors her, and I believe he wishes for her to favor him in return. So, yes... he was respectful."

The answer should have been reassuring. But the way Willis delivered it—too smooth, too calculated—put me on edge. Beneath his steady tone, tension rippled through him, stiffening his posture. He was uncomfortable. And he was watching me, as if bracing for my reaction.

A cold dread slid down my spine.

My body went rigid. "What are you not telling me?"

Willis hesitated, just for a moment. Then, finally—

"The Siddhe King did, however, try to kiss her."

15

ARIANA

Nerves prickled my skin as I stood there, just outside the room that housed the party.

Olive fretted over my hair while we waited. She had re-done the stones that were braided and looped into the left side of my head, while the right hung freely with loose curls.

"For not growing up as a Bavadrin, you are quite skilled at this," I commented as her fingers did a last check of the work on my wild mane.

Olive smiled. "I never back down from a challenge of design, whether it be a gown or something else." Suddenly she straightened as if she heard something that I did not. Large, warm eyes turned to me as she practically bounced on her toes. "It's time!" She spun me around and gently pushed me through a door.

I didn't have a chance to ask if she would join before entering an enormously beautiful ballroom. Pillars supported a remarkably tall and skillfully painted ceiling. Artists crafted the entire palace into an enchanted castle.

Tables filled half the room, while the other remained free for dancing and mingling. At the far end of the chamber were massive archways framed by soft, flowing fabric leading to a balcony. As I moved into the space, it felt like hundreds of eyes landed on me, but I saw none of them, for my attention snapped to the Siddhe King.

"Ariana, the Leader Superior of the Bavadrins." He announced, and though he simply spoke the words, all heard his voice.

Clause's icy gaze traveled down the length of me, taking in the deep red fabric clinging to every curve before flowing to the floor. A chill raced through me, stemming from everywhere that his eyes touched, before rising to meet with mine once more. He tilted his head towards the table at his side, a silent command to join him and the others already seated. Half of them with necks nearly breaking to get a good look at me, their King's new puppet.

Gritting my teeth, I closed the gap between us. Those still standing parted for me, providing a path to their King. Somehow, besides the immense space of the room, I found myself at his side in hardly any time.

He wore black, of course. I tried not to dwell on what Edda once told me, that black was best for hiding blood. I'd learned that firsthand, helping an injured child at the orphanage. Head wounds bled more than I ever imagined. The little girl was fine, thank the Spirit, but my dress had been soaked. Was that why he favored the color?

"Olive outdid herself. You are absolutely stunning," Clause commented, taking my hand in his and bringing a knuckle to his lips. Though the touch was fleeting, I barely resisted the urge to yank my hand from him.

His presence was commanding, even without brute size. Broad shoulders narrowed into a lean waist, and his long legs moved with an effortless, fluid grace. As if he was more feline than man, all quiet strength and lethal elegance.

"Thanks. Maybe I will take her with me when I leave," I said with a tight smile. This was now a strange game I played, tiptoeing an edge where I wondered how far his hospitality towards me would go if I continued to stand my ground without apology.

It did not bother him in the least. Instead, a smirk curled at his lips, and he gently led me to the table where he introduced me to several men, none of whose names I cared to commit to memory. The only familiar face was that of Malavika, someone I had not seen since my arrival. She flashed a smile at me, though the hate in her eyes was palpable.

I sat in the seat directly at Clause's side. It was the first time we didn't have an entire table between us while we ate, and I missed having that buffer. For the first several minutes, the men practically kissed the floor their King walked on with their words. Praise and agreement were the only things thrown Clause's way.

Useless yes men, all of them. The worst part was they did not appear to possess any useful knowledge of the lands or their King. The smartest of Clause's minions at the table was likely Mal, and given our previous encounter, I doubted she would be easy to discretely pull information from.

They droned on and on about absolutely nothing of importance. My gaze drifted to the side, looking at the balcony and the darkness beyond. I craved to be out there, for the freedom the night air offered, instead of being surrounded by these fools.

"So, are all Bavadrin leaders as beautiful as you?" The Siddhe sitting before me asked.

Ugh.

"I'm sure some found Fraser pretty," I commented with a shrug. My hand tightened around my fork in annoyance.

"Shit leadership seems to run amongst the Bavadrins," Malavika stated abruptly, speaking for the first time during the torturous dinner.

"What?" My gaze narrowed, turning to her while she threw daggers with her eyes. The Lysian sat diagonally from me, placing me easily in her line of sight, as was her King.

"I heard your father could not produce the only heir he has ever wanted, because of his soft spot for his wife." She smirked, vicious darkness dancing in her eyes.

"Malavika," Clause warned, the tone firm.

My ears burned hot from the heat moving within and I leaned towards her. "Soft spot?" Was she delusional? Fraser had brutely murdered my mother.

She sat back, keeping her focus on me. "He didn't kill his wife soon enough, and instead allowed for her to abort every single son he impregnated her with."

Clause's hand slammed the table so hard that we all jumped. "Leave." His gaze pinned her.

She looked at him in shock. "Are you serious?"

"I will not tell you again." It was his only response. The words clipped.

Mal stared at him for another moment, as if hoping he would reconsider. Her neck turned blotchy and red from the emotions she was doing her best to keep bottled, but a look of hurt still sliced through before she stood and left. She not once looked at me again.

Aborted every single son he impregnated her with. Ridiculous. And yet, it suddenly became difficult for me to draw breath. Why would she have said something like that? The world around me closed in, sending a jolt down my spine.

My stomach twisted. I was going to be sick.

"Excuse me." I stood without waiting for a reply of any sort and dashed to the balcony. Faces blurred past me as I rushed towards the outdoors.

The night greeted me, though because of the moon and the snow reflecting off the higher mountain peaks, it was not dark. I could see far over the city and terrain. No longer closed in by walls and strangers, I finally found myself able to gulp down deep breaths.

A gentle breeze tugged at my hair and pulled some of the fiery anger from my body, taking it on a journey across the Siddhe mountains. I wondered how much bitterness and pain was trapped amongst those glistening peaks.

Something in the air shifted, turning stagnant. The sensation caused my shoulders to stiffen, for there was only one who harbored such an effect that even the air dulled around him. Suddenly, stolen was my sliver of freedom.

"How did you know someone approached?" Clause asked when he came up beside me. "Your entire body tensed as soon as I stepped out onto the terrace."

"It's impossible not to notice when you are near," I commented.

"Is it your conjuring?" He asked, as if he did not know.

I turned to him then in surprise. "Are you serious?"

Confusion touched his features. "Why wouldn't I be?"

I would have laughed if I was not in such a foul mood. "I think it's *your* conjuring."

"*Mine?*" His brows drew together as he stared at me, waiting for more of an explanation.

Was he truly serious? "There is this stagnant presence around you. Like nothing can move freely close to you. Your control is so consuming that it even stops the wind."

He looked down in thought. "Interesting. I never knew this extended out to those close to me. I always thought it just affected me." He then turned to me, observing my face. "It bothers you?"

I released a breath. "It's suffocating." My skin crawled because of it whenever near him.

His hand wrapped around the railing. "I apologize." He looked over his city. "I have been like this for so long, I don't even need to try to maintain it anymore. It is just second nature."

The presence began lessening. It was as though the hand holding me underwater finally eased up, allowing me to surface. Allowing me to breathe and feel the air once more.

A breeze cut through the stagnant sensation, obliterating it. Clause's eyes slid shut just as a gust ruffled through his hair. He drew in a slow, steady breath. "I forgot how sweet fresh air could smell." His words were soft, like an afterthought to himself.

When his eyes re-opened, his attention found mine. "Is this better?"

"Much. Thank you." And I truly was thankful. If I had to spend time around him, then at least with the shackles he had on the surrounding air gone, it was more bearable. "What caused you to create that stagnant space in the first place?"

His gaze left mine, again looking over the mountains. "A

funeral. It was freezing, the wind bitter that day. It sliced through me with such ease." He blinked, the moment lasting just long enough that it was clear whatever that day was to him, it was a painful memory. "So, I stopped it. I stopped everything, at least as much as I could. Since then, I haven't felt the brush of the breeze on my cheek." He turned those dangerously silver eyes to me. "Until now. I had forgotten how nice it could feel."

It was very recently that I myself had the displeasure of attending a particularly cold funeral. My throat ached at the thought of Landin. At the fact that I stood here, staring at the man who had stolen him from me.

I considered asking Clause whose funeral he was referring to, but decided against it, instead choosing to ask about something else. "Was there truth to what Malavika said?"

He sighed. "I didn't wish to discuss such things tonight." His response was answer enough. He *believed* those things.

"She would never have done that." I shook my head. "My mother would have protected all of her children. She broke after every stillbirth. She couldn't have possibly been responsible."

"Just because someone kills, does not mean they cannot also mourn the loss." Clause replied, his gray eyes not once straying from me.

Desperation tightened around me, fueled by the wish to not believe any of his words. And yet, I wanted to know. "Why would she ever do something like that?"

"As I said, the Spirit of light and dark gifted you with conjuring. Your mother had gifts too, from the dark Spirit. She could sense future things, but only for herself. A mild flicker of a gift, like a light just before it goes out by the blow of a breath. And with a child in the womb, she could sense their futures too.

The males would have grown up to be a threat to the world, so she protected it by eliminating them."

I stepped away from him, as though his words shoved me. "No. She wouldn't. Children are not born evil. She would have guided them, taught them. I would have had siblings." It was an effort to keep my eyes from lining with tears. What he was insinuating could not have been true, and yet I felt myself responding as though I believed these lies about my mother.

The moonlight danced in his eyes, somehow making them colder, causing him to appear even more dangerous. "This is why you need to better protect your heart."

"What?"

His hand rested lightly on the railing, angling his body towards me. "You see others and welcome them into your heart freely as long as they don't appear a threat. Yet, they are. Anyone who you hold power over is a threat, even the weakest of them. They are not your equal. They can and will betray you, even if they love you. For they may even think what they do is for your own good, but ultimately it is for their own selfish desires they act against you."

"I don't believe that."

"And yet, it is still true."

"What happened in your life that made you believe something like this?" I asked. The question was insanely bold, but I continued to test his patience with little caution.

His lips curved into a sad smile. "Your conviction in this belief that people are innately good is a rare and beautiful thing. It will be a sad day when you will lose it."

Well, he didn't have to worry there. "I will never give up on people."

His smile faltered. "Yes, you will," he said it as though it was a promise, a truth that he believed in.

And at that moment, I understood something. We were both playing a similar game.

He believed he was giving me the freedom that would ultimately stifle my views, causing me to see things his way. While I was trying to take that same freedom and use it to smother him in return. We both were playing with a lot of rope and both expected to come out victorious. But that was impossible.

One of us had to lose.

16

ARIANA

As I weaved through the small crowd, I finally made it back to the table. A pitcher of newly replenished wine sat before me, and I poured it into my goblet.

After my bizarre interaction with Clause on the balcony, I left him out there in favor of a drink. The room buzzed as more and more people took to the dancefloor. Those of all races lingered together without prejudice, and I couldn't help but appreciate the beauty of that.

"You truly are a fine creature," someone said, drawing my attention to one of the King's many advisors who did anything but actually advise. Instead, they kissed the ground Clause walked on, hanging off every word he spoke, and nodded so fiercely they likely scrambled their own brains.

"You call all Bavadrins creatures?" I eyed him while facing the party. Music twirled around the room, giving the space a lively feel.

"I did not mean any disrespect by it," he said, eyes glossy from having one too many drinks already. He then stepped to me, getting a little too close. "Care to dance?" Alcohol drifted from his breath as he offered his hand.

"I'd rather scrub the floors of the castle with a toothbrush," I said with a polite smile. The last thing I saw was the dumb expression on his face before I downed my wine, set the glass on the table, and left him standing there.

I didn't want to sift through the people at the party again, but I also did not wish to entertain Clause's minions. Was it too soon for me to take my leave?

A familiar face snagged my attention. Timothy, one of the servant boys who helped Gorm that day I found the servant's building, was gathering empty glasses on a tray. Shocked, I turned and made my way towards him.

"Fancy seeing you here." I smiled as he looked at me in surprise. His gaze dropped, then rose once again, taking in my gown and appearance. I also took in his. He looked clean, his hair brushed, and the dark jacket and pants he wore made him look older, dapper even. "Don't you look handsome this evening," I stated.

His cheeks instantly turned red, and he stared at me with wide eyes.

Someone came up beside the boy, bumping into him, before leaning down and whispering loud enough for me to hear. "I think this is when you tell the lady she looks beautiful tonight." Gorm glanced at me and winked.

"Ah, yes, of course. You– You look– beautiful." Timothy's face grew redder by the moment, nearly matching my dress.

"Thank you." I smiled and turned to Gorm. "How is this possible? That you both are here tonight?" Typically, they worked jobs outside of the main palace. From what I knew, they never stepped foot inside.

Gorm absentmindedly scratched his elbow. "Well, the King requested we help with the party if we so wished."

"And you wanted to?"

"Are you kidding?" Timothy's eyes lit up. "You do not know how good the servants within these walls eat. This has been amazing compared to our usual work."

I smiled yet turned to Gorm in question. "Did something happen to the usual servants who work at such events?" Clause didn't strike me as someone who typically allowed for such a service change. To take those given a rough cut and place them in polished roles.

"The King did it for you," Gorm answered with a lifted bushy brow.

"Me?"

"He knows you are not close to many at the palace. You spend most of your free time with us or at our housing lodge. So, he invited us to work the event, to offer you a familiar face and hopefully a bit of comfort amongst this uptight madness." Gorm smiled knowingly.

His words took me aback. The act of inviting those who I found comfort in was surprisingly thoughtful. Especially for someone who also believed finding favor and friendships with others was a threat. This must have been some sort of tactical move. Somehow this helped Clause get closer to his goals, but how?

"How is your foot?" I asked Gorm, needing something else to focus on.

He groaned. "You need to quit fussing over it. It has healed already, thanks to your care. Though I am afraid that the memory of that nasty foot being in your hands has permanently burned into my mind, leaving scars that even you cannot heal."

A laugh bubbled out of me, and I slowly felt myself relaxing. "It's really alright. I wanted to help."

"You did." He nodded.

The music shifted, a new happy beat moving around us. Something about the melody reminded me of home. And suddenly I felt even more at ease.

"Dance with me." I turned to Timothy, who nearly dropped the tray he held.

"Wh– What?" He shook his head. "Surely there is someone you would prefer over–"

Gorm's dramatic gasp cut the boy off. "You refuse a dance with the Bavadrin Leader Superior?" His eyes grew large, as if he could not believe what he was hearing, and it was an effort for me to stifle a laugh.

Timothy turned to him, eyes rounded like moons with alarm. "No! Of course not, it's just... I am carrying this tray and–"

Gorm took the tray out of his hands. "I will take it to the kitchen, no problem."

Timothy's enormous, panicked stare turned to me. "I– I wouldn't know what to do. I don't want to hurt you."

I laughed, holding my hand out for him to take. "Trust me, you won't."

He hesitated before ultimately accepting it.

Gorm winked once more before disappearing into the crowd, carrying the tray away.

Timothy timidly led me to the dancefloor. He lightly touched me, one hand on my hip, the other holding mine. He was nearly trembling as he slowly began shifting me across the dance floor.

I pulled on a cord within, the one tied to my conjuring. My chest warmed before I sent the sensation down to my feet. A thin layer of mist coated the floor, too light for anyone to slip or notice, but enough for me to use.

"Seriously, you are fine," I whispered, and his gaze dropped to the ground. Monitoring his feet to ensure he did not step on mine. "Don't worry, you won't step on me." A bit more of the mist took to the sole of his shoes. This was winding up to be a wonderful practice for me.

"I wouldn't be so certain," he muttered.

I leaned towards him, voice dropping. "I am using my conjuring to monitor your movement and where your feet are going. Trust me, you won't step on me." And if he did, then that meant I needed to practice a lot more.

Timothy visibly relaxed then, not completely, but it was an improvement.

My gaze drifted to someone watching us from the sidelines. The man who had asked me to dance, and I refused, stared at us, face red, eyes filled with anger and hatred. I made an enemy. It was something I should have avoided.

"How's your night been?" I asked Timothy, trying to take his mind off what he was doing.

His gaze darted around the room before settling on me. "It's been pretty great, actually. We got to eat some of the leftover food, and it has been the best thing I have ever tasted in my life. The palace servants really have it good." He had such enthusiasm, despite the difficulty life dealt him.

"I'm glad you're enjoying your work."

"We have you to thank for that."

"This has nothing to do with me."

Large, bright eyes sparkled as he viewed me. "Without you, we would still be out there, and Gorm might be without a foot."

The song ended too soon, and our movements stilled before the next one took the room.

"Thank you for the dance." I released him at the same time that I released my control of the mist, letting it fade away into nothing.

"It was my honor." He dipped his head, cheeks bright red when he met my eyes. He then disappeared into the crowd. Leaving me to sift through it before ultimately being pulled towards the balcony again, in need of an escape.

I paused on the threshold to the terrace, for someone was already out there.

Clause stood with his back to me, viewing his capital and the mountains surrounding it. The stagnant feeling was still thankfully removed. A gentle breeze cozied up to him, running through his hair before disappearing, as if afraid that he would force a barrier once more if it lingered too long.

Without that suffocating pressure around him, he almost seemed normal.

But he was anything but normal. With one touch, he took Landin from me.

I hated him.

And yet, I needed to exist near him if I wanted to find the best way to destroy him.

"Do you wish to be alone?" I finally asked, breaking the silence. Was he out here the entire time since I last left him?

Clause turned, viewing me, a soft curve to his lips when he met my gaze. "Not at all."

I approached the railing, stopping beside him. "I am surprised to find you out here and not enjoying the party."

"I like the way the breeze feels," he stated simply, looking back over his lands. And suddenly, a part of me felt sorry for him. He kept everything at arm's length, even the air he breathed. Letting no one get close enough to know him, to even matter to him. He built a cold and lonely existence around himself. It was a strange thing, to feel sorry for a man you wished to kill.

"Do you have any friends?" I asked.

He chortled, glancing at me. "How do you define *friend*?"

The question baffled me, for how to define such a thing? "It's a relationship between two people. Someone who gives you the freedom to be yourself and loves you all the more for it."

He released an amused breath. "That is but a fantasy."

It was impossible to argue with him because he honestly did not understand. How could he? It was something he clearly had never experienced. And without knowing how such a relationship affected someone, he couldn't even understand what taking someone like that was like. He did not know the impact he had made when he so easily took Landin's life.

Even so, I refused to back down. If he blinded himself, then I would help him see. "It is as real as you and I."

"How many friends would you say you have?"

"I don't know. Several great ones."

He arched a silver brow. "Several. And you believe none of them prefers to change you. All of them simply give you the freedom to be whatever you wish, do whatever you please, and they love you all the more for it?"

I sighed. "It's not that simple. I oversimplified the definition of the word. Of course, friendships have their struggles. But ultimately the trials strengthen the bond."

"You do not know how dangerous it is to place such faith in so many people. Most in this world do things for their own self-serving reasons. You should not place your trust so easily in others." He pressed his lips into a thin line, clearly displeased by my view of the matter.

I shook my head. "Maybe if you trusted more, then you

would understand that there are some out there worthy of that trust."

He viewed me before glancing at the room where the party still raged. Gray eyes met mine once more, and he inclined his head towards the room. "Allow me the pleasure of a dance with you?" It was an obvious change of subject, one that also made me uncomfortable.

My stomach clenched when he offered me his hand. I was fairly certain I pissed off all of his right-hand men and so them seeing me dancing with their King would likely offer me some level of security. I doubted any of them would ever dream of doing anything that may upset their King, and so as long as I held his favor, that offered me protection. Would I still hold his favor if I embarrassed him by turning down the invitation for a dance?

It was clear Clause wanted me to understand him, to view the world as he did. For some reason, the King cared about my opinion of him. And that was something I could use.

"Under one condition," I stated, and his hand fell to his side.

"What may that be?" Though his voice was soft, it sent a jolt down my spine. This game, whatever this was that we were playing, was dangerous. Even more so because I felt as though I did not know all the rules.

"Tell me the story of who hurt you." I asked for something deeply personal. Something I doubted he felt comfortable sharing. Especially given his inclination to keep everyone at a distance.

"Who hurt me?" He framed it as a question.

I elaborated, "For you to believe friendships are not real. That people are too selfish for such notions."

He took a moment to view me, his expression completely unreadable. I half expected him to refuse an answer. And yet, he began speaking. "I'll tell you of the first person who thoroughly taught me this lesson, but to do so, I suppose I need to give you some background information." He paused, as if waiting for me to agree.

"I have nowhere else I need to be." I shrugged.

Gray eyes studied my face before turning from me altogether, looking out over the balcony. "This is a beautiful land. It can be cold and harsh, but here, surrounded by the mountains, it is an oasis."

"There is certainly something special to it." I moved to stand beside him, viewing his lands.

He continued staring out at nothing in particular, his gaze drifting along the horizon of mountains. "My father loved it here. Loved his people, his family. Until some close to him betrayed him, trying to seize his throne for another. His inner circle, his so-called *friends*, were nothing more than poison he let into his life."

I frowned. For this seemed like a story about his father, not him.

"That was the beginning of my father's change. He became paranoid, crazed at times. Me, being his heir, I was always with him, and saw it firsthand. But my mother, she did not get that joy. My father kept her caged to her room. Isolated. Alone. He feared letting her out, that someone would get to her and use her to harm him. So instead, he placed her out of reach. Hiding his weakness behind doors. She became a prisoner."

"That's awful," I murmured.

Clause nodded. "She was weak, simply obeying, no matter what he did to her. But she was a Queen. She gave him an heir.

She could have stood her ground, and fought for what she believed. Instead, she just took it. Every day, losing more of herself. Every day pulling away from even me. Like a flower hidden from the sun, she wilted."

He drew in a breath, releasing it slowly. "I was fifteen years old when I found her laying on the floor of her room in a pool of blood, her wrists cut."

His hand wrapped around the iron railing, knuckles turning white. "She was supposed to be my *protector*, my *friend*, my *mother*." He said those words harshly as if they were dirty. "Instead, she was a selfish coward who left her only child to suffer at the hands of his mad father." Pain settled in the space surrounding him.

"She probably saw no hope of an escape from the prison she found herself in," I said, imagining what she possibly felt.

Cold gray eyes sliced to me. "She was a mother." There was venom in his words. "And she left me with *him*." Anger charged the air between us.

Her actions hurt him, and still hurt even so many years later. And with my comment, I made it seem like I agreed with her choices, that I stood on her side instead of his. My words upset him, and I seem to have unintentionally found a boundary of his I didn't even know existed.

I never truly saw Clause mad, with that anger directed at me. Yet now, it charged the air I breathed, burning all the way through my lungs. My muscles tensed as I held his stare, suddenly uncomfortable with looking away. He was dangerous, and I finally upset him.

I usually tried to push Clause's boundaries, never have I rushed back toward them. What was the best way to soothe the hurt and anger of someone who trusted no one?

I reached out, my hand covering his before I changed my

mind. Touch was a powerful thing, especially for someone like him, and so I used it. "I'm sorry. I didn't mean to upset you with my comment. You were a child, and it is a parents' duty to protect their young. They should have protected you. I can't imagine what it was like to find her like that."

My thoughts immediately traveled to my own mother, her lying dead on the floor. Perhaps I could imagine it, but Fraser took my mother from me. She did not do that to herself. Or did she? If it was true that she could sense her future, if she somehow induced stillbirths, then perhaps even our mothers shared more in common than I ever imagined.

Nausea settled in my gut at the thought. I had to force myself not to think of it, not to believe it or risk becoming ill.

Clause's features softened, and his gaze dropped to my hand, the one resting on his. The tension between us softened, the edge growing dull as the anger dissipated. He released the railing, his hand flipping over and gently grasping mine. "Well, did I earn myself a dance?"

It took all my willpower to not rip my hand out of his.

"Lead the way." I offered a tight smile and allowed the murderer of my best friend take me towards the music.

Before I knew it, we were on the dancefloor, and the eyes of every person raked over me as the Siddhe King tugged me closer and began moving me across the floor. His steps were smooth, like fluid, precise. Those gray, cunning eyes, had not once left mine. They trapped me.

"I didn't mean to frighten you on the balcony." He broke the silence between us.

"You didn't." I offered him a small forced smile, trying to pretend confidence into existence. The moment on the balcony was uncomfortable for so many reasons.

His lips tugged down. "I got angry, but that was misplaced. I apologize for it. Normally, I do not let my emotions get away like that."

My eyes widened, for he always exuded a confident poise. I suddenly was not sure if he knew what it meant to be emotional. It was clear the conversation upset him, that it was something difficult for him, something I doubted he shared with many.

I realized that most of his demons lingered beneath the surface of a calm water. He never dealt with them properly, and instead forced them to submerge, keeping them out of sight. Yet they remained idle, waiting. The King was not as whole as he made himself appear. Maybe that was something I could use to my advantage.

I thought of how to respond. "Showing an emotion does not mean they have gotten away from you. It makes you more real, and relatable. It was a sensitive topic, and you have every right to feel angry." Perhaps if he allowed himself to feel, to heal, then he could one day be comfortable building bonds with others. He could learn. Maybe he could be a better King for his people, one capable of compassion.

Surprise touched his features.

My stomach twisted. What was I thinking? *Be a better leader?*

I forced a smile that I hoped looked natural. "Why do you look stunned?" Nothing I said was new or worthy of surprise. My thoughts however, those certainly shocked me.

His brows drew together as he continued to guide me across the dancefloor. "I imagined you scolding me for feeling angry. That you would want me to relate to my mother's suffering."

My smile faltered. Did he really think that his feelings had no value? Had no one ever held him or shielded him from anything? Had no one shown him the power of positive bonds and interactions? I thanked the Spirit for Edda, for when I was young, she was all those things for me and so much more.

My gaze fell away from his, pulled down by a sudden sadness sifting through me at the thought of Edda. I forced my attention back up to meet his eye. "She was not the only one suffering."

His hold momentarily loosened on me, the only sign of his surprise at my comment.

"My mother suffered too," I whispered, my gaze dropping till I stared at nothing but his shoulder. "My father was not a good man. I have no memory of him ever being kind. She was shackled to him, a monster. Yet, she remained there for no other reason but to shelter me from him." My eyes watered. How much of my words were even true anymore, if Malavika was right about what she did...

Suddenly I realized it must sound like I am rubbing it in his face that my mom loved me while he thought his abandoned him. My gaze rose. "I'm sorry."

"Don't be. I'm glad someone protected you from the cruelty of the world," he whispered. I half expected him to add something about how doing so, they unfortunately also sheltered me from the true selfishness of the world. Yet, he didn't.

"I wish someone had protected you, too," I said, and meant it. How different could he have been if the circumstances were better?

We stopped moving without my realizing it. Clause stared at me, cold silver eyes holding me captive. A strange tension circled us, the air buzzing with it.

His gaze dipped to my lips. One of his hands still held mine, while the other remained on my lower back. A dangerous man surrounded me, looking at me in a way I never expected, with desire.

My stomach dropped. *No.*

Suddenly Erik was in the foreground of my mind. He was the one I wanted to dance with, to touch me, to look at me with desire. He was the one I felt safe with. The one who had spared Landin's life only for Clause to take it.

The Siddhe King moved closer, stepping into me, his powerful frame enveloping me even more. I nearly forgot to keep breathing, while my heart forgot to pause between beats.

He leaned in towards me till his breath caressed my lips.

"Please," I managed to whisper despite my throat closing.

He stilled.

"Don't." The word barely a desperate murmur, yet he heard.

Hungry silver eyes rose to mine for a moment that lasted an eternity. I would have been shaking if I had not completely frozen in place. A fear so potent sliced into me.

Finally, he stepped away from me.

I sucked in a breath, and somehow when I spoke, my voice sounded steadier than my mind. "May I take my leave?" I didn't even know why I asked. I should have just left. But he was a King, someone who probably often got the things he wanted, and I did not know how he would react to what just happened.

Clause dipped his head. "You may go if you wish," his voice was gentle.

That snapped me into action, and I began moving at once. However, when I went to step past him, he reached out. Fingers wrapped around my forearm, smoothly bringing me to a stop. I could only look ahead and wait for whatever would come next, while Clause towered at my side. His gaze roamed my face. I didn't even have to look at him, for I felt it. And suddenly it was difficult to breathe again.

"You do not need to fear me," he said softly before releasing me.

No one stopped me again as I practically fled from the room, ran down the halls, and hid in my room, thankful for Shay's presence when I entered. She was my piece of home, keeping me grounded as the world shifted all around me.

17

ERIK

Every night I dreamed of her.

Somehow, I'd forget reality when I was there. They were the most vivid dreams I have ever experienced in my life. They were visceral.

I felt the heat of her body pressed against mine, the way it fit so perfectly. Smelled the wild flowers of her hair. Tasted the salt of her skin. Heard the breathy way she moaned my name, as if it belonged to her lips alone.

It was so real. Too real. And every morning, when I opened my eyes to find her gone, the loss hollowed me out a little more. It only fueled my desperation to get her back. To keep her from slipping through my fingers like sand.

In my dreams she began asking me to claim her. To mark her. Did she even really know what that meant, the gravity of such a thing? But in that realm, I was all too eager to both please and possesses.

"Where do you want it?" My teeth skimming her flesh, teasing, promising.

Goosebumps chased my touch as she trembled beneath me, her fingers twisting into my hair. "Anywhere." A breathless plea. "Everywhere."

So I marked her. My teeth sank into her skin as I laid claim to her.

That dream nearly destroyed me.

I woke into the nightmare of an empty, cold bed. Into the reality that she was gone, in danger, while I remained trapped in the safety of her home. Never had I felt more powerless. More useless.

The dreams that followed that one were worse. So much worse.

I could no longer touch her. No longer feel her, speak to her. But I could see her and the shadow that haunted her. The Siddhe King.

An invisible force held me back, as if I were locked behind an impenetrable wall. I was there, but I was nothing. Unable to act. Unable to save her.

I watched as she ran from him. As he caught her. Fire exploded through my veins, burning through the barrier that bound me. But still, I could not reach her.

SHE SCREAMED. And my flames receded—just enough for me to see.

See him pinning her to the ground. See him climbing over her body like a beast.

Rage unlike anything I had ever known consumed me, too vast, too limitless to name. I roared for him to stop. Ordered him to let her go. I threw myself at the barrier over and over again.

But they didn't see me. Didn't hear me.

But I heard everything.

Heard the way she begged him to release her. Heard the laughter that rumbled from his chest, dark and delighted at her struggle, at her fear.

His movements were slow, deliberate, savoring the moment. He leaned towards her, closing the space between them.

She twisted, trying to turn her face away, and when she struck out, her hand meant to slap him, he caught it.

Her wrist snapped like a dry, hollow twig.

The scream that ripped from her shredded me. Tore me open, filleted me to the bone.

Tears streaked down her face as he caught her scream with his mouth.

And I lost my mind.

Lost it so completely that it ripped me from the dream.

I woke gasping—drenched in sweat, my room scorching hot.

The sheets beneath me had charred to ash.

18

ARIANA

Shay's nails scraped across the stone as we rushed down the palace halls. I turned the corner and hardly stopped in time before running into the Siddhe King. My hand flew to my chest in surprise, while my heart nearly jumped out of my throat.

His lip curled at the side. "I'm sorry. I didn't mean to startle you." He stood outside the door to the room where we always broke our morning fast. Typically, I entered to find him seated and waiting for me. This differed from what I quickly grew accustomed to. "Are you hungry?"

I woke feeling a bit ill that morning. The thought of forcing food down my throat was not appealing. "Honestly, no."

He glanced down at the wolf before meeting my gaze once more. "Care to go for a walk through one of the gardens instead?"

I peered down at Shay.

"Your wolf can join, if you wish," he added, extending the invitation.

I swallowed, forcing my attention back up. "I would like that."

We moved through the halls side by side, an awkward silence surrounding us. My heart not once slowed, even as I tried intentionally drawing steady breaths through my nose.

"That stagnant air around you has not returned," I commented, desperate to fill the space with words. As if they could provide some sort of buffer between us.

"You didn't like it," he said with a shrug. "And I don't think I care for it much now, anyway."

He opened an unimpressive door that led to a very unusual garden. The area was small and private. A little pond glistened in the center, a single large tree with a bench beneath it, and blooming flower beds, despite it being winter, filled the area. A curved path weaved around the small quaint space.

"You expected something grander?" Clause asked with a smile, observing my reaction as I absorbed everything I saw.

"No. Well, yes, I suppose. But this is truly lovely." And it was. There was something warm about it, safe, even nestled in the walls of the castle that imprisoned me.

"Care to sit for a bit?" He directed us towards the bench bathed in warm sunlight.

"Sure." I took a seat and watched as Shay took it upon herself to explore the small space. Her nose sniffed as she made her way around the perimeter. All her attention and focus appeared to be on her surroundings, though I knew she kept a tab on me the entire time.

"Last night," Clause began, only to pause. My heart instantly went wild against my ribs as a nervous energy settled in my bones. "Why did you pull away from me?"

I needed more time to think of a response, but the panic coursing through me made it harder for my brain to string coherent thoughts together. "What do you mean?" I asked, playing dumb and regretting the question as soon as it slipped past my lips.

His attention heavily remained on me, though flew over my face as if searching for something. "Last night we shared a moment, and you pulled away," he stated. "Is it fear of me?"

My throat suddenly felt scratchy, the sun uncomfortably warm as I did my best to not squirm. How to answer such a question? One thing was certain. Clause expected those around him to lie for their own selfish reasons. If I wanted to reach him, to possibly ever help him see the world for the better instead of the cold, dangerous place he assumes it to be, then I needed to be honest. I needed to show him he could trust me.

My body heated with discomfort. "That's part of the reason. Anyone would be stupid to not be cautious when around you."

His head tilted. "And what is the other part of the reason?"

I sucked in a deep breath, holding it for a moment. "You mean other than you killing someone important to me?"

He nodded. "If there is another reason."

"My heart belongs to another," I told him my truth.

A smile took his face before he tilted his head back and laughed wholeheartedly. His response threw me off. When his eyes landed on me once more, there was a challenging glint to them. "That's what you believe? That whoever this person is who you think holds your heart is your match?"

My entire body tensed. "Why wouldn't they be?"

Laughter took him once more. He strangely seemed almost *relieved*. As if he worried more about my fearing him than this. His gaze met mine again. "You are so much more than whoever this person is. They are not your partner, your other half. They could never be." He spoke with such certainty that it was offensive.

I scoffed. "I can't expect you to understand."

"And why do you think not?" Gray eyes met mine with a challenge.

"You keep the world at such a distance. You do not know love or what it means to care for another." He couldn't possibly understand.

He viewed me, some of his joy disappearing. "You are wrong. I know what it is to love." The way his voice softened had me nearly believing him.

The response took me by surprise. "You do?"

"I have had a mate." His lips curved into a sad smile, and he turned from me, looking out over the small pond. "She was exquisite."

I couldn't imagine it, Clause loving someone, choosing to let someone come close, caring for one another. "What happened?"

He turned back to me. "She was a lot like you. Spirited, fierce, never afraid to challenge me." He smiled softly at whatever memory those words triggered for him. "We loved one another. She was my partner. My equal."

"A conjurer?"

He nodded. "Yes. Mist, like you. She could become it, as I think you can too."

"Become it?" My eyes grew larger as I viewed him. He was divulging so much information, breadcrumbs thrown left and right. I did not know which trail to follow.

"She also had a gift from both the light and dark Spirits. Sometimes there is a perfect mixture of both. To where your soul ties to the dark spirit's world as a tether, allowing your body to dissolve with the light Spirit's conjuring without losing your life. It is an incredibly rare gift, a perfect balance, but some elemental conjurors can channel enough to leave their bodies. To become the thing they command."

Could I really do something like that? It sounded unreal, though the way Clause spoke with such conviction, I couldn't help but wonder. "She sounds... remarkable," I mumbled a response while my mind tried to make sense of everything.

"She is." He turned to me, eyes softening. "She was." There was pain there, loss.

"What happened to her?" I asked, not knowing if I should. Yet this was a rare opportunity to learn more of what made the Siddhe King into the being that sat beside me.

Clause took a deep breath and turned from me once more. "She challenged me, and I loved that about her. My father hated that she did that. Someone bold enough to challenge his heir must be bold enough to plot against the King."

My stomach dropped, and I feared I knew where this story would go.

"One night, after finishing my day's duties, I returned to our room. She laid on the bed, unmoving." His eyes slid shut, but he continued talking. "The air was charged with darkness. It was so heavy. I knew, before even seeing her, that something was wrong." His eyes opened yet continued looking forward, focused on nothing in particular. "I approached the bed, finding her throat slit, blood everywhere. The sheets drenched with it."

My hand moved to my mouth, though I made not a single sound.

"I took her into my arms and her body was still so warm. Whoever had done it must have just been there. I ran out of the room, rushing to alert my father. When I entered his chambers, he was washing blood off his hands. He didn't even try to hide it. Instead, he told me he took care of the threat. That I would be all the stronger for it."

Clause released a strangled breath. "She was not the only death that night." He paused for a single heartbeat. "I killed him. My blade cut through him so smoothly despite all the things inside of a body. I sliced into him over and over until his blood drenched the floors."

He finally turned. Cold gray eyes settled on me. "So, I know what it is like to love."

My mouth dried. "I am so sorry." I didn't know what else to say.

His gaze softened, and he lifted his hand. The backs of his fingers brushed my hair back over my shoulder, pulling it away from my face. "You have nothing to apologize for. Eventually, you will understand that whoever this person is, who you think holds your heart, they are not strong enough to hold it."

My ribs felt like a cage, keeping me from being able to breathe effectively. "And you think you are?" Was that really what he was insinuating?

"I know I am." His voice was soft and certain. Not a threat, but a promise.

I shook my head before rising to my feet, putting distance between us. "And what if I refuse you?" How long would his patience last? Did he expect me to sell myself to him to ensure the protection of the Bavadrins and Lysians?

A brief look of disgust passed over his features. "I would never force a woman to be with me if she didn't desire it. You are free to refuse for as long as you can bear it."

As long as I can bear it? He was delusional. The certainty that he knew the outcome would be in his favor was preposterous.

My hands balled into fists at my side. "And if I never want you the way you wish for me to? Would you kill me?" If he saw me as possibly being able to grow into being his equal, then letting me live when I opposed him would be a threat.

His eyes narrowed. "I will never kill you." Another promise spoken into existence. The finality of it felt in my bones. He meant those words. Or he was remarkably good at pretending.

My entire body tensed. "How can you say something like that?" How could a King who kept such a distance from all allow me to wander so close to his heart? And then promised protection when it came to my life. He knew almost nothing about me.

He got to his feet, rising to his full height. His face was unreadable, no trace of emotion in those cold eyes. "Someday, you will understand."

There was more to the story. Things he was not telling me. "You do not intend to shed light on this right now?"

His lips curved into a smirk. "No. Not today."

19

ARIANA

Deep red droplets curved around the edge of the table before dripping onto the floor with a small splash, followed by another and another. Too quickly, it spread.

Blood covered the worktable in the closet of a room where I spent the majority of my time helping the servants, tending to wounds and ailments. This, however, was not something I was prepared for.

"Can you help him?" Soren asked, his brown stare pinning me.

Grabbing a blade, I sliced through the boy's pant leg, just below where a piece of fabric was used to cut off circulation to prevent blood loss. Whoever had done it did not do it effectively, for blood continued pouring out of the wound. Removing the fabric from his leg, I got a good view of a deep gash in his thigh.

I shook my head. "Clause can help you. He has healers in the castle."

"He won't help him." A muscle twitched at Soren's jaw.

"By the Spirit," someone whispered from the door to the small room, pulling my attention to Timothy, whose massive eyes stared at the boy on my table. The boy who looked just about his age, far too young for this to be an ending to his life.

Timothy turned to me, shock melting from his gaze into determination. "What can I do?"

"Grab the thread and needle," I said, turning from him and rushing to get other supplies for disinfection and healing, amongst other things. Timothy moved through the space, quickly and efficiently, careful to stay out of my way.

He handed everything over to me, and I began disinfecting them, as well as the wound.

"Will we need to hold him down?" Timothy asked.

I glanced at the wounded boy's face. His skin was pale, and a sheen of sweat coated his forehead. I reached for his wrist, the pulse hardly even there. "No. I am afraid that he lingers on the edge of death. No amount of pain will pull him out of that lull right now."

Timothy stepped back, yet remained in the room.

I began working at sealing the wound, to keep him from losing even more blood. "Why would Clause not heal this?" I asked Soren, without looking up.

"The Siddhe King only uses his healers for those who have made their place, showing him their benefit to being kept alive. This boy has not yet had that opportunity," he answered. "He has not even completed all the Clan markings that would shield him from such an attack."

Slowly, the wound began closing with every pass of the needle through his skin.

"How did this happen?"

Soren did not answer, and I quickly glanced at him, meeting with his heavy gaze before turning back to my work.

"Is it you who does not wish to tell me? Or are you frightened you will displease your King by sharing that information?" I asked instead.

"We were outside the mountain walls." It made little sense. Outside the mountain walls, it is still Siddhe territory.

"Your own people did this?" My fingers moved swiftly to finish the stitch and tie it off.

"Those who are outside are not cared for, not the way those in here are. Some have tried to rebel. We are sent to keep the peace." His words were cryptic, for keeping the peace likely meant killing.

"Why are the conjurors kept separated from those who are not?" I asked, pouring more disinfectant over the stitches before applying a salve that would help the healing. The boy was lucky I had it already prepared, for it nearly worked like magic compared to every other healing ointment in the world.

"I cannot answer that," Soren said with a frown.

I untied the wrap around the boy's leg. All that could be done for him already was. My attention shifted to his face. He looked terrible. Skin pale and moist, cool to the touch as he lay there, unresponsive. His pulse felt thready, rapid yet incredibly weak.

"Will he make it?" Soren asked.

I shook my head. "I don't know, but his outlook is not good. I think his body is in shock from the blood loss."

My gaze lifted, and I saw fear in that usually unreadable gaze. "Who is this boy to you?"

"My nephew," Soren answered, brows drawn.

Thoughts ran through my mind of what more could be

done. We could have avoided all of it if a healer was available to them.

An idea crossed my mind. "Timothy, grab two needles and the blood tubes." My gaze lifted to Soren. "I will ask you a question. As a leader to your people, you can speak for them. I need you to tell me the truth. What you feel. None of this will get to Clause, to anyone, but it needs to be your truth." I pulled my sleeve up and tied off my upper arm with a rubber cord before splashing disinfectant onto my skin. "Are you a Bavadrin?" I asked Soren, just as Timothy placed the supplies before me.

I grabbed a tube and needle, connecting the two before disinfecting the tip.

The needle nearly bit into my skin before a hand grabbed my wrist, stopping me.

"What are you doing?" Soren asked, hand still preventing me from moving.

We were working against time to give the boy a fighting chance. "I need you to answer my question. Are you a Bavadrin?" I pressed.

There was a pause. All of us suspended in a single moment of time.

"Yes." He finally breathed out the response, hand falling from my wrist, and by the look in his eyes, his answer surprised even himself.

The needle cut through my skin into my vein. My blood ran through the tube to the other end before I sealed it, keeping it from running out. I pressed my fingers into the boy's arm, searching for a vein that was nearly impossible to find. "I am the Bavadrin Leader Superior. My blood runs through the veins of my people." Finally, I found a faint cord beneath the flesh. "I am giving this boy a chance of surviving this." I sent the needle of the other end into his arm and, by the Spirit's blessing, found my mark.

My blood began running into the boy.

"What if I lied?" Soren asked, his voice soft, as if afraid.

"You didn't," I answered with certainty.

"But what if?"

"Then he may very well die. My blood possibly killing him." I glanced at Soren, who nodded yet said nothing more. "This is the Spirit's way."

The three of us remained in that room, standing around the boy lying on the table. Time trickled past and nothing outwardly changed. The boy still did not move, the three of us still stood in somber silence. Slowly, I began feeling the weakness as it came over me. My head going dizzy. I shifted, placing my hands on the edge of the bloody table, distributing my weight.

"Maybe we should stop?" Soren asked, his gaze torn between duty and love. He wanted his nephew to live, but he also likely was not supposed to allow harm to fall upon me. But I was not in harm's way.

"I can go a little longer." I sounded more confident than I felt.

"Maybe you should sit down? Want me to bring a chair?" Timothy moved closer. His hand reached out as if to touch my shoulder, though he hesitated, uncertain whether he should touch me at all.

"I'm okay. Thank you." I began swaying when I looked up, trying to meet his eye.

Soren reached out for the tube connecting his nephew and me and pinched it, cutting off the flow. "No. That's enough."

"Okay." I suddenly lost my will to oppose him and pulled the needle from my arm, pressing the clean fabric to it. I went to take a step, but my vision turned blotchy, and darkness took over. Timothy's arms circled me, keeping me from falling to the ground. Then everything went black.

I WOKE WITH A START. The room blurred into focus, *my* room.

"Hey, welcome back to the land of the living!" Olive rushed to my bed, her eyes large and hopeful. "You gave us a scare there." She smiled.

I pulled myself up into a sitting position and leaned against the headboard. The effort such a small thing took was extraordinary.

"What happened?" I asked. My head spun, worsened by the shock of being in my bed, not knowing how long I was out or what transpired after the darkness took me. Was everyone alright? Had Clause harmed any of them for my actions? My throat closed up as panic coursed through me, chest tightening.

"Hey." Her hand found mine. "You are safe. Everyone is." Her voice soothed, and the tension left me, replaced by a calm. It happened so quickly that it felt unnatural.

"Did you just calm me?" I looked at Olive's hand covering mine and she removed it.

A small guilty smile warmed her face. "I did. Sorry. You are still weak, and I didn't want you to worry yourself into passing out again. I know I should have probably asked first."

I moved past what she did and into what pulled at my heart. "The boy?"

"Alive."

Relief moved through me. "And Soren?"

Olive tilted her head towards the door. "Waiting in the hall outside your room like usual."

The calming sensation she washed over me became a real one. My muscles loosened.

"What are you doing here?"

She shrugged, taking a step away from the bed. "Clause wanted someone to stay with you, so here I am. He intends to bring you some food in case you are hungry. I drew you a bath, in case you woke soon. You have enough time to relax and clean up some if you wish to before he arrives."

"Thank you." I slowly rose from the bed, surprised to not feel as dizzy as expected. My gaze drifted to the bath, steam invitingly rose from the tub.

"Do you want for me to stay?" She asked, drawing my attention back to her.

"No, I'll be okay, thank you." I walked her to the door. It was a relief to find Soren standing in the hall.

He gave a slight nod of his head in recognition, and I couldn't help but smile at him.

"Didn't believe me?" Olive glanced at Soren and raised a brow as she turned to me, likely sensing my relief.

"I'm sorry. I don't mean any disrespect. Yet, hearing and seeing for myself are two different things." I still was uncertain of whether to trust her. She seemed nice, but that meant little when we were strangers, and she appeared loyal to her King.

She shrugged, a smile splitting her face. "No worries. I get it. Rest well." She hugged me. "Good luck."

"Why would I need luck?" I asked as she pulled away from me.

"For when the Siddhe King comes to visit," she stated it as though it were obvious.

My brows pulled together. "I don't understand."

"He was not exactly happy that you decided to endanger yourself."

"I didn't..."

She held up her hand; the action cutting me off. "You do not need to waste your energy and breath explaining it to me. But you should probably think about how you want to explain it to him."

"Thanks for the warning," I murmured, wondering what explanation the Siddhe King needed other than a boy's life was threatened and that I could help.

20

ERIK

"We will move our forces into the Siddhe land." Willis began the meeting by dropping new information. "My wolves have scouted the territory. It seems that the Siddhe never venture between their city and their borders. Staying hidden amongst the forest and mountain range should not be an issue as we slowly close in."

His gaze drifted around the room, landing on the several of us privy to such meetings as we sat around the wooden table.

"And what if the Siddhe have someone like you? Someone who uses animals to monitor and spy," Eislyn asked. She joined us several days ago, and her mind has been invaluable since.

"Then they already know what we have been doing, but I do not think that is the case," Willis answered with a frown.

"I agree," Kiora stated in support. "From what Shay has shared with us, Clause seems fond of Ariana." My blood boiled at the mention of his name as the young Sparrow continued, "Maybe even obsessed. Yet he did not know of her existence until she displayed her power for all to see and took back control of the Bavadrin lands. He likely has spies, but they are probably not animals. They are people. They know the common knowledge and not much more."

"You think he only knows common knowledge? Care to wager a bet on that?" Iver smirked.

Kiora snorted softly, hazel eyes sliding to Iver. "You have nothing to offer which I desire in order to place a bet."

He tsked softly. "Is that so?" Earning an eye roll from her.

"Why move our forces now?" I asked Willis, getting back to the point. The Bavadrin turned to me and hesitated. Something was happening. He refused to give detailed accounts of Ariana's whereabouts and experiences anymore. Only things he deemed pertinent to our success moving forward. Though for him to now wish for us to advance into the Siddhe territory meant something.

"Did something happen?" Kole leaned forward, resting his thick forearms on the table, when Willis was not quick to reply. Everyone looked at him, waiting for a response.

"Nothing of concern yet. But there is a strange tension rising. Shay senses it. The wolf fears for Ariana. I believe it is time to move closer in case she needs us to act. We have learned a lot since her time there, and we have prepared for what is to come." His brown eyes held my stare.

"Why do you hold back what you know?" I pressed. Under the table, my hands formed into fists as frustration heated me from within. The Bavadrin Ariana left in charge pulled back on his knowledge, and all that it did was anger me.

"I share what is needed."

"We are on the same side," Kole stated.

Willis shrugs, turning to him. "Does not mean that every detail of the Leader Superior's time there needs to be recanted for everyone here to judge."

"What is there to judge?" I asked, my voice deceptively even, portraying a calm that I did not feel.

Willis turned to me, lips set in a firm line.

I released a disheartened breath. "You think I would judge her? For doing all she can to survive in that place?"

Iver sighed, turning to Edda, whose gaze remained fixed on the table, not present in the moment. "What about you, Seer? Care to share what you see?"

Onyx eyes lifted towards my youngest brother. "Everything is drenched in shadows. Nothing is as clear as it should be."

"Ah, you Bavarians and your cryptic replies." Iver remained focused on her. "You see something. You just wish to keep it to yourself, much like your little friend here." He nodded towards Willis before turning back to her. "Say we move into the Siddhe land. Will that further endanger Ariana?"

Her lips thinned. "No."

"And if I enter the city to find her?" I asked.

"Absolutely not," Willis stated, a hard edge to his voice.

"Shay has found a way in." I turned to him. Using a bit of detail he happened to inform us of. "An entire army could not take that route, but I could. And I am one of the strongest conjurors you have."

"Are we forgetting about me?" Iver grinned, though he placed a hand on his chest as if offended.

"He said *one* of the strongest." Eislyn cut in. "And you can't help but stick your nose into trouble, Iver. So that means you get to stay with the rest of us."

"Ah, still bitter towards me, I see." He smirked at Eislyn, who shook her head at him.

I turned to Edda. "You did not answer me."

Her frown deepened. "I see two hazy paths before you. If you go, that is. One will help her, while the other will destroy her. You hold the answer to your own question based on your decisions alone. I must warn you, if you go, it will not be easy for you or her. You will see her experience pain, and you will need to refrain from trying to protect her from it or the outcome will be catastrophic."

"So, my going could be helpful?" I leaned towards the old woman, as if hanging off her words. A spark of hope shot through me even though I swore to myself I would never trust her sight.

"Or harmful," Willis stated the other path.

"What of your future?" Eislyn asked Edda. "It is clear something troubles you. That your mind is elsewhere most of the time."

"At this point, I am trying to also not do harm," she stated with a frown.

"What's that mean?" Kole looked at her like she was a foreign animal. It was the only way he ever viewed her.

She released a low hum before answering. "There has been a block on my future for a long time. I cannot see it. For the first time since I can remember, I am moving through the world completely blind. To clear my sight I am going to need to leave. A few days in isolation should recenter things."

"A few centuries in isolation would be preferred." Kole muttered under his breath.

How was she blind if she knew that some of her choices could cause harm? It made no sense, though she hardly ever did.

I turned to Willis, focusing on something potentially more fruitful than entertaining the old-timer. "I am going to Ariana. No more waiting."

His stare pinned me, cold and unyielding. "Did you not

hear the warning? Sure, you can help, but you can also make it worse."

"I won't make it worse." The words were uttered through clenched teeth.

"Do not be so certain," Edda spoke up. "Iver kept what he was from you because of hesitation regarding your response to learning his truth. Even your own family is cautious of you and now you wish to enter a highly volatile environment where a single breath in the wrong direction can bring the castle crumbling down on top of Ariana."

A ripple of anger scorched me from within. "I am not some boy who cannot control himself. I would never bring her any harm."

Edda's black eyes narrow on me, challenging. "What if you get there only to learn she wishes for you to leave? That her heart now favors him and not you. What would you do?"

The room turned icy cold at her insinuation. My muscles contract and it was an effort to unlock even my jaw in order to formulate a response. "Is that true?"

Edda tilted her head, viewing me. "We are stuck in a layered web, all of us. Each move comprises potential repercussions."

It was not an answer, yet the table did not wait for her answer, but mine. All eyes focused on me.

What if Ariana wanted the Siddhe King? The notion never crossed my mind. In all my thoughts of her and him, I always viewed him as an enemy, someone forcing her to stay there. Keeping her from returning to me.

I will find you. Those were the words I promised her. That I would come for her. That I would bring her back with me. But what if that was not what she wanted?

A sharp pain cut through me at the possibility of a reality I never considered.

"I would leave, if she wished for me to," I finally answered.

I would find her. I would keep my promise. Though she never promised me she would return with me. And if she wished to stay, I wouldn't stop her.

The thoughts rushing through my mind nearly choked me.

"You would follow her lead in this?" Kiora asked. "No matter what? Ariana has been in there for weeks. She knows what she is dealing with more than any of us. If you go there and she tells you to do something, or not do something, you think you can follow without hesitation?"

I turned to the Sparrow, thankful for her question for pulling me out of the spiraling of my thoughts. "If it helps her, then yes."

Kiora turned to Willis. "The decision is clearly yours. But if sending him gives her any edge of coming out of this better..."

Willis nodded, gaze withdrawn in thought. Waiting for him to reply was grating. Especially when I was not sure I would listen if he forbade me from going to her. I did not promise to follow the Bavadrin's second in command without question. Finally, he said, "If your actions make this worse for her, then you make yourself a threat. You will be eliminated without hesitation."

"Have you lost your mind?" Kole's eyes nearly popped out of his head. His head snapped so quickly to Willis, that his neck was bound to feel it the next day. A heavy tension settled in the room, weaving itself through the space. A thread connecting all of us.

Willis ignored him, gaze locked on mine. "If that is a risk you are willing to take."

Kole rose from the table, stopped only by Eislyn's hand, grabbing his wrist. She shook her head gently, stilling him.

"I am willing," I stated.

"Be not mistaken." Edda pinned me with a stare. "You are to be a wallflower. There for support, but not to intervene on your own accord. If Ariana needs you to do something, she will say. Otherwise, you do nothing to change the path of fate as it weaves around her. Be a wallflower, or you doom her."

"Noted."

Edda stood, walking towards the exit. "I need to clear my mind. Hopefully then I will be able to see more." She paused at the door for a moment, as if intending to say something else, before walking out without another word.

Iver released a low whistle. "Love makes people agree to the wildest things. Even Kings may be willing to fall for it." He said *Kings*. As if someone other than I may agree to things for love. As if Clause perhaps could. Though there was no way that was what this was. Clause might have thought he loved her, but it was mere infatuation. He did not know Ariana enough for anything more.

"As if you know anything about it," Kiora mumbled under her breath, drawing Iver's eye.

"Care to find out what I know?" He smirked.

Kole turned to Iver. "Are you ever serious?" His words were a growl. Anger radiated from him, hating how things were turning out.

"So, it's settled," I stated, getting the room back on track. "I am going." Though it was a statement, I looked at Willis for confirmation.

He dipped his head while his lips remained pressed into a displeased line. From his view, this was a gamble. A possibility to either help or harm his leader. But I would not allow for that harm to be because of my actions.

"When do we all leave?" Eislyn asked.

Willis said, "Prepare your forces now. We leave at dawn."

Standing from the table, all eyes landed on me once more. "I am leaving tonight." I turned to Kole and Eislyn. "And I am going alone."

They both didn't like it, apparent by the frowns on their faces, but nodded in understanding.

With anticipation, I turned and headed towards the exit.

I was going to see her again, to be near her. Despite the doubt the Seer planted in my mind, there was also hope. I could help Ariana by going to her, which meant that she wouldn't send me away. For if I arrived only to be asked to leave, then how would that offer her any benefit? It wouldn't.

I would go to her, keeping my promise, and bringing her home.

"One more thing." Willis's voice stilled me just before I reached for the door. "There is something all of you should know." I turned to face him. "Ariana finally learned why the Siddhe King keeps conjurors separated from those without the gift."

21

ARIANA

Cold silver eyes meet mine before sliding down my figure. Taking in the robe I wore, covering the thigh-high nightgown underneath. After bathing, I put on something comfortable and crawled back into bed.

Clause's gaze stopped at my face and softened with a tinge of concern. "Did I wake you?" The plate in his hand lowered at his side. He seemed truly apologetic at the notion of disturbing my rest.

My hair swayed gently as I shook my head. "I tried to rest, but it never came." I eyed the plate, filled with food. "Thank you for bringing that, but I am afraid my head is still spinning, and I am too nauseous to eat anything."

His unyielding stare held mine. "I can leave it in your room, in case you change your mind." It was a request to enter the chamber without actually asking the question.

The two of us had spent plenty of time alone, so why did this feel more uncomfortable than what was typical?

"Okay." I stepped aside, letting him in. Knowing that he

wished to speak about more than the food, and so did I. There were questions burning through me, demanding answers, preventing me from rest. I gently closed the door behind him.

He walked to the bedside table, lowering the plate onto it, before facing me once more.

"You were reckless today," he said. The words sounded so simple from his lips, yet carried a strange weight.

A power drifted out of him, one that commanded the very room he stood in. It came from a dark place. He was the shadow that snuffed out all the light. The shadow that took no prisoners. The shadow that pulled everything into a dark abyss from which there was no escape. Except I refused to move, refused to allow him to cast that shadow over me.

An unease roamed through the room, sending my pulse climbing.

"I wouldn't have had to be if your healers actually healed your people," I stated, refusing to let his presence rattle me.

His jaw twitched, the only sign of his displeasure. "That has to be earned."

"A boy's life hung in the balance." I took a single step towards him, my words a challenge. Why was he so stuck in this way of thinking?

"If he is too weak to survive, then he is too weak to serve. This is the way of life. The strong remain, the weak do not."

Even though Clause once said he saw me as his potential equal, it was clear he also saw me as weak in caring for others. His views drove me mad.

Anger simmered under my skin, heating me. The rush of emotion made my head spin even faster. I didn't have the energy to oppose him in his deepest thoughts. So instead, I asked for something else. "Why do you keep the conjurors in this city and the others outside?"

His gaze narrowed.

"I have been honest with you this entire time. Can you say the same?" I pressed when he didn't answer.

He approached, shoulders moving with each step, like a stalking panther, stopping just out of reach. His jaw set, features strong and regal. "You already know the answer. You just have not connected the dots."

I sucked in a deep, steadying breath. "Why not help me then? Because right now, I am too tired to connect much of anything." It was an effort just to stand without swaying.

His lip curved into a crooked smile at my words. "Sometimes, those who are the weakest are the greatest threat," he stated, something he had already shared with me before.

My brows pulled together. "Non-conjurors are a threat to conjurors?"

Clause pivoted, his attention drifting towards the window, and he paced towards it in a few steps. The candlelight flickered, highlighting the sharp features of his profile. "My father was not a conjuror. It is the reason I had to spill his blood. Forced to use a blade, over and over." A look of disgust curled his lip. "It is a filthy thing, taking life in such a way, staining my hands with someone so... undeserving."

The shock of what he was saying settled over me.

"You are afraid of them." My words were a whisper. The massive mystery of why the separation existed, explained by the Siddhe King's fears. It made sense. Clause could take the life of a conjuror with a single touch, but those who had no gifts stood a chance against him, and he feared that.

Having so many conjurors in the Siddhe city overwhelmed me because I saw them as a great threat. Yet, it is those without gifts that threatened him. Conjurors were a shield he easily controlled. That meant those without gifts could become the blade that would be his undoing.

Clause turned to me so quickly; I flinched back. "I know my weaknesses, and I remove them," he stated, voice cold and cunning. He stood before me, a pillar of strength, yet deep within he was afraid, like the rest of us. But he didn't have to be.

I shook my head. "You do not have to live this way." He was allowing his fears to control him. If only he gave those outside his city a chance, and treated them like his own, then they likely wouldn't fight against him, would have no need to. They were an enemy of his own creation, and he was too nearsighted to see that.

He sighed, bringing a hand to rub his temples briefly before dropping it to his side. When his gaze met mine once more, it lost some of its edge. "You continue to believe this notion that you are safe, even with weakness flowing around you." He shook his head. "You are blinded. It is not possible to be surrounded only by good. Trusting others is not enough. Fear is the only way to rule. You must have power over it. You must control the fear of others, and you must exterminate your own."

He took a slow step, entering my space. Lifting his hand, his fingers brushed my cheek, warming it. The touch was so strangely intimate that it rendered me immobile. "You have been living in a fantasy and though it is beautiful, it is not real. I can clear the shadow of this illusion. I can bring your world into the light. If you want it." His hand fell to his side, head tilting as if waiting for a reply.

"What do you mean?" A danger circled me, an uncertainty stalking me. It paced through the space, rubbing up against me before settling into a crouch, waiting to strike.

He stepped even closer, and with him, that dangerous sensation grew. "You need to decide what you want, Ariana. Do you want the truth?" A darkness misted over his eyes. "I must warn you, I take no pleasure in bringing you pain, but that is exactly what I will do, if that is what you need. I can free you from the shackles of this fantasy you live. I can show you your world for what it truly is."

My throat closed up, a tremor running down my spine. "What truth?"

"Do you wish to know?" There was something captivating in the way he asked the question. Like it was a promise instead of a question.

"Yes," I answered softly.

"Even if it may destroy a part of you?"

My heart skipped a beat. Why was this conversation having such an effect? Did I believe I lived in a world surrounded by lies? No. And yet, nervous energy vibrated under my skin.

"Yes," I finally said, not understanding what exactly I agreed to.

He nodded, gaze briefly cast down in thought. "The day after tomorrow, we will not break our fast together. At noon, come to the throne room. Exactly at noon, no sooner. I will leave the door open for you, feel free to linger in the hall and listen in for as long as you wish. And if you choose to enter the room, you are welcome to do so."

I swallowed, my head reeling. He seemed to sense my uncertainty and stepped even closer, his eyes softening with concern. Was it a concern for me or for something else?

"You are so beautiful." His hand found my cheek once more. I should have stepped away, yet my feet remained planted firmly beneath me. "The purity of your soul, the curiosity you have with the world."

I could no longer breathe right, causing the room to spin even more than before.

"It is your weakness, but it is also one of the things that has always drawn me to you." His words were gentle and though I didn't quite understand them, they did something to me. Warmth spread through my chest at his proximity. At his touch. "If I have to help destroy that part of you for you to live on, then without hesitation, I will." His gaze dipped to my lips. "I just want to taste you, once, with you still like this. With you surrounded in hope."

No.

"Clause." His name was hardly a whisper slipping past my lips. It was a warning. And instead of causing him to hesitate, it was as if I called him closer.

I did not get a chance to voice the rest of my words. The *please don't,* that died in my throat.

All the distance between us vanished. The Siddhe King's mouth pressed to mine, arms circling me in an instant. I was immediately overwhelmed by him. My heart felt as though it exploded in my chest. My brain made little sense of anything as if his touch turned it to sludge. I pressed my hand to his chest, a halfhearted effort to push him away. And though I couldn't think clearly, I felt *everything.*

Our breaths mingled moments before his tongue slipped into my mouth, colliding with mine. There was not a bit of hesitation when it came to the way he kissed me. None of the typical exploration of each other that would have been expected for a first kiss. Instead, he simply devoured me. As if starved. He took me as though I had always been his for the taking. And the way his hands gripped me, moving over my flesh with need, my body responded.

It was as if his soul somehow whispered to mine.

His touch burned through me with a strange certainty. Fingers traveling across my skin, over the contours of my body.

No. I needed to stop this. Some shred of my brain worked enough to know this, but it was as if some sort of spell was cast over me. I was not myself, at least not entirely.

His fingers slid up the back of my neck before spearing through my hair.

A moan slipped past my lips.

Suddenly, we moved two steps back, and he pressed me against a wall. His mouth was relentless as it consumed me. His leg forced its way between mine, causing my robe to part and the nightgown to ride up on my thigh. One of his hands drifted up over my breast before stopping at my neck.

Fear sliced through me, of what I was allowing to happen. And with it came a trickle of clarity.

His other hand released my hair and found my thigh, gripping it possessively. When his fingers started rising higher up my leg, a burst of energy moved through me and my hand found his wrist, stilling him.

Finally, he pulled back, our lips parting. Though he didn't remove his body from mine, keeping me trapped between him and the wall.

I was nearly panting, trying to catch my breath while I viewed him, uncertain of how he would respond. *Afraid* of how he might respond.

Sadness tainted his eyes as they searched mine. "I will free you from the lies that have surrounded you from birth. I will show you how cold the world truly is. And know that when you need shelter, when you need truth, that I have been one of the few in your life to truly give it to you." His hand found one of mine, and he brought it to his lips, kissing my palm. The act was incredibly tender. For someone capable of so much cruelty, I was stunned by the moments when he was gentle.

He then stepped away, releasing me completely.

I remained there, leaning against the wall, unable to move or even speak.

He took another step back before finally breaking our stare, glancing at the tray of food. "You should eat something if you can stomach it." He peered at me when I didn't reply. "Good-night Ariana." He dipped his head before excusing himself from my room.

I couldn't respond to anything he said. Instead, images of what we did replayed in my mind over and over. It was just a kiss, but why did it feel like something deeply disturbing? It was wrong in every way. And yet, it was as if my blood responded beyond my control.

I did not want him. Not him.

Thoughts of Erik slammed into me with such force that I choked.

Tears lined my eyes, and I slid down to the floor.

What in Spirit's name was I doing?

22

ARIANA

"Ugh, do you have to do this? Why are you even here at this hour?" Gorm's voice grumbled through the space as I placed a salve on his foot.

"I am meeting Clause at noon today instead of this morning," I commented with a frown, choosing to ignore his first question. Unease settled over me like a fine blanket at the thought of the Siddhe King's truths. The things he said would open my eyes to the lies of my life. And that was not the only thing that troubled me regarding him.

Gorm jerked, bringing my attention to his grumpy face. "Hold still," I instructed.

"It tickles!" He mumbled a few words I could not make out before saying, "Seriously, I am fine."

The angry inflamed wound on his foot said otherwise. "No, you are not, you injured yourself. Again. And it is infected. *Again.* I told you to check your feet before bed every night and to come to me if there are ever any issues." I had no idea how anything tickled the man who could hardly feel a thing at all where his feet were concerned.

He grunted. "You think I am this young and limber fella, do you? Well, I'll have you know I am an old man. And I cannot bend like I once could. It's not easy for me to see my feet every night."

"I'm going to secure a mirror to the floor by your bed, then." I snapped. It was actually a decent idea.

He snorted in response. As I continued working on finishing up with his foot, we fell into a silence that allowed my mind to wander. It was the day Clause believed would change my world. He intended to show me something that he thought proved his way of life superior to my own.

But no matter how much I considered the possibilities, the outcomes always were the same. I loved those who I trusted, those who were closest to me. I would never turn my back on them. The Siddhe King was wrong.

I knew it in my bones that he was wrong. Yet, a dark cloud hovered over me, trailing me. It rumbled with thunder, on the edge of a downpour that had not yet come. Being suspended in that moment of waiting for some unknown horrors to unfold was torturous. It twisted my stomach, poisoned my mind, and stole my sleep.

And then there was the moment I shared with the Siddhe King. What happened between us made no sense. How I could have responded that way, why my mind was so slow to register everything, to react. To push him away. Something within felt a belonging being in his arms, but that feeling was foreign. It was wrong. And it was enough to frighten me.

What little control I thought I had begun slipping through my fingers without my notice. Leaving me with nothing but air to grasp at.

I wanted to go home.

I wanted the safety of arms that I chose to find comfort in. Not ones that circled me when reality strangely merged with something indescribable. Something was happening and I couldn't understand what it was.

What I would give for a single day back home, in my room, surrounded by friends. What I would give to see Erik, to remember how good life could be even in the darkest moments.

Paws scraped across the floor as Shay ran into the room, coming around to stand beside Gorm where she seemed to dance excitedly.

"Hey girl." I smiled at her, my one piece of home. "You never came back last night. I was getting worried." Typically, she always returned in the night, sleeping in my room. It felt uncomfortable spending the night without her.

She whined as though apologizing.

"What's a girl like you doing in a place like this?" A voice sliced through the room, stealing my breath. A memory moved through me, flooding my mind with the image of Erik and the sound of those same words spoken to me the first time I met him.

Had my thoughts of him brought forward a cruel illusion?

Gorm glanced from Shay to something behind me, before angling his head as if encouraging me to look.

Fear settled under my skin then. A fear to hope. A fear of being fooled by a trick of a distraught mind.

I rose to my feet and slowly turned, wishing to remain suspended in that moment of uncertainty longer. For at least there was still hope nestled in it.

Warm blue eyes met with mine.

Erik.

Breath left me.

He stood before me.

His clothes were simple, nothing to mark him as the King he was. But there was no disguising him. No hiding the presence that bled from his skin, thick and undeniable. Power rolled off him in waves, filling the space, pressing into me. It wrapped around me like unseen hands, his strength an intoxicating force, the heat in his stare a slow-burning fire.

A single heartbeat stretched between us.

And I was caught in it.

Those predatory eyes pinned me, held me captive in their depths. *Is this real?*

Then, my heart beat again, and I was released.

My body moved before my mind could catch up—drawn to him like the tide to the moon, pulled without hesitation, without resistance.

Powerful arms closed around me. One wound tight at my waist, anchoring me to him. The other skimmed up my back, fingers pressing into the delicate skin just above my nape.

The scent of him surrounded me, and I breathed him in—desperate, hungry, filling my lungs with him. My pulse pounded against my ribs, but in his arms, I could feel it—his heartbeat, slamming just as wildly as mine.

It is real.

The familiarity of him unraveled me. The safety of his embrace shattered the last fragile thread of strength I clung to.

A sob tore from my throat.

Tears fell freely now, and his hold only tightened—as if he could somehow keep me from ever slipping away again.

I shattered as he collected the pieces, not letting a single one fall to the ground.

"How is this possible? How is this real?" I whispered, unable to release him. Afraid that if I let go, he would disappear.

His head dipped and his breath moved over my neck as he spoke. "Shay found a way in through the mountains."

My arms tightened around him. New tears flowed at the sound of his voice.

It is real. I couldn't stop telling myself this.

"You are here," I whispered.

"I told you I would come for you." His voice was so gentle, so safe and warm. Had it always harbored such a tone? One that caused my heart to trip over beats.

A cough from Gorm somehow infused me with the strength I needed to release Erik and step away enough to view him. He towered over me, capable frame tense while his gaze explored my face, as though afraid that *I* would vanish.

He raised a hand, the pad of his thumb smearing the last tear that slipped past my eyes.

"What now?" I asked, stunned by the change of having him before me.

Erik glanced at Gorm without replying. Suspicion tainted his stare.

The old man chuckled. "Young fella, this young lady has touched my dirty feet on more than one occasion. And I already know she plots secret plans right under the Siddhe King's nose. I would never betray her. She has done more for me in her short time here than that King ever did."

My lips pulled up lightly at Gorm's comment. "We can trust him." I half expected Erik to refuse and force us to find more privacy.

Sapphire eyes turned back to me, and they nearly took my breath away. The strength in his gaze was overwhelming. "The forces have moved closer. They are likely about a day away now, if they were to be needed."

I nodded, brows pulling together. "Did something happen?" Why did they move closer?

Erik tilted his head, his muscles tensing, his body growing rigid as if bracing himself for something. "You tell me. All Willis would say is that Shay sensed a change, and that danger seemed to surround you more. It was enough to spook Willis into action."

Clause. Flashes of what happened invaded my mind, stealing the moment. Robbing my relief at seeing Erik.

My attention dropped to the floor as guilt wrapped its hand around my throat and squeezed.

"Did something happen?" Erik pressed, tension seeping into his voice.

I swallowed, unable to look at him as my mind raced.

He stepped towards me, yet I stepped back, gaze colliding with his once more.

"Why are you here?" I asked.

He looked baffled and confused. "I came for you. There is no other reason."

My chest tightened with a horrible unease. It was the day Clause intended to open my eyes to some sort of lies. The same day Erik happened to show up.

I took another step back. "You are certain?"

Erik's thick brows drew together, and he viewed me as though looking at something he didn't understand. "What is this about?"

"Clause said..." My voice trailed off, suddenly uncertain how much I should even share. What if whatever Clause was insinuating had to do with Erik?

My heart rate spiked. A cold sweat came over me, my stomach growing queasy. I was going to be sick.

Erik searched my face, though he made no move to close the distance. "What is happening? Why are you afraid?"

My fear– he smelled it.

I couldn't answer him. Instead, I stood before him like a silent coward.

"Are you... are you afraid of me?" His voice grew low, a look of disbelief passing over him.

I shook my head no, though was uncertain. "I just... I don't know."

"What don't you know?" He went completely rigid.

"The timing of your arrival, it..." I tore my gaze from him and looked at Gorm. "Would it be noticed if he stayed here for a little bit?"

Gorm snorted. "No one would notice. He can even come to work with me tomorrow. A big healthy guy like this would be useful."

I glanced at his leg. "Not with your foot like that."

Gorm grunted. "Young lady, you think Clause will ensure I get fed if I do not work?"

"I'll make sure of it." I turned to Erik, who was still staring at me. Uncertainty dug its talons into me.

"Should I leave?" He asked, his voice so low I was uncertain I heard correctly.

"What?" My throat closed up.

"Do you want me to leave here?" Pained eyes searched mine for an answer I could not fully provide.

"No I–" I looked at the ground, trying to collect my head. "The timing of your arrival is just... I'm sorry. I don't know what's going on." I was drowning in the uncertainty surrounding me.

Erik stepped towards me, reaching for me. I moved back before he could touch me. A look of hurt flashed across his face and it ate me alive. Guilt wrapped around me so tightly I could hardly draw in a breath.

"Will you stay here?" I asked.

"Where are you going?" Confusion painted his face with a frown.

"There's somewhere I am needed. I hope it will help clarify some things for me. And then I will explain as much as I can. I just need you to wait here. Please." I paused, searching his face, but found nothing threatening. I trusted him. In my gut, at my core, Erik was the truth. Yet, my mind somehow became poisoned, and I doubted how much of my gut to trust. "Will you wait?"

He shrugged. "I have nowhere else to be." He seemed at a loss for words.

I glanced at Gorm who said, "I'll keep an eye on him. He will be okay here."

I nodded. "Stay off the foot." I turned, glancing at Erik. "I'm sorry. I'll be back." I left the two of them in thick, uncomfortable silence.

My heart raced, pulse throbbing in my head.

Unease coated me in a heavy film that I could not shake. Something was happening. Though I could sense it, I was also blinded by it. What was going on?

I would have been shaking if I were not moving quickly down the hall, heading towards the secrets Clause believed he could unveil. My steps were swift and silent, fueled by a mixture of adrenaline and fear.

I turned down the hall the throne room was off of and saw Soren at the end, standing guard by the open door. His jaw clenched when he glanced my way, noting my approach. Something about it only worsened the dread coursing in rivers through my veins.

As I drew closer, voices seeped out.

I paused by the door. Holding my breath so that I could hear the next words clear as day.

"Are you sure you wish for this? Our agreement was made long before her birth. Whether she knows it or not, you are, after all, Ariana's last living relative," Clause said, voice as smooth as silk.

My entire body tensed, and the dread coursing through me melted into something so much worse. Something that had not even a name. I had no living blood relatives, at least none that I knew of.

"Yes, I am certain. It's time you give me what is owed." A gravelly voice answered, robbing me of breath. My heart stopped in my chest at the sound of it, at the sound of *her* voice.

Edda.

23

ARIANA

I couldn't move, let alone draw in a single breath.

Instead, I stood there. Mortified.

Millions of thoughts rushed through my mind, none of them making sense, none heard clearly enough to even try to decipher. My world shifted.

Only when more words were spoken beyond that open throne room door did my thoughts go silent. The storm stilled enough that the ocean inside of me turned flat and waveless as I listened.

"You haven't even asked about how she is doing. Do you not care to know?" Clause asked.

"She is alive. That is all I need to know. Will you stop dragging your feet and give me what you owe?" Edda replied.

"This will destroy her. You vanishing like this. It isn't too late. You can live out the rest of your life at her side. I will welcome you here if you wish to stay."

"She has been here only a few weeks and already you have turned sentimental?" By her tone, I easily imagined the arch in

Edda's silver brow that accompanied the comment. An invisible dagger of emotion pierced my heart.

Clause released a sigh. "Very well. How young are we going for? Your early twenties again?"

Again. A word meaning that this was not the first time they exchanged things.

"Yes," Edda confirmed.

There was a moment of silence, and then her voice, but it wasn't hers, not quite. A new youthfulness held her tone. "Was that so difficult?"

The Siddhe King chuckled darkly. "Not at all."

"Well, I would love to say this was a pleasure, but it wasn't." Edda quipped.

"Your kindness could kill." Clause replied, his tone light.

She snorted, and suddenly footsteps echoed through the throne room, approaching the exit.

My body acted before I ever gave it a command. Suddenly my back straightened, shoulders squared, head held high. I moved down the rest of the hall, turning into the room without missing a beat.

My gaze slid to her. Onyx eyes I could recognize anywhere stared back at me, but a face and body much younger. She was beautiful, her hair black as her eyes, not a single strand of gray. Skin void of the timeless wrinkles that were once permanent fixtures.

She glanced at me, yet her face portrayed nothing. Her steps did not falter as she hurried towards the exit. I slowed as she approached, the space between us closing quickly.

"Do I know you?" I asked, voice certain and strong. It portrayed nothing of the mass of emotions wreaking havoc within.

Her attention flickered back to me. "Sorry, girl. I don't know you." Her lips curved down disapprovingly. She did not even hesitate as she breezed past me.

I froze in my tracks. She saw me and addressed me, yet acted as though I was no one to her. It was such an exceptional act that I nearly doubted everything I heard moments ago.

My gaze locked with the gray eyes across the room, Clause's features unreadable. It was impossible to know what he thought or felt at that moment. A perfect facade, just like Edda's.

Another pulse of energy shot through me. I whirled around.

"Edda," I called her name.

The woman stopped mid-step then. Her head turned, not quite looking at me, eyes cast down. "I do not know anyone by that name." She twisted away and continued towards the exit without waiting for a response.

Pain melded with my conjuring, condensing within, before traveling to my palm. My hand shot out before me, and with it, a wall of mist formed, blocking her path and the door.

She spun around, eyes blazing, as they met with mine. They harbored accusations. However, none of it made it to her lips. As if too surprised to actually speak.

"Why?" My voice wavered, the only sign of the terrible hole in my chest.

Her jaw clenched. "Girl, have you been hit in the head? I do not know you or what you speak of."

Clause tisked softly from somewhere behind me. "Oh, C'mon Edda, why not answer her question?"

Her eyes widened just a fraction in shock, gaze cut to him, sharp as any conjured blade. But no conjuring could ever touch him. "How dare you?" Her lip curled.

"How dare I?" His voice grew colder. "You have kept her

from me for how long? You knew she existed this entire time, yet kept us apart."

I shook my head. "What does that even mean?" I looked over my shoulder at him. "Why me? You have plenty of conjurors. You do not need me for anything." Why did he pretend I was so important to him?

His attention moved to me, drifting over my face, dipping to my lips before rising. "You are wrong. I have always needed you." His tone remained firm, yet grew a gentle edge when addressing me.

"Don't listen to him." The venom in Edda's youthful voice was potent, drawing all of us to her. "He will destroy you if you let him." Her onyx eyes blazed as they often had when I was a girl and Fraser did something terrible to me or in front of me. Yet now that cold, judgmental look should have been reserved for no one but herself.

I wanted to hate Clause, yet a part of me felt sorry for the Siddhe King. His views of the world and people isolated him. The life he lived was a sad shell compared to what it could have been. It didn't help that since my arrival, he primarily only showed me kindness. I began harboring a strange compassion for him. A difficult life path led him to such a sad belief.

"How?" I asked.

"How?" She looked at me, baffled.

"Yes. How exactly will he destroy me?" I asked, gaze narrowing. Clause did not obliterate my heart, did not tilt the world beneath my feet. She, however, did.

I felt as though I was falling into a bottomless pit. My stomach wedged in my throat, my heart no longer beating.

Edda scoffed. "Have you forgotten already of your long-lost friend Landin?" She took a step towards me, eyes burning with a viciousness I knew all too well, but from a face I hardly recognized. "What, out of sight, out of mind? You wept for a few days and now have found a home in his murderer's arms?"

"How dare you." I shifted on my feet out of pure shock. Red misted over my eyes, becoming the only color I saw. The blood rushing through my veins boiled, and when it traveled to my heart, a sharp pain tore through my chest.

"You are in a mess of a situation right now, and you need to get your head on straight." Edda's gaze narrowed, completely unapologetic.

"You think you are the one to give me advice?" I shook my head. "Why did he owe you this..." My gaze traveled down the length of her body. Fat was redistributed into all the right places. Curves filled out her dress, and long limbs gave her a willowy look. She was beautiful. "...this favor?"

She didn't answer.

My teeth ground against each other. "I asked you a question. What did you pay for this favor?"

The silence broke when Clause spoke. "This time, her payment was helping me acquire conjurors."

I could have laughed. The lie of the conjurors being chosen by the Spirit, being taken for a higher purpose, was propagated by her. She stole our people and sold them to the Siddhe King for youth. How many families were torn apart because of her? How many lives were stolen? The entire Dunes Clan was erased from our lands because of *her*.

My eyes burned and I shook my head in disbelief. "Why?"

No response.

"Why?" I pushed the word through clenched teeth. The rage within grew till I trembled with it, unable to contain it within my body. For the first time, I felt too small for everything. Incapable of controlling the feelings coursing through me. Failing to control even myself as I navigated through the world.

Clause sighed and answered for her. "To gain youth. Edda here is nearly as old as I am. I guess you can say she is one of my oldest friends. We have been trading in favors for a long, long time."

I shook my head, breath leaving me. "Did you ever care for me?" I asked Edda.

She stepped in my direction before stilling, and her gaze for the first time softened. Though I no longer believed what I saw in her eyes. "You are the only thing I have ever cared for in my entire life. I was too late to save my daughter, but you, I protected, however I could." Clause had said she and I were blood relatives when he spoke to her before I entered the room. With her current comment...Was her daughter my mother?

"You raised me to care for others," I stated. My whole life, she taught me kindness and patience, amongst other things. Yet her actions the entire time were anything but. They were callous and cruel. She played the role of the warm caregiver, yet was a monster underneath. A nightmare dressed up as a pleasant dream.

Not an ounce of remorse colored her dark eyes. "I raised you to not be like me." She nodded. "To not destroy the world, like your brothers would have if your mother had allowed them to be birthed. If my daughter had allowed them to be birthed."

Tears lined my eyes, despite my anger. "Everything is a lie."

"My love for you is true," she stated. The worst part was that she believed her own lies. The way she said it, the certainty in her voice, in her stance. She truly thought she loved me. But how could one love fully without letting the other person even know them? She was a stranger. I cherished a shadow that never existed.

"How can you say that?" My voice broke, tears sliding down my cheek. I didn't even try to hide them. Didn't care if they made me look weak. "Why are you doing this to me? Why didn't you just disappear?"

"You don't think that's what I was trying to do?" She said, gaze cutting to Clause, accusing him of the situation we found ourselves in.

"You are a Seer." She knew this was how our story ended.

Edda scoffed. "So, you assume I see crystal clear? I have to make sense of broken, fragmented storylines that are interwoven with lies. And my future, in particular, had been shaded for a long time. As soon as it happened, I saw myself for the threat I could be to you. And I tried to protect you the best I knew how."

"The time with the Lysians," I whispered. "That's why you were so cruel?" The reason she pushed me away.

"I needed you to stand on your own, to not rely on me so much. To show you that you did not need me, not really, not anymore. I never wanted to hurt you, but in the event I disappeared from your life, I wanted you to know you were ready to continue on your own. Without me."

"Do you now see?" Clause said while my gaze remained on her. "How trust is so easy to be betrayed by those we least expect. And how they claim it is for the greater good, for your own good even."

My eyes slid shut, hot tears running down my face. I couldn't argue with him any longer. He was right.

"What now?" I asked the Siddhe King when a strange numbness settled over me.

He approached until standing at my side. His attention moved over me. I was thankful that he did not try to touch me. "This fairytale I broke for you. It is now up to you what you wish to do with the pieces, discard them, burn them, free them. I will let you decide." He turned to Edda. "The Seer is yours to do with as you see fit." His head tilted as he viewed her. "You tried to fool me, Edda. That will never happen again. You meddle in things you know nothing of." His words were a cold threat, even without the promise of death.

What to do with her? I couldn't just let her go. But death? Could I have her killed for this? No. I didn't know the right path. I needed more time.

"I take it you have a dungeon or cells or something I could have access to?" I asked, my voice cold and foreign.

He nodded.

"Ariana." Edda stepped towards me.

"No!" I whirled towards her. "Keep my name out of your mouth. I don't know who you are. You were never more than a cruel illusion."

The wall behind her fell when I released my hold on it, and Soren moved, blocking the exit.

"Lock her up," I stated.

Soren gave me a single nod and closed the space between him and Edda, slipping a hand under her arm.

Her shoulders sagged, sadness misting over her fiery dark eyes. She didn't even try to fight him.

Edda spoke with her chosen parting words, her tone that of a warning from a Seer. "Before you decide anything more, remember who you are, Ariana. Remember what even started this entire thing, the answers you sought. If you search again, then this time you will be granted answers. But I warn you, there will be no going back. A chain reaction of events will be put in play." Her eyes actually lined with silver. "You will break, and yet you will remain whole." She then turned her dark gaze onto Clause. "He thinks he opened your eyes to the lies while he is no better than I." Her attention sliced back to me. "Allow me to return the favor and show you who he is."

I didn't want to listen to her, yet I heard.

I didn't want to trust, yet I believed the warnings.

What did that make me? A complete fool?

"Take her away," I said by way of goodbye.

24

ERIK

I sat on a bed that old man Gorm stated was free to use, and kept to myself until he asked, "What should I call you?"

"Erik." My attention drifted to him, and he offered a polite smile. I did not return it.

He nodded, though continued looking at me. "You know, Ariana has been quite the welcoming presence here."

The knot in my chest eased at the mention of her and the positive light she seemed to emanate even in the Siddhe lands. "She is a welcoming presence everywhere she goes."

"Is she leaving us?"

I eyed him. "I don't know."

"She has been pressing her luck since she got here. And somehow things have always worked out for her." He shook his head, a solemn look casting shadows over his face. "The tides have changed, though. I can feel it in the air."

"Are you a Seer?"

Gorm laughed, his entire upper body shaking. "Oh, spirit

no. I am but a simple air conjurer, probably no more powerful than Ari's Sparrows. But the wind speaks to me, to all of us. We need to simply learn to listen to the whispers."

"How much do you know?" Ariana seemed to trust this man, but I did not know him.

He smiled. "If you are asking whether she has told me anything, she hasn't. But I keep my eyes open. And despite my age, the brain in this skull is still kicking." He tapped a finger on the side of his head.

I eyed him uncertainly. Proceeding with caution was the best bet at this point. Especially with how withdrawn Ariana seemed. Yet, my curiosity got the better of me. "How's she been?"

He smiled warmly at my question, as though pleased by it. "She is good, growing stronger every day."

"In what way?" I leaned back in the bed, hoping some of the tension would leave my body.

"Her conjuring for a start. The Siddhe King told her of how she harbors a gift from both the Spirit of the light and of the dark. To where she can become that which she commands, and if she did, then her soul would remain intact, tethered to the world for her to reclaim."

If Gorm knew of this, then certainly the wolf would have too. Why would this have been something Willis did not share with the rest of us? "And she believes this?"

He released a low, throaty laugh. "Son, she is doing it." My jaw unhinged in surprise. "Not completely. She can just manage her fingertips right now, but soon and with practice, I have no doubt she will do it to her entire body."

"You're serious?" I stared at him. He didn't seem bothered by the weight of my attention, the edge as I considered him.

His smile remained, not at all offended by my doubt of what

he said. "Sure. Though you do not know me, and I have no way of proving anything." He shrugged a single shoulder. "You'll just have to ask her to show you."

We fell into silence then.

My mind only thought of her. Of how she viewed me before leaving, as though afraid. The uncertainty in her eyes cut me deeper than any blade, leaving a wound that festered with worry. I stepped into a world I knew little about, one that she seemed to have started thriving in, growing more powerful. For a moment, with my arms around her, it felt as though nothing changed. Then a strange cold cloud settled over her, and a wall of ice separated us.

Day turned into night, and others began trickling into the servant's room. Some of them looked at me as though I didn't quite fit in despite my ragged clothing. Others completely ignored me. All of them, however, left me alone.

Suddenly Ariana entered the space without an ounce of hesitation until her gaze landed on me and she stopped in her tracks. It was then that even those who ignored me finally took notice.

I stood at once, yet lingered by the bed I had sat on, uncertain whether I should approach, whether she even wanted me near her.

Her brows crinkled, and it looked almost as though she were fighting back tears. "I–" Her voice broke, and she cast her eyes down. "I need a minute." She stated before turning and rushing into another room behind a closed door.

I followed until a scrawny boy stepped between me and where I was going.

"The lady said she needs a minute," the boy boldly stated, chest puffed out as if it could make him look the least bit intimidating.

"Step aside, kid." I shifted to the right to go around him.

He moved with me.

My brows shot up in surprise that this kid had the nerve to remain standing in my way.

"Timothy," Gorm's grave voice snapped the boy's attention. "This is a friend of our Ari. Let him pass."

Timothy's eyes narrowed, and he turned to me. "Friend? How come I have never seen you then?"

"Timothy!" Gorm yelled out, louder than before. "Don't make me get up out of this bed. If you do, Ariana will be upset with both of us. Let the poor man pass."

Timothy eyed me once more but stepped away. Clearly displeased, yet respecting the old man enough to listen.

The floor creaked as I moved to where Ariana disappeared. I pushed open the door, the hinges squeaking in loud protest, and then again when I shut it behind me.

Ariana stood with her back to me, hands on either side of a sink. She had to have heard me enter, though made no move to acknowledge it. Her posture was stiff with tension, rigid in a way that was not typical for the woman who was made of quiet composure and confidence.

"I want to help you, but I do not know how," I spoke instead of physically going to her. Something strange settled in the space between us and the last thing I wanted was to give her any reason to retreat from me more than she already had.

There was something so fragile about her.

"I do not deserve your help," she said, her voice low. Sadness enveloped her. She did not elaborate, leaving my mind to race with what this could have possibly meant.

"Why would you think this?" I asked after a moment.

"He kissed me," she murmured.

Was that what concerned her? "I know. At the party, he tried to kiss you, but you stopped him."

She released a shaky breath. "No, after that. He tried again." She swallowed. A tremor racked her body. "Except I didn't stop him."

The heart in my chest missed a beat, and then another. Air pressed out of my lungs and somehow kicked my pulse back into gear. My skin suddenly felt too tight, blood too hot.

The poison of anger snared my heart. Trapping it to a small cage where it hit its confines with every beat, sending a pulse of pain through my chest over and over.

My hands balled into fists at my sides one moment. Only for my fingers to spread wide the next, claws sliding out.

Rage shot through me, wild and hardly contained. My veins burned, and I wished more than anything that I could release it. That I could burn everything around me.

"You must hate me," she whispered, her voice small and frail. Still, she did not turn, did not look at me.

My hands shook.

I tried to center my thoughts in order to respond somehow. "Edda warned me..." My voice trailed off. The effort to keep from exploding required too much focus. Though the Seer warned me, I unquestionably believed that my connection with Ariana was strong enough to withstand whatever unnatural pull Clause might have had on her.

"Warned you of what?" Ariana's voice turned cold and sharp. Something about it drew my attention to her, and the way she went completely rigid.

"Before I left, Edda found me." My voice was rough, the words like sandpaper in my throat. "She said there's something tying you to him. That the two of you affect each other. That in the end..." I swallowed against the bitterness rising in my chest. "That you might choose to stay."

I needed to fucking leave. Right now.

Ariana stood there, frozen, until finally turning. Red-rimmed, swollen eyes locked onto mine. "I don't want to stay," she whispered, her voice fragile, laced with a misery that shattered something inside me.

The tightness coiling in my chest loosened just enough for me to breathe.

"I don't want him." Her gaze didn't waver, though it brimmed with pain so raw, so consuming.

Relief flooded through me at her words.

"What do you want?" I asked.

She hesitated before answering. "Someone I am unworthy of having." She paused as if trying to collect strength, before whispering, "I'm sorry."

The way this woman could unmake me was unlike anything I had ever known.

"I forgive you," I said nearly at once. Ashes, I hated this. But I had seen firsthand what this sort of thing could do. I refused to allow my path with Ariana to travel the same road Kole and Eislyn fell down. There was no world in which I would not hear her out. Would not try to understand.

A breath hitched in her throat, her gaze dropping to the floor. A shudder ran through her, her entire body trembling as she whispered, "Why?"

"If Edda is correct, then something else, something greater that we do not even understand may play a part in all of this. A conjuring of some sort, a spell. I can't say that I don't feel like burning the entire castle down with him inside of it. That the fact that he touched you...I want him dead." I took a step and stilled. "I meant what I said. That I would always recognize you, no matter what happens, no matter what you do. I will see you. I would want you, because I trust you, Ariana."

"And what do you see in me because I am not sure I recognize myself anymore?"

"I see a woman, still standing strong even under so much pressure."

She released another breath, shaking her head, eyes filling with tears anew. "I am not strong."

I moved towards her. "I see a woman who has been placed in such difficult positions that most would have long crumbled by now." The tears dribbled over, falling down her cheeks, and I took another step. "A woman who cares for others so deeply that she risked her life to save a Lysian who kept her prisoner." Another step. "A woman who held my heart in her hands then, and still does today."

Her eyes slid shut, and more tears fell. It hurt seeing her so defeated.

"May I touch you?" I asked, uncertain of her state of mind.

She nodded yes.

Another step and all space between us evaporated. My arms circled her, and she shuddered at my touch. She embraced me in return, clinging to me.

"I have missed you so much," she whispered. "I am so sorry."

"I'm here now." My chest expanded, and I filled my lungs with the scent of her. I savored the feeling of her against me. The way her skin warmed my own. The way she leaned into me. All of it filled me with relief.

I was right. Edda was a fool to fear Ariana's choice, for her heart brought her back into my arms.

Whatever this tie Clause had to her, I was going to sever it.

Permanently. Whatever it took. It was going to be obliterated out of existence.

She moved to look up at me with those beautiful large eyes that draw me to her, and my lips instantly found hers. A soft surprised gasp slipped between us before my mouth took hers. Her body instantly relaxed against mine.

My hand tangled into her hair, the other keeping her pressed to me as we shared a moment I had long craved for. She tasted better than I ever remembered. Better than my dreams. However, the kiss did not last nearly long enough. We parted and she kept her eyes shut while her pulse raced, matching my own as our bodies pressed together.

Sliding my eyes shut, I leaned down, our foreheads touching, breaths mingling in between. We stood, holding one another until the both of us regained our composure.

"Will you tell me what's going on?" I finally asked, pulling back slightly to study her face.

She tensed before releasing me and stepping away. "Clause said the life I lived was a lie. He said he would show me the truth today."

Was this why she suddenly withdrew earlier? "And you thought I was that lie?"

"I didn't know what to think. I feel like a fool. He is messing with my mind in ways I never expected."

"What was the lie?"

A tremor moved through her, and suddenly emotion left her altogether. "It was Edda. She's been working with him."

A cold dread descended over me, for the old bag knew everything. All of our plans.

"Also, apparently, she is my grandmother. That little detail I never knew." Her voice was dry.

I ran a hand through my hair. "So, Clause knows everything," I stated, though that made little sense. Edda knew I was coming to find Ariana. Yet no one stopped me. Even now, there was no doubt the Siddhe King would have done something if he knew I was there.

"I don't think so." Ariana shook her head. "She seems to think she loves me. It looks like she did not tell him of anything to do with the army or you."

"What do you want to do now?" I asked, certain that this changed things. Sure, Edda might have stayed quiet for now, but how long would that remain?

Determination settled in Ariana's eyes. "I am done living here. I want to leave, but first, there is something I need to do."

"What?"

"All of this started because of your sister." She mumbled under her breath and looked as though she suddenly understood something. Turning, she moved towards the door.

"What are you doing?"

Calm eyes found mine. Despite the chaos surrounding her, she suddenly seemed strong. Her footing somewhat regained. "Going to ask where Iona is."

My brows pulled together. "But you already have. They won't tell you."

"They will this time. For Edda has seen it." She swung open the door and marched into the room.

The hum of conversation died at once, and all turned to her.

"I want to know where Iona is," Ariana stated.

One of the servants snorted. "This again. Listen, you want to rub the old man's feet, knock yourself out. But we are not getting involved with your mess."

Her jaw clenched. "Is everyone here so afraid?"

"If you were smart, you would fear too."

"Are you truly ready for this?" Gorm cut in with a question directed at Ariana, searching her face for something.

"Ready for what?" She looked at him with surprise.

He nodded as though she answered, though she never did. "I will take responsibility for whatever comes next." He announced to the room.

"There's going to be serious blowback for this." Another man snapped.

"Ariana and I are prepared for that, aren't we?" Gorm asked her and she responded with a nod.

"What kind of blowback?" I asked.

"The kind you don't want." The first man muttered and leaned back in his bed.

I didn't have time to ask anything else before Gorm answered Ariana. "You will find Iona at the House of the Velvet Wildfire."

25

ARIANA

I stood before a small building with a wooden sign hanging above that read *House of the Velvet Wildfire* painted in red letters. My hand hesitated by the doorknob while I took a moment to collect my wits before entering.

Erik opposed my going alone to the place Gorm said I would find Iona. Yet he did not fight me as hard as I expected, stepping back and allowing me to ultimately decide. Understanding that I couldn't protect him, couldn't protect anyone if things went poorly. However, I had Clause's promise of never killing me as a shield, which offered a small bit of comfort.

With a slow exhale, I pushed the door open, entering a small, dimly lit room. A bell on the door chimed, alerting whoever to my presence.

On inhale, I drew in the scent of sex and musk that was poorly covered by vanilla-scented candles. My stomach turned at the smell. Disgust coated my insides, before bubbling out of my pores and likely only adding to the stench.

A woman entered the small space from behind a beaded partition drape. Her movements were far too graceful for such an establishment. She had her blond hair pulled back into a sleek ponytail. Blue cold eyes met with mine and sharp teeth peeked through as she smiled viciously. Her icy gaze moved over me. There was something almost familiar to the sharp features of her face.

"I think you are lost, little lamb," she said to me.

There were no chains on her wrists. No discomfort written on her face. Nothing that portrayed a person forced to be in such an enterprise.

"Iona?" I asked, a gut instinct telling me it was her. The Lysian before me was the correct age and certainly looked beautiful enough to fit in flawlessly with a royal family.

The smile dropped from her face. "Who are you?"

"My name is Ariana. I am the Bavadrin Leader Superior."

Her stony gaze held mine. "You are the Siddhe King's little pet?" She stepped forward, into my space, beautiful and intimidating as she leaned towards me. "Better run back to the King's lap, little lamb. This is no place for a girl like you."

"And this is a good place for a Lysian princess?" I didn't need her admitting who she was to know I guessed correctly.

Her eyes narrowed. "There are no princesses here." Her attention flicked to the door as she nodded towards it. "Get out of here."

"What if I could offer you freedom?" I challenged her, certain she would choose to accept.

She tilted her head back and laughed. The motion caused her shoulders to shake. "Look around, little lamb. This is *my* establishment. I chose this, and I would choose it again. I have all the freedom I could ever need."

My eyes widened in bewilderment. "This is a whorehouse."

A smirk curled at her lips. She brought a hand up in the space between us. Fire moved over her fingertips and she viewed me. "You should run along now." The entire act was intended as a threat.

Pity for her, I knew tricks too. It would take more than fire dancing in her hand to startle me.

I snorted, moving my hand out in front of me, sending mist to circle the flames, snuffing them out till all that was left was smoke. "We have been looking for you, trying to find you and bring you back home."

Her gaze narrowed. "Who is *we*?"

"Your brothers, amongst others." Did she really not think her family wanted to bring her home since the moment Clause took her from them?

She tilted her head, assessing eyes raking down the length of me. "My brothers have befriended the Bavadrin Leader Superior?"

"They thought we had something to do with your disappearance." I always believed they were wrong, however with the revelation regarding Edda, the Lysians were right to view us as a threat. The thought made my stomach clench.

She stepped back, folding her arms across her chest. The movement like a barrier. She wanted to place distance between us, retreating. "Listen. I can see this has caused you some trouble finding me, but that isn't my problem. I didn't ask for you to come here. And I am in no need of your services. I am where I want to be."

Soft moans drifted into the room, coming from somewhere beyond the walls that separated me from the rest of the whorehouse. My insides curdled with disgust. Iona glanced at the space behind her, beyond the beaded partition. When she turned back, a smirk lifted her lips.

"You truly want to live like this?" I asked.

She snorted. "And what do *you* get for opening your legs, *Great Leader Superior*?" Her gaze narrowed. "My guess is not much of anything."

My mouth dried. Did she really believe what she insinuated? "I get a choice."

Her eyebrows shot up. "So do I. So do the ladies working under me." Her lips flattened into a thin line. "It was not always this way. In this *establishment*. I took over and offered protection for the ladies here. I do not hurt them. They have the power to turn down offers if they wish. What you hear right now are moans of pleasure, not screams of pain or fear. They are safe."

There was something in her eye that darkened when she said they were safe. A hidden lie.

"You are saying everyone here is by their choice?" I asked.

She viewed me, jaw ticking. "Mostly."

So, it was not all roses and pleasure. Iona tried to overlay an ugly image with something more beautiful. Yet, the original bled through underneath. She couldn't completely paint over it. "Who isn't?"

"Listen, little lamb, run back to wherever you came from." She pointed her chin towards the exit. "You do not want the King as an enemy."

The King? "Does he..." I stumbled over my words in shock. "Does he come here?" Disgust slithered over my skin.

A smile split her face, sharp teeth peeking through. "Would you be jealous if he did?"

More like appalled.

She continued without waiting for me to respond. "Clause does not need to come to such places. Now, his right-hand men do enjoy a visit from time to time. One of them provides oversight." She paused, eyeing me. "So, it would not be wise to stick your foot into this."

"Who is kept here against their will?" I pressed anyway.

She scoffed, unfolding her arms and dropping them at her sides. "I tried to be nice and give you advice. If you do not wish to take it, that decision is yours. I certainly will not be laying a finger on Clause's favorite pet. But, you should know that your choice here will have consequences, despite who you are to him."

Her use of certain words was peculiar. "And who am I to him?"

"You don't know yet?" She chuckled, shaking her head. "I am not getting involved in that. However, I will say that you coming in here and creating trouble will ensure that trouble returns to *you*. All of that does not matter to me. However, if I answered your question, it would bring trouble for *me*, and I refuse to subject myself to my King's wrath."

"Your King?" My jaw nearly dropped at how smoothly she called Clause *her King*. As though she belonged to no other. "You so easily turn your back on where you came from?"

She shrugged, completely indifferent to my comment. "My father never came for me, did he? Never wanted me or fought for me. He just let me disappear."

"But you think Clause fought for you?"

"I'm here, aren't I?"

She was delusional. Drinking the poison water Clause seemed to pump through the people he acquired from lands that were never his to farm from. I didn't have the time or patience to sway her mind. I was not sure I even wanted to if she had people kept against their will at such a place.

"Where is the person who does not wish to be here?" I asked instead.

"The girl belongs to one of Clause's men." She paused as if allowing time for her words to sink in. "You sure you don't want to disappear and pretend you never stumbled onto this place? If you intervene, we will alert Clause at once."

"Show her to me."

Iona shrugged, as if it truly made no difference to her. "Very well." She moved through the beaded partition, keeping a hand up to leave an opening for me to step through into a long, dim hallway. Doors on each side, eight of them. Eight rooms. All were probably used as places for services exchanged, all except for the one she led me to. The last room.

Iona tilted her head, indicating that through the threshold was the answer to my question.

I reached for the handle and opened the door, surprised to find it unlocked.

A Siddhe woman lay on a mattress, her pointed ears peeking through dirty-looking brown hair. A small groan escaped her lips at our presence, yet she did not stir, did not even open an eye. Chains circled each wrist and each ankle, binding her even though she looked too weak to even stand.

"Does she get food or water?" I asked, unable to move, to actually enter the space. The scent of sweat and rot assaulted my nose, but didn't stop there. It traveled down my throat, taking hold of my stomach. I *tasted* the revolting air.

Iona shrugged, eyeing me as if more curious to see my response as opposed to what hid behind the door. "I do not know. I do not enter this room, for it is the one area in this place that does not belong to me. For whatever reason, this girl was brought here. I do not care to know why. I do not involve myself."

"You are disgusting." I turned to her. "This is happening right under your nose, and you do nothing."

"And what do you wish for me to do? To free her?" Iona dared to smile as though *I* was the foolish one. "Let me know how well that turns out for you. I am not here to rescue anyone outside my means. I can help the women here, those in the other rooms. Their protection is my sole responsibility. We all have limits, little lamb. I know mine. You had better learn yours before you are put on a spit and roasted alive."

I did not respond, instead turning my gaze to the emaciated girl.

Mist shot out of my fingertips, like vines drifting through the air, over the bed, to each of the shackles. It entered the space meant for a key, curving around the metal compartment, pushing and pulling until all four locks snapped open.

26

ARIANA

I lowered the girl down onto an open bed in the servant's bunker. She weighed close to nothing. It took far too little effort to wrap her in a blanket and carry her from that torture room and through the city.

Shay found me as I walked the streets and followed us to the servant's compound in silence, releasing a soft whine only after I placed the girl on the bed.

"Who is she?" Erik asked, looking over at her as the blanket fell away from her face, revealing one that did not belong to his sister. His shoulders sagged a touch with relief at seeing a stranger in such a state and not Iona.

"They kept her chained in a whorehouse," I said, running to get a cold compress to hold to her forehead.

"You should take her back." One of the servants stated coldly. "This will only bring trouble."

I froze, turning to view a Siddhe man with a scowl curving

his lips. "I could not just leave her there." Eyes of the entire room were on me.

My attention settled on the wolf as I decided. "It's time. Go."

Shay released a throaty rumble and ran out of the room at once. The time of suffering under Clause's rule would not continue. His people were going to get a choice of the kind of life they wished to live.

It was going to start soon, within the next day my army would arrive. Those trapped and wishing for a different life would be liberated. That was my only demand. Freedom.

"Your bleeding heart is going to be your downfall." The servant stated boldly.

"Shut it." Erik snapped at him before turning to view me. "What of Iona?"

I pulled my lips into my mouth, taking a moment to ponder how best to reply. "I found her, but she did not wish to leave."

"What?" Disbelief tainted his voice. He even stepped away, as though the words blew him back.

My heart hurt for him. All of this, the scars on his back, were to get to this moment, to find her and rescue her. He sacrificed his body for her. Yet she was no damsel waiting for rescue. Instead, she entered the dragon's den willingly and made a home there. "Iona said she runs the whorehouse and is happy there. She knew they kept this girl in one of her rooms and did nothing to help."

"I suppose all of that is close enough to the truth." Iona's voice sliced into the room just before she sauntered in. Her stony gaze moved through the space like a serpent's eye until landing on Erik. "Brother."

Tension flooded the space, and everyone turned to view the cause.

Erik froze, eyes wide, moving over his sister, recognizing

her. He was stunned into silence, and Iona used that to her advantage as she stepped deeper into the cabin yet remained by the door. "What are you doing here, Erik?"

"I came to help free our people," he stated, staring at her as though seeing a ghost.

Her jaw clenched. "Well then, I am sorry, but you have wasted your time. Please let father know he should be wiser than to send his heir into a world he knows nothing about."

Erik shook his head. "Father is dead."

Iona's eyes widened. For the first time, a look of troubled surprise painted her features.

"What, expect *your King* to have filled you in on that detail?" I stated, moving to stand at Erik's side.

He glanced at me as my words sank in and he then turned to Iona. "Your King?"

The trouble melted from her eyes, replaced by a mask. She shrugged, feigning indifference. "He actually wanted me. While dad never came for me."

The air around Erik warmed, as though he burned beneath his skin. "Father had an entire people to care for."

"And you don't?" She tilted her head in wonder.

Erik tensed. "I do, yet I am here, aren't I?"

Her gaze narrowed, sliding to me. "Are you?" She turned back to Erik. "What are you doing with Clause's little lamb?"

He went completely rigid at her word choice. "Ariana is not his." The tone in his voice was absolute and cold, plummeting the room deeper into an icy tension, while the temperature in the space sweltered.

None of the servants made a sound or moved a single muscle. They simply stared in our direction.

Iona slowly shook her head. "You do not know what you are

messing with. Don't tell me you actually care for this Bavadrin?" She pointed a long, thin finger at me.

"That's none of your concern," I said, growing tired of her meddling. She wanted me to leave her *establishment*, and I did. So why now was she here?

Iona's eyes doubled in size, looking at me. Her hand fell to her side. "You are going along with this- this fantasy?"

"It is real," I stated.

She snorted. "And I thought I was the one who messed with the hearts of others." Was that a comment about what she had done with Kole and Eislyn?

"If you do not want to leave this place then why are you here?" Erik asked, eyes narrowing.

She shrugged. "I was curious to see what the little lamb was up to. And maybe get a front seat to the show."

"What show?" I asked.

"I told you there would be a punishment for taking the girl. We have already sent word. Clause will probably be here in no time, with his favorite entourage in toe." She turned to Erik. "A word of advice. If you actually think you care for her, leave. Unless you are already so integrated into this bunk that your absence would be noted."

"I'm not going anywhere." He stepped closer to me as if to make a point. His muscles coiled, ready to act towards a threat that had not yet even arrived. Too ready to act. And I was not the only one who noticed.

Iona chuckled, eyes dimming. "Tell me, if the Siddhe King decided to bend the little lamb over one of these filthy beds and make her his in front of your eyes. What would you do?"

Erik stopped breathing, as did the entire room. I reached for his arm before he had a chance to respond. His skin was burning hot. However, his gaze remained trained on his sister.

"Erik," I said his name, hoping to earn his attention.

Iona spoke again. "Tell me, what would you do?" She had a disgusting way of getting her point across, yet I understood it for what she meant.

"I would kill him before it got to that," he said, voice deceptively soft.

Iona chuckled. "You are a fool and if you wish to live, that is the wrong answer."

"She is right," I whispered, finally earning his gaze. "If you stand against him, you can't win. Not on your own. Your conjuring can't affect him and all he needs to do is touch you and you're dead."

Iona licked her lips, as though hungry by this excitement. "Not to mention what would happen to all the good people here in this room if you were to upset him too much. It would be so much blood on the hands of a dead man." Her gaze slid to me. "A burden I don't doubt the little lamb would take on to herself, only to be crushed by it."

"Stop." I snapped at her before turning to Erik. "Maybe you should leave."

"I am not leaving you," he turned to me, eyes blazing.

"Ari is right," Gorm stated, joining the conversation. "If you act too rashly and your life is taken, then you can never help her when it truly matters. Instead, you would be dead, and Ari would be on her own. No matter what happens next, you must not intervene if you wish to have any hope of survival or helping Ariana."

"You see me so weak?" Erik asked, turning to me.

"You are one of the most powerful people I know," I said. "Yet part of being strong is knowing when you are outmatched. Alone against Clause, you are outmatched. All of us are. We need to be smart."

"Funny." Iona tilted her head, viewing me. "I feel like I just said almost the same thing to you before you decided to get involved in things that shouldn't concern you." Her gaze drifted to the girl made of bones and skin lying on the bed near me.

I gritted my teeth. Forcing myself to focus on Erik. "Clause cannot know who you are to me." A look of confusion passed over his features before I pressed on. "He knows there is someone important to me. If he found out who you are to me." My voice broke, sliced by fear. "That cannot happen."

He look pained, actually pained. "Ariana."

Iona turned, looking behind her. "Oops, looks like time is up." She smiled, excitement twinkling in her eyes.

"Move to the back of the room, and stay there unless I say otherwise," I instructed Erik. "Please, do not get involved. I will tell you if I want your help. Do *nothing* unless I say."

Strain etched into his face, flattening his lips. But he nodded.

I turned to Timothy. "Stay with Erik. Make sure he doesn't intervene."

Erik cared for others. He had a decent heart. If his actions would jeopardize a young innocent boy like Timothy, I hoped that he would think twice about it. Hopefully, it gave him enough pause to clear his mind sufficiently to make a decent decision.

When my gaze met with Gorm, he sent a reassuring nod, lips curving into a sad smile that did not touch his eyes.

No one else made a sound in the bunker.

I focused on the girl on the bed and stepped towards her, not fully reaching her before others walked in.

Iona moved aside, allowing free entrance. "I came to make sure no one here left."

"Good." Clause paced into the room. His cold gray eyes

immediately landed and remained on me. Though still gray, a potent darkness swirled within them.

The weight behind the gaze, the anger, it rendered me immobile. I froze mid-step.

Three other men entered on his heel, flanking him when he stopped. Iona remained lingering in the back, leaning against the wall, giving no indication of leaving anytime soon. Soren appeared in the doorway, stopping there, as though blocking the exit. A frown etched into his face.

I was the first to break the silence. "What crimes has this girl committed to warrant being strapped to a bed in a whore-house without food or water?"

"That is none of your concern!" A man to Clause's right snapped.

"Dragal." Clause silenced him with just his name.

The man's mouth snapped shut, but his face turned red with anger.

Clause remained where he stood as he addressed me. "In this life, you are not yet my Queen. We are not yet true ruling equals. Therefore, when you act against my wishes, it cannot be ignored. No one acts against the Siddhe royalty." Darkness emanated from him, potent and heavy. It vibrated through everyone and everything, stemming completely from him. There was something terrifying about it. Unhinged.

"But the girl–"

He cut me off. "I do not care for the girl. She does not matter outside of the weight you foolishly placed on her life. And for what purpose?" His sights narrowed, though remained solely on me.

Behind him, Iona's gaze slid to Erik before returning to me.

"Her life matters," I stated firmly.

He nodded while a frown pulled at his lips. "I told you to

not go looking for Iona." His gaze finally left me and moved over those in the room. My heart stopped when it focused on where Erik stood before continuing through the space. "Someone here gave you information on where to find her." He turned back to me. "And you took it and directly opposed my wishes." His voice was so deceptively calm, but I *felt* the danger in it.

I stood completely rigid before him. "You act as though I have never opposed you before."

"With your words. I will allow that with you. But with your actions?" He slowly shook his head. "You forget who is King here. I have tried to be patient with you, but apparently, some lessons will need to be learned sooner rather than later." He clasped his hand behind his back and moved further into the space, walking a small circle as he again looked over the servants in the room before returning to where he started. "It seems like you brought a girl here, but there are simply not enough beds."

That was not true. There were plenty, two still open, even with the girl added to the room.

He continued, "So now that you took a life from me, I expect you to give one in return."

My mouth went dry. "What do you mean?"

He lifted a hand, gesturing to the space. "Choose one servant who stays in this room and take their life using only your conjuring." He shrugged, icy gaze centering on me. "A fair trade."

27

ERIK

Ariana's entire body stilled. She did not even draw a breath, did not blink as her wide eyes held the stare of the Siddhe King.

Dread engulfed the room, and with it, the scent of fear emanated from nearly every being. They made not a single sound.

Timothy hid his hands, tucking them behind his back to veil the shaking while his attention remained glued on Clause and Ariana. The boy swallowed and locked his legs to keep them from trembling.

"You cannot be serious." Ariana's voice drifted out of her, soft with disbelief.

The Siddhe King titled his head. The movement somehow came off threatening. "I very much am. You have two minutes to decide who you wish to make the payment with."

"I accept the punishment." Gorm's rough voice pulled at the attention of everyone. He looked at Ariana. "I told you where

Iona would be, and in doing so, I accepted responsibility for my actions."

Ariana's face paled as she viewed her friend. "No." She turned to Clause, approaching him. "You don't have to do this."

He released a breath, eyes dimming with a mixture of determination and something else. "Maybe there's a different way to teach you and your friends here this lesson. But this is the punishment I chose. It is already done. I am a man of my word and will not go back on a decision," he said with a cold detachment.

"They don't deserve this." Ariana shook her head, brows drawn. "These were my actions. I accept responsibility myself. They do not need to suffer. Not fo—"

She never finished voicing the thought, for the man at Clause's side abruptly shifted and backhanded her. The movement was so sudden; I didn't even register it in time before it was too late. My attention had been focused on the King and her.

A deep, voracious tension shot through my body. My ears muffled, my claws slid out of my fingertips, muscles strained to not immediately act.

Ariana's neck snapped to the side due to the power behind the blow, her hair fanning out from the movement. When she looked up, her eyes met with mine and they alone were the only thing keeping me from moving from my spot and peeling the skin from Clause and his men.

Her gaze held determination. The force of it kept me in place.

Ever so softly, she shook her head no. Telling me to stay put.

Blood swelled at the corner of her mouth.

My legs locked beneath me in an effort to maintain my position. To not rip the man to shreds with my bare hands.

The man had drawn her blood.

My gaze centered on him, and I committed everything about him to memory. From that point forward, he was living on borrowed time. I was still staring at him when his face morphed into one of agony, though he made no sound. His arm, the one that hit Ariana, was in Clause's hand.

"You do not touch her," Clause simply said.

The man's wrist crumbled, as if the bone within disintegrated, his hand flopping to the side, no longer held up by anything that attached to his arm other than soft tissues. When Clause released him, he cried out then, pulling his arm to his chest, holding his hand with the other. He did not make another noise. Sweat coated his pale face and his knees nearly rattled against one another.

Ariana focused her sights on only Clause. Completely ignoring what had occurred. "I'm sorry," she said. "Please."

She then fell to her knees in front of him and bowed her head in pure submission.

My jaw clenched so hard that I did not know how my teeth did not splinter. The sight of her before him like that made my stomach turn. The blood in my veins that already boiled nearly evaporated altogether from the heat burning beneath my skin.

Never had I felt a more profound hatred for someone.

"I beg you. Don't make me do this." She meant her words for only him. "Punish me. Not them."

He frowned, reaching out for her with the same hand he just destroyed a man's bones with. She didn't flinch away from his touch as he grazed her chin before forcing her head up.

Moisture lined her eyes. "Please."

Something about him shifted. His gaze warmed, though his

frown deepened. As if this somehow pained him to see her like this. "Choose someone, Ariana. And this will end sooner."

A tear slipped out of her eye, rolling down her cheek. "I have never killed anyone with my conjuring before. Don't make me do this. Don't try to turn me into this."

My heart stilled, crushed by an invisible fist. Ariana was in a position I could not find a way out of. A sense of helplessness clogged my throat.

Clause squatted before her, lowering himself to her, the two of them eye level. Something about the way his hand remained under her chin, gaze searching her face, seemed so intimate. And it was by the grace of the Spirit that I somehow kept from engulfing the world around the Siddhe King in flames.

"Then this will be your first kill," he said, his voice gentle. He withdrew his hand from her face. "If you do not choose right now, then I will take a life myself. And I will keep doing so as long as you drag your feet until every servant in this room is dead. And then we will move to the next servant compound, and the next, and the next. Until you complete your punishment."

A look of shock passed over Ariana, and the only response she could manage was a small shake of her head. As though this was something she never imagined him capable of.

Clause sighed, his gaze hardening. He rose to his feet but didn't stop there. In several steps, he approached the closest servant to him.

Ariana's eyes widened, too slow to register what was going on. She jumped to her feet. "Wait!"

Clause reached out to a young Bavadrin boy who looked no older than Timothy. The boy's massive, shocked eyes only enlarged as the Siddhe King reached for him, fingertips grazing a forearm.

The boy dropped dead. His young life, taken. Just like that. As if it were nothing.

Beside me, Timothy stopped shaking. His entire body stilled as he viewed the boy on the ground. When his eyes met the Siddhe King, the scent of fear no longer surrounded him.

He then lunged.

Ariana reacted nearly at the same time, her hand shooting out towards him. A wall of mist formed around Timothy at once. It muffled his screams as he threw himself at the mist barrier, over and over. His balled-up fists pummeled Ariana's conjuring to no avail. The entire thing lasted only seconds. He abruptly stopped, the energy leaving him as suddenly as it came. Timothy fell to the ground, bowed his head in defeat, and wept.

"That was just a boy. A child." Ariana's voice turned cold as she addressed the Siddhe King. "He had a life to live. People cared for him. He was someone's family."

Clause turned from Timothy to her, looking unimpressed. "I told you the rules."

"Ariana," Gorm called her name. When she glanced at him, he closed his eyes and nodded. "Come, sit with me."

She viewed Clause again. Pain and rage etched into the lines of her face. "I will *never* forgive you for this. I want you to know that. If you make me do this, I will *never* forgive you." There was a shard of desperation in her voice. As if despite what just happened, some small part of her hoped that her words could move him to reconsider. As if he might have cared.

She must have concluded that there was no other way but to accept his punishment. A conjuror could not fight Clause with their gifts. And hand to hand, he had an enormous advantage with his power. She believed his threat, and after what he just did, so did I. Desiring to save as many lives as possible placed Ariana in a terrible position when it came to his demand. Given how easily Clause just took an innocent boy's life, the lengths he would go to in order to make her into someone else was clear.

Clause's lips curled at the side. "Yes, you will. And it is because of this that you will grow strong enough to survive this world."

"Ariana," Gorm grumbled.

That time, when she looked at the old man once more, her feet moved. Everyone watched as she approached him, and she settled into a seat beside him while he still lay on the bed.

Gorm reached out, taking her hand in his. "I always knew the risks. I told you I accepted the consequences."

She let out a shaky breath. New tears fell down Ariana's face as she held his gaze. "I can't."

"Yes, you can. You will." He glanced around. "Look around you. I am the oldest here. I have less life left to live, anyway. My feet are falling apart. I am withering away. And, at least this way, my death means something. We get to protect everyone else in this room. No one else needs to die."

More droplets rolled down her cheek. "I am so sorry," she whispered, voice hardly audible. She tried to remain strong, but her shoulders curved with agonizing defeat. Her voice lost its strength, her gaze filled only with painful regret.

She was breaking before me.

It was unbearable to watch, yet my eyes remained fastened to her.

"I would have likely died from that last foot infection if it weren't for you. You coming into our lives has been wonderful. Never regret that. This situation is not your fault." He paused.

"Now, get on with it." He nodded encouragingly. The old man faced death without an ounce of hesitation.

Time continued moving, and the longer they took, the closer the Siddhe King came to taking another life.

Ariana slid her hand over Gorm's, and he wrapped his fingers around hers.

She took a deep breath before her eyes shut. Tears streamed from them in rivers before falling from her chin. Her brows furrowed, lip quivering. She released a shaky breath, and I realized she was trembling.

The silence spreading through the room was so profound it was deafening. Solemn darkness encased the space.

Gorm's body tensed, his eyes closing. He exhaled, then made a gagging sound. It didn't even last a minute, but felt like an eternity.

Ariana's shaking intensified.

Gorm twitched several times before finally stilling.

His fingers loosened on her hand.

His heart ceased beating.

Keeping her eyes closed, Ariana leaned forward. She pressed her forehead into his chest. Her words were barely a strangled whisper. Her voice cracked, breaking, as she said, "I am so sorry, my friend."

She then released him, hand letting go of his, and sat back up, her eyes finally opening. An awful hollowness shone in them as she stared ahead.

Clause approached her and kneeled at her side.

Ariana's distant gaze tracked him as the backs of his fingers brushed her cheek, smearing the last of her tears.

"You were exquisite," he said to her, as though to compliment her on a task well done.

She did not reply with words, though her eyes promised of death.

His lips twitched, and he rose to his feet. "I'll see you tomorrow morning for the breaking of our fast," he said to her before he and his men left, one of them cradling their broken wrist.

They left two bodies in their wake.

One life taken by the Siddhe King, the other by Ariana.

28

ARIANA

A numbness settled over me first. It narrowed with a crushing force, and strained against my ribs, tightening around my lungs. Strange coldness coated my skin, my fingertips growing numb, my mind vacant.

The conjuring within, the feel of my mist, the power beneath my skin.

"Ariana?" Erik lowered himself beside me, yet all I could do was stare at nothing. There was a void of space before me, filled with an invisible darkness that was very much felt. It flooded the room, seeping through my skin, and poisoning me.

Voices spoke, telling me they would take care of the bodies.
Bodies.

Two lives were taken because of my decisions. Two souls forever gone.

A tremble slithered down my spine, the sensation odd amongst the detached shock of it all.

A boy no longer drew breath.

Gorm. His final breath stolen by my mist.

I felt it. How his lungs tried to expand, to draw in oxygen while my mist prevented it. The twitch of each muscle as it thirsted for air. I felt it when he stilled. When his soul left his body.

My eyes slid shut.

The numbness enveloping me began to crack.

It was all too much.

My muscles shuddered uncontrollably as if vibrating. Was I shaking?

Hands gripped my shoulders and forced me to my feet. They guided me to the room where I often did my work healing the servants. *Healing.* Never did I think I would be responsible for their deaths.

A door clicked shut and suddenly arms surrounded me, holding me while I numbly stood there, unable to move.

"Ariana," Erik's voice cut through my thoughts. "Don't let him win." Warmth from his chest seeped into my stiff body. "This will not break you." His heartbeat thumped strong and true, felt against my ear as he held me. Warmth and life radiated out of him while I stood cold and lifeless.

"Then why do I feel broken?" I mumbled, eyes filling with tears anew.

My friend. I took his life.

He was one of the first to show me genuine kindness in the Siddhe lands. And where did that kindness lead him?

Into a grave.

"Because you care. Because you are nothing like the Siddhe King." Erik's arms tightened around me. "We will free the people of these lands."

I wished to believe him. "How are you so certain?"

"The air whispers secrets. All you need to do is learn how to listen." His words sounded like something Gorm would have said.

A wave of pain crashed into me, swallowing me whole. I sobbed as my knees buckled. Erik held me while I fell apart. He took my pain, my shame, and offered only love in return.

Warmth surrounded me. A strong heartbeat spoke to my own, coaxing it into a more natural rhythm. Slowly, simply by holding me, life began trickling back into me.

He held me till my tears dried and there were paw scratches at the door.

We finally parted, though he seemed reluctant to release me. I went to the door, opening it enough to allow Shay to enter before closing it behind her.

The wolf released a whine, a look of concern in her eyes.

"You already got the message to them?" I asked her.

She snorted a confirmation. My gaze met with Erik's and we both turned to the wolf.

"I need to know how far out the forces are. Will they be here tonight?" I asked her.

A soft whine, which I took as a no.

"Around dawn?"

Another soft whine.

"By noon?"

A snort of a confirmation.

"By ten?"

Another snort.

"By nine?"

A whine.

I was leaving this place.

This gave me something to focus on.

I sealed away the pain of what I had just done. Locking it deep within myself and turned to the future. For that was the only way to see this through. We did not have time for me to mourn. To feel.

The determination to bring all of this to an end fueled me. Erik brought me back to life, but Shay fed the flame within.

I turned to Erik. "How ready are we, really?"

"We are prepared. Iver has been training everyone to take down Malavika. We know non-conjurors are Clause's weakness, and we are prepared to use that to our advantage." Fire blazed in those blue eyes of his. "We will win."

I ran my tongue over my teeth, a plan formulating in my mind. "Clause rules his people ultimately. No one can hardly sneeze without permission from him. All decisions go through him. It is absolute. No one speaks or decides for him. That means that without him, they fall apart. I can keep him distracted around the time of the attack so no one can get direction from him. Buy our forces some time, an advantage to make way into the city."

Erik's brows furrowed, forming a prominent wrinkle that seemed to come more and more easily. "How will you distract him?"

"I'll go to him before the scheduled breaking of our morning fast, which is often around ten, anyway. My goal is to keep him secluded and prevent any contact with his people. I'll surround the room in mist if I must."

Erik's gaze broke from mine as he thought it all over. "I don't like this."

"I know. But you cannot be anywhere near me during this. If he gets an inkling that I care anything for you." The fear of this possibility nearly had me shaking. "I am telling you. That can *not* happen."

"Will he hurt you?"

"He won't kill me." I said with certainty, though perhaps

Clause keeping me alive was a worse outcome. What type of torturous punishment would he see fit for what we were about to do? I couldn't let my mind run down that road of possibilities. Not when this was our best chance at potentially freeing the imprisoned conjurors within the capitol. I had to do this.

Erik searched my eyes. "I am not leaving without you."

I stiffened. "If I cannot get away from him then I do not want you coming anywhere near him."

His lip curled in anger, flashing those elongated canines. "I am not leaving without you."

Shay lowered her head, ears back, a low growl rippling though her throat in warning.

Erik ignored the wolf completely, and instead took a step towards me, crowding me against the table. "I. Will. Not. Leave. You." He spoke slowly, his words a threatening caress, an oath.

"Fine." I hoped that if I ended up in a position where I could not get away, that perhaps Iver would be strong enough to stop Erik from killing himself to get to me. "But I am going alone in the morning and you are staying far away from Clause."

Heat swelled through the room, stemming from the Lysian King. Claws elongated from his finger tips for the briefest of moments before receding. "Fine." He stepped back.

I had expected more of a fight for he clearly hated this. But for some reason he agreed, choosing to follow my lead. Except when it came to possibly leaving without me.

"I'll help as many people here fight or flee as I can." He ran a hand through his dark hair. "But I am not leaving this city without you." Midnight blue eyes met with mine and I saw the fear within them.

"I have put you through so much," I whispered the words, saddened by them. No matter how much weight pressed down on him, he remained strong and true, sheltering me the best he could. But there was no shelter powerful enough to withstand the darkness that loomed. Darkness slowly wrapped itself around me, sliding over my skin before seeping into my bones.

"*You* have gone through so much." He took my hand in his, tugging me into him. Gone was his anger, as if burned away in a flash. Leaving something more desperate. His hand grazed the small of my back, before slowly following the curve of my spine up to my neck.

I leaned into him, not wanting to let go. I just wanted to hear him say 'let's go home' and for us to walk away hand in hand. But that was nothing more than a fantasy, and reality left little room for that.

"I probably won't return before everything starts," I said. My arms circled his waist as I pressed my cheek into him.

He nodded, chin moving against my head. "Be careful."

"You too." We released one another, yet did not step away.

Erik's knuckle grazed my cheek, as if craving to feel my skin once more. I leaned into the touch, wanting to take it with me. To take *him* with me. My eyes closed, remaining in that tender moment. Firm lips pressed into mine, surprising me with an eager passion that ended too quickly.

When we finally parted, I pivoted and opened the door, needing to get away lest I fell back into those arms and remain there for eternity.

I walked into the room and paused. The bodies were removed, leaving behind a dark and heavy cloud that expanded through the space, sifting into every crevice. My gaze met with Timothy, who sat on his bed. His pained and swollen eyes met with mine, void of the light he always carried.

"I am sorry," I said to those in the room. My attention

snagged on the empty bed where the girl had been. "Where is she?"

"One of the guys took her to get food."

I turned to the male who had warned me against finding Iona. "She is awake?"

"A healer came by, barely touched the girl before rushing away. She still looks like shit but certainly was more lively than before. I guess the King promised a life for a life. It wouldn't do him any good if the girl didn't even survive the night."

I swallowed.

And then left them to remain in the pain that I brought to them.

Shay followed me with nearly soundless steps as we moved towards the castle, and then through it. When we got to my room I did not enter, instead going to stand before the Dune Clan's leader stationed outside my door. His lips pressed into a firm line when I approached him. Dark eyes filled with unspoken words. Whatever mask he normally wore had cracked, allowing the turmoil within him to peek through those solemn eyes.

I wondered where he would stand come tomorrow.

"I need you to take me to where Edda is kept," I said to Soren.

His jaw clenched, and he nodded, though did not offer a verbal response. When he began moving, Shay and I followed. Eventually the halls Soren took us down became less ornate and bare stone surrounded us. He stopped at a door on one of those dark halls.

"I will wait out here," he informed. "She is in there."

I nodded, glancing at the wolf at my side. "Wait here."

Shay grunted and sat down beside Soren.

Following a deep inhale, I entered a dingy space. The scent

of wet rock permeated the space. A single torch lit an area that had three cells, however, only one was being used.

My jaw clenched when I viewed the woman I thought I knew better than anyone else in my life. Though I no longer recognized her physical appearance, nor the soul within the body, I felt a sense of relief at seeing her unharmed.

Edda sat on the floor, leaning against a far wall. When her onyx eyes met mine, she jumped to her feet, swiftly moving to the bars that separated us. Her gaze traveled over my face, causing her brows to furrow. "You set it all in motion already. The truths are being revealed to you, but there is one more left for you to uncover."

She was always the seer. I was not about to ask her what the last truth was. If she intended to tell me, then she would have.

"Did you know he would take the life of a child and what I would be forced to do?" I asked her, my voice somehow remaining firm despite the blade of torment wedged between my ribs.

Her frown deepened. "No. I never knew the details, just that it would be painful and eye-opening for you."

Silence spread between us as I held her stare. She was still so much of who I remembered, yet at the same time, completely unrecognizable. How was it possible to be that? Foreign yet reminding me of home.

"Do you believe me?" She asked.

"For some reason, I do."

One of her hands released an iron bar. She hesitated before reaching out for me, as if to touch my arm. I stepped back, staying out of reach.

Sadness swirled in her young yet ancient eyes as she pulled the hand back to herself, holding it close to her chest. "Why have you come?"

My ribs constricted. "You are not innocent. You disgust me, and yet my heart still fears for your safety. With what happens next, I do not know what Clause will do. I will not have your death on my hands too, another person powerless to make a choice, to defend themselves."

My conjuring hummed to life within me. Mist shot out of my fingers towards the lock, keeping her caged. Edda's eyes grew larger as she stared at my hand.

The iron pen keeping my grandmother in creaked open.

My *grandmother*. Even thinking the title hurt.

I spoke before she took a single step. "If I ever find you standing on the opposite side of me again, I will not grant you freedom again."

She nodded. "What do you want me to do?"

"Stay out of my way." I turned to leave, only to have her hand take mine, stilling me.

"I only ever wanted to protect you," she said, a strange sorrow staining her voice.

I looked at the foreign fingers wrapped around mine before setting my attention on her youthful face. "And I only ever wanted those closest to me to never manipulate me."

Her hand fell away from mine. "I will help you."

I did not have it in me to waste more of my breath on talking to her. I only needed one thing from her.

"Just stay out of my way." I then turned and exited the room with Edda a step behind me.

Soren's eyes widened at the sight of us.

"She is free to go," I said to him. "Will that be a problem?"

"No." He frowned, looking at Edda while my attention remained on him.

"Good. I am going to bed now. Tomorrow will be a long

day." I glanced at Edda, "I take it you know your way around and will have no issue slithering out of the castle?"

"I'll be fine." She answered with a sad smile I did not care for.

Turning on my heels, I made my way to my room with Shay, where we found no rest.

My mind was a mess of turmoil. Thinking up awful scenarios and possibilities, my dreams wild with dark creativity. I could not control the thoughts, as they wreaked havoc on my mental state.

Why was the night always the worst for such thoughts?

I paced, stared out my window, and closed my eyes for brief periods without slumber until finally, it was time.

I bathed and dressed in a lovely lavender blouse and brown pants that allowed for effortless movement and maneuvering.

When Shay and I left the room, we went our separate ways.

A thin layer of mist coated the floor in my wake, creating an invisible web, and I the spider who would sense any disruption.

I made my way to the room I long ago marked in my mind, yet stayed far away from until now.

Guards flanked the door, a look of surprise passing over them at my approach, yet they said nothing, continuing to face forward as I marched up between them, to the door.

Three quick hard taps of my knuckles and my heart skipped a beat.

Distract him as long as possible. I repeated these words a thousand times over in my mind ever since sunrise. They were my mantra, the thing that kept my mind from running wild.

Footsteps approached the door.

Fate thickened the air. Time drew near, causing a prickling sensation to dance over my skin in anticipation.

With a click, the door opened.

Clause's eyes landed on me and instantly changed from irritated to surprised.

Tension coiled like a snake at my feet before gliding around me, slithering over my skin until it was nearly all I felt. "We need to talk," I said to him.

His lips curved at the side, not at all upset by my icy demeanor. Gray cold eyes drifted over me. "You look lovely, as always." He then stepped aside. "This conversation was not one I expected to have yet, but I suppose if you have sought me out, then you are ready for it."

Apparently, we each had conversations we wished to have with one another. I could only imagine how different they were going to be.

I stepped into the room and froze.

Breath slipped out from my lungs, my muscles rendering me immobile.

"Wh- What is that?" I hardly forced myself to murmur the words out.

Before me was a wall with a floor-to-ceiling portrait. Clause looked exactly the same as he did now, except there was a brightness in those eyes, a warmth that never surfaced. A handsome face, silver white hair, gray eyes, sharp jaw, and even the commanding presence seemed to come across the painting. His hand rested on the hip of a woman, her ears pointed delicately, showing she was Siddhe. That was the only difference between her and me. Her face appeared as real as if I were to look in a mirror.

The edges of the painting were pulling away from the portrait slightly, showing the age. It was old, incredibly so. Yet the person in his arms was... I could not even think.

"It is my mate." Clause answered from somewhere behind

me. The door gently clicked shut, locking me in with him. "It is you."

29

ERIK

I did not sleep that night, nor any night, it seemed like. Being on this side of the Siddhe mountain walls made nothing better. I was a fool to imagine it would. As if seeing her could have smothered the unease, or at the very least lessened it. Stupid fool. If anything, witnessing what I had made everything worse.

I was being whittled down to a sharpened edge that burned for release.

Shadows surrounded me before tunnelling into my consciousness. The darkness begged for bodies. For retribution. As if that were even possible. My conjuring blistered beneath the surface for days, burning to escape, to incinerate the Siddhe King and his court. To scorch them out of existence, out of storybooks, leaving not a dusting of his influence on this world.

I sighed, attention shifting to the boy in the bed near mine. He did not sleep either. Just laid there, staring at the ceiling.

"Hey, kid." I kept my voice low so as not to wake every servant in the barrack.

He did not respond, eyes remaining unfocused, staring into oblivion.

I sat. The bed creaked as my weight shifted. I leaned towards him. "Timothy," I said the name I heard Ariana call him.

"What?" He did not move to meet my eye.

How much do I say? Anything? Ariana seemed to care for this kid, another way for Clause to torment her. Breaking her heart. How much could she withstand before sinking into hollowness so profound that she couldn't escape it? I refused to allow my thoughts to continue traveling down that vein. No matter where she went, I would find her, even in that darkness. I would carry her out of it.

"What do you know of what is about to go down?" I asked. My question met with silence. I exhaled slowly. "Some shit is about to go down." Cautiously so not to make much noise, I rose to my feet. "My suggestion is to lie low. Do not engage in the fight, and if you see an opportunity to run and escape this place, take it. And don't look back. Or, if you feel an urge to fight, then feel free to come with me." I left the kid with that parting advice. Hoping that he was smart enough to heed my warning.

He did not follow me.

Carefully stepping out of the servant housing, I met with fresh, crisp air. Not a guard was in sight, as if they were not needed in the city at all. All of them circled the perimeter. They would soon learn of the errors in that line of thought. We only needed to pierce their defenses and then had a clear path to their King.

The sky lightened before the first rays of light cut over the horizon.

Paws approached, drawing my attention to the wolf who

would guide me into position. The short cave that opened into the Siddhe lands was close to the city. Following the wolf, I headed towards the beginning of the end of this nightmare.

By the time we arrived, two Siddhe guards lay crumpled by the entrance, their blood pooling into the dirt. Kole and Eislyn stood above them, blades glistening with fresh crimson.

"It's good to see you." Kole's gaze swept over me, ensuring I was unscathed, before darting back to scan the surroundings.

"I take it Ariana is doing well, seeing as you are standing here, and the city is not burned to smithereens?" Iver approached with Willis through the cave.

"No, she isn't," I replied flatly and everyone but Willis turned to me with heavy stares. The Leader Superior's Second observed the forested area before looking at the main castle and our ultimate target.

"As soon as the army funnels through this cave, they'll know we're here," Willis stated, steering the conversation toward strategy.

I nodded, turning to Iver. "You, Kole, Eislyn, and the Sparrow are a part of the extraction team."

Iver grunted. "I haven't forgotten. Though I am shocked you do not demand to be a part of those retrieving our Bavadrin."

The decision to follow her lead in this graded on me. And even though Edda turned out to have been a snake in all of this, I trusted her when she said that following Ariana's direction ensured the best outcome. Edda cared for Ariana, even if she did not care for any other soul, she cared for Ariana.

"Get her and get out of there." My voice somehow remained steady even though I felt caged. I understood why Ariana wanted me no where near Clause, but that did not make any of this easy.

Iver tilted his head, his eyes narrowing in scrutiny. "And if she decides she doesn't want to leave?"

"She will," I answered, refusing to entertain any alternative.

"And if she doesn't?" His tone sharpened, testing the edges of my resolve.

"Iver." I spoke his name in warning.

Willis moved towards us. "Then you do what she wishes." His gaze bore into me, challenging not my authority but my intent.

For a fleeting moment, surprise flickered across Iver's face before he schooled it back to neutrality. I held Willis's stare with a cold one of my own. "I will not stop searching until I find her," I stated.

"If she wishes-" Willis began.

"I promised her," I cut him off. "I promised her I would find her. "

Willis studied me for a long beat before inclining his head. "Very well."

We were wasting time discussing this. Ariana was likely already with *him*. The monster who did not belong in this world. "Let's go," Willis said just before the sounds of wolves howling came from the other side of the cave. The signal.

The ground beneath us trembled as our army surged forward, their footsteps reverberating like a drumbeat of war.

Tension shattered as the vanguard broke through the cave's mouth, spilling down the hilly slope, past the brush, and into the Siddhe streets, led by one of the wolves. We melded into the stream of solders. Chaos erupted—shouts cut through the air as the Siddhe scrambled. Moments ago, the streets had been eerily calm; now, they seethed with uproar. Most fled in terror, a few chose to fight.

My heart thrummed with power. Adrenaline sharpened my senses.

I felt it before I saw it—the unnatural shift in the wind, a subtle warning honed by my time among the Sparrows. My body reacted instinctively, jerking back just as the glint of a blade sliced through the air where I had been standing. A second later, two more knives came flying from the shadows. I spun away, narrowly evading one, but the other buried itself in the shoulder of the soldier beside me.

Following the trajectory, my attention locked on the male who poised to throw more knives. Flames sparked to life in my hand, ignited by the familiar pull of my power. Before the male could throw another, I unleashed a torrent of fire. The blaze surged toward him with force, engulfing him in a searing wave. The crackle of flames swallowed his scream, and when they subsided, only ash remained where he had stood.

We pushed forward, weaving toward the castle. Every step brought us deeper into the city.

Yells echoed off the narrow alley walls as more opposed us. The sound blending with the clash of weapons and the heavy thud of bodies falling.

I used my flames sparingly. They were potent, but reckless in close quarters where my own men fought alongside me. Fire had a will of its own, eager to consume indiscriminately. And though I had the precision to direct its wrath, that required a level of focus that I did not think was even needed due to the ease we advanced into the city.

Instead, my sword became an extension of my body—sharp, swift, and reliable. It cleaved through the Siddhe defenders who dared to stand in our way. Flames danced along its edge for a heartbeat before extinguishing, adding a point of terror to those who met my gaze.

I could feel the pull of the castle, its towering spires looming above. Clause was there—I was certain of it. But so was Ariana. My grip tightened on my weapon.

Warriors near the front grunted around. Some of those in the line froze, abruptly halted, before falling to the ground. Dead.

There were glints of weapons that vanished as bodies dropped to the ground after being impaled. *Malavika.*

Rage burned through my veins, fire, yearning to be set free.

"Use the Ribbons!" Iver yelled to the front lines just before another dozen stopped in their tracks, as if running headfirst into something, or in this case, chest first. Blood soaked their leathers from the blades that appeared just before they impaled themselves, going down.

"Pay attention!" I growled. Iver's plan better work, or we were going to lose too many of our forces to Mal.

I pushed forward. Another wave of soldiers crumpled around me. My warriors.

The seal on my conjuring shattered like glass under a hammer.

I unleashed myself on those who stood in my way, placing themselves between me and Ariana. The fury within promised death. Conjured fire licked my skin before I sent it forward and out, clearing a path ahead.

My mind became a blur, almost silencing the chaos within. Eradicate the threat. Get to Ariana. End the monster. Those three thoughts consumed me, leaving no room for hesitation or mercy. Acting on brutal instinct, I faintly even sensed the souls I destroyed in my wake.

That rage, born of fear, burned hotter than any flame I could conjure. The terror of losing her for good, of failing her, drove me forward, each step fueled by desperation.

Something attempted to smother the flames lining the road as I pressed on, clearing our path. My focus shifted, hand raising to obliterate whoever dared to block us. Moisture caused the flames to hiss. A water conjuror. I concentrated on the spot where the fire hissed, willing it to burn hotter.

Voices screamed beyond the hiss. I could not make sense of it over the roar in my ears.

The moisture lessened. And when it nearly went out completely. I withdrew the flame from that section, wishing to see what stood on the other side. My gaze dropped to a–

"Please! Please spare him!" A mother cried, arms wrapped around a boy, tears streaming down her face behind her pressed-shut eyes. Fresh burns marked her arms as she did all she could to shelter the boy's body with her own. Angry and frightened eyes of a boy no older than eight years of age held my stare, refusing to look away.

A boy. A *child*.

The sight drew a clarity that nearly brought me to my knees.

The child fought to free a hand from his mother's hold. Water floated around him, responding to his movements. This was who stood against me? A mere child?

"Please! I beg of you. Not my baby!" The mother's borderline hysterical screams were like acid to my ears.

I looked around, truly noting the battle. Half of those standing against us were simple civilians. Defending their homes, not knowing that we wanted to help them, not destroy them. We were here to free them, not take from them.

This was wrong.

30

ARIANA

Clause's words echoed in my mind, as if my brain were a chamber made to hold and recite them over and over.

It is my mate. It is you... It is my mate. It is you... It is my mate. It is...

"This isn't possible." My response was a numb whisper on my lips as I stared at the image of myself with pointed ears. The painter captured the small curve of her lips, the glint in her eyes. She was happy in his arms. And he... I tore my gaze from it, staring wide-eyed at the ground, trying to process the enormity of everything. "I am not her."

"But you are." Clause came around me till he stood before me. A finger nudged my chin up, forcing my gaze to lock with his. "The way you move, the way you speak, even your conjuring. The way it feels to be in your presence. You are my mate. I feel it. My blood *sings* at your existence." His hand moved, tenderly brushing against my cheek. "And I think you can feel it too." There was something nearly heart breaking in his cold gray eyes.

My throat tightened.

I stepped back, breaking contact with him.

He was right, partially. There was always something strange moving through the air when we were near one another. When he had kissed me, it was not normal, nor was it right. Whatever tied me to him, I did not want. I rejected it.

I examined the painting again, desperate to understand. Clause's eyes were warm and welcoming in it. He seemed different. "Are you the same person as the one depicted in that image?"

"It is a painting of me." He observed me as the wheels in my head spun.

"But are you the same?" I glanced at him. "The person in this painting feels warmer, hopeful almost. Whereas you have a brutality that is not conveyed in the canvas."

He took a step towards me, and I moved away. "When I lost you, things changed." Gray eyes burned into mine.

Fear clogged my throat. I needed space, air. But there was nowhere for me to go, to run.

I caged myself with him, with this secret. It was difficult not to choke on the disgust. The Siddhe King and the Spirit itself were cruel and twisted beings, and I was never more than a pawn. In all of this, my fate was sealed. I was something to be used.

I tried to force a steady voice, but it wavered. "So. If you are correct and my soul is the same one you claim it to be–"

"It is. I feel it in every ounce of my being."

I glanced at the image. The warmth radiating from the man in it. "Then in my past life, I fell in love with someone who no longer exists, mated someone who is no longer real."

Clause's gaze narrowed. Tension connected us, the cord amazingly strong as it coiled around my wrists and ankles, tying me to him. Anger washed over me. For the Spirit played with my fate like this.

That resentment fueled me.

I spoke the next words with certainty. "I have said it before. My heart is not yours."

He tilted his head, viewing me with calculating eyes. "It is, Ariana. You are mine, and I, in turn, am yours. We will always be that."

"I do not want this version of you," I boldly stated, and the room grew colder, darker.

"Would you have the other?" He peered at the painting, at the man he no longer could be. The person he himself destroyed.

"After last night?" I shook my head. "It is impossible."

His lip curved slightly, as if not swayed by a challenge. "You will come around. You will see. Our mating was unique, changing us on a mystical level. Nothing can shadow the bond we share. It is eternal."

"Except perhaps the most powerful conjuror can." I stared at him pointedly. "You shadow that bond by your actions." My back straightened with my resolve. I was not some puppet with no choice. "What you forced me to do, the way you took an innocent boy's life without a second thought, it is disgusting. No amount of pain or history from your past excuses those actions. If my soul loved you in another life, then I am truly saddened to witness the monster you have become."

His jaw clenched, a dangerous edge cut through his gaze. "Like I said, you'll come around."

"No. You are going to relinquish your control, or I will not stop till you are put down, or I am dead," I stated. It was a warning of truth I hoped he heeded.

"You are not going anywhere, certainly not the afterlife." He took a step, and I remained where I stood, refusing to back away again. "The reason you died was because you trusted those you shouldn't have. You were not prepared for what came for you. You were too soft for this world. I will now help you withstand anything and everything. I will not allow you to slip away, to *die* again." Pain accompanied those words, attempting to pull at me.

He cared about only his own pain, no one else's, not even mine, his *precious mate.*

I dared to scoff at his words. "You are a fool to believe that your actions are hardening me towards the world. The only person they are hardening me against is you."

The tension tightened around me, pulling me, yet I refused to move.

He stepped closer and nearly all the space between us vanished. Dipping his head, I felt his breath on my ear as he spoke. "Tell me you feel nothing when I am close to you." His hand found my wrist, pressing into it. "Tell me your pulse does not race for me." He released it and his hand traveled up my arm before finding my neck and pausing there. He pulled back and his eyes burned as they met with mine. "Tell me you do not crave this." He leaned towards me, but his lips never found their mark.

With my heart thundering in my chest, I backed away. "You sadden me nearly as much as you disgust me." There was an anguish to him when it came to me. A blindness. He secluded himself from everyone, remaining untouchable. But there was one who could cut through his defenses, one who he would open the door for, and the Spirit used that to their advantage.

It was cruel, really. To wrap a curse in such a package, one he would never refuse. One he would welcome as a gift instead of as his potential undoing.

It was my birth that was the curse; the spirit had said at my ascension. I now understood what it meant. I was a curse that could cut to the heart of the most heartless being in existence.

My attention momentarily strayed from Clause and moved beyond the room.

The web of mist outside his door tugged at my concentration as feet rushed down halls, heading in our direction.

So, it has started.

My heartbeat thumped even stronger in my chest as new nerves traveled down my spine.

Without a single twitch of a finger, I conjured. Mist surged around the room we stood in, pushing up against the doors, walls, and windows until no crevice was left. It sealed us in, just in time for the first set of fists to pound on it just outside. The mist absorbed all sound.

My focus re-centered on Clause. "How many lives have you taken since your mate's death?"

"Plenty," he answered, likely not even knowing the number.

"I am afraid we are at an impasse. We stand on opposite sides. Your people deserve better than you as their King."

His silver brows furrowed before he offered me a glimmer of a hope. "Perhaps you can help me be better."

I recognized that hope as the lie that it was. He wished to placate me for the time being.

I shook my head no. "Maybe I could have, but not anymore."

He chortled. "You place more value on the lives of those you hardly knew compared to the friend you brought here when you first came to visit? You warmed up since then, yet now have decided that it is impossible for us to meet each other."

"Every life has value," I snapped. "I miss Landin, but in part, I could perhaps try to understand your position. He drew his blade on you more than once." My brows furrowed, and I looked to the ground for a moment in thought. "You are right. There is something that ties me to you. That is why I wanted to understand you. I also wanted to help you see you did not need to keep living the way you have been. The world can be cold but can also be beautiful and warm, yet you hid yourself away from it. You keep the cold out, yes, but also the warmth. And what kind of life is that?" My eyes watered. "Then last night happened. The lengths you will go through to hurt me is extraordinary." My heart broke not only for Landin, for the boy, for Gorm, but also for the King standing before me. Perhaps, there could have been a different outcome. But he stole that chance when he turned me into a murderer.

Clause took a measured breath. "That is me protecting you by making you strong."

"No. That is you trying to *ruin* me."

He sighed. "You don't understand."

Of course, if I did not see his way, it meant that I simply did not understand. For how else could I stand on the opposite side of him? This thought was condescending.

He was infuriating.

"Just like your mother didn't understand when your father forced his ways on to her?" I snapped, not caring if it brought wrath.

Clause's jaw twitched, hands clenching and unclenching at his sides. "I never caged you."

"Cages do not have to be physical. You wish for me to not find the warmth I need from this world. The warmth I need to truly live. You wish to force me into an icy darkness, and keep me there."

"No."

"Yes. You wish to smother me, to turn me into something I am not. To care for nothing or risk you brutally taking it from me. A prison wholly constructed of your actions and decisions, because I am not free to decide for myself how I wish to live or who to care for."

"Stop."

There was an assault on the mist surrounding the room. Several rhythmic jabs all over, such as that from a sword. *Malavika*. Relentlessly, she attacked, trying to break through the barrier.

I continued, a new thought spurred by her presence. "Why not bring Malavika happiness and make her your Queen, for she is the type of person you truly wish to stand at your side, not me. You think you love me, that you love your mate, but that is a lie. You wouldn't try to change me in such ways if you truly did."

Suddenly he lurched forward, pushing me back till the wall prevented me from moving. Hands came on either side of me, trapping me. "Stop pushing me, Ariana." His voice was a soft snarl. A warning.

My spine remained straight as an arrow. "Or what? You'll kill me? You'll destroy everything I love and care for till there is nothing left of this version of me?" His gaze pinned me, but he did not answer, so I continued. "Did you stop pushing me when I asked you to? When I fell to my knees in front of you and begged you to have mercy, to show me kindness?"

The assault on the mist wall continued, and it was an extraordinary effort to maintain the barrier without splitting my attention between it and the Siddhe King. I needed to take a deep breath, and I needed him further from me.

I touched Clause's chest, and his breath hitched as my fingers slid over the soft fabric of his shirt till resting in the center, over his sternum. His warmth seeped into my icy hand. "Instead of showing me compassion, you shoved me off a cliff and turned your nose up at me." I pushed him away from me.

His hands dropped, and he stumbled back a few steps. "How do you not see how much I love you? How I miss you? How my actions are intended to protect you?" His head pivoted, looking at the painting with longing. "I have missed you for nearly as long as I have lived. For centuries, my heart has only beat for you. I waited for you." He turned, those cold eyes finding me once more. "You are the only thing important to me in this world. I would give you the world. Why do you fight our bond?"

"You are lying to yourself if you believe that. Because you would only allow for me to experience *your* world, not the one outside these walls, and not the way I want to experience it."

"You'll change your mind," he said, his eyes shifting to my tightly clenched fists. Those observant eyes then scanned me, resting on my hairline a moment too long, probably noting the moisture building there from silent effort. Cold gray eyes pinned me. "What are you doing?"

"What is right," I answered.

In two long strides, he was before me, a hand at my throat. He did not squeeze, yet kept me pressed to the wall as his power invaded me, stealing away my conjuring. The mist around the room fell. A rush of people crashed through the door into the room.

Clause's eyes remained on me, his jaw clenched.

"There's been an attack. Our walls are breached," Malavika stated.

"Go to your perch and kill them all," Clause answered without even looking at her.

I dared to break eye contact with him and glanced at the door, finding Soren and two guards standing there, looking uncertain what to do next.

Clause's hand moved, releasing my throat, only to run his thumb across my lips tenderly. I reacted, trying to push him away.

With ease, his free hand captured my wrists, trapping them in front of my chest.

Dizziness overcame me, taking my fight. My knees weakened. "What are you doing?" I drew a deep, shaky breath as gray eyes pierced into me.

Clause leaned towards me, his breath hot on my neck. "Forcefully slowing your heart so that you are less likely to cause trouble." When he pulled away, his hand gripped under my arm, taking me with him as he moved me towards the door. "Soren, take her to the bird's nest balcony so she can have a delightful view, as everything she *thinks* she loves crumbles beneath her feet."

Soren slipped a hand under my arm, taking the brunt of my weight, for I could no longer hold myself upright as the world somersaulted around me. But before we moved, Clause's hand reached behind my head, gripping my skull and forcing me to face him.

He leaned in, his lips just shy of mine when he spoke. "Were you anyone else, I would have killed you for such a stunt."

And that made me his perfect curse, something that even he was incapable of destroying.

But *he* was not *my* curse, and in that moment, I very much wished to end him and his horrid reign.

31

ERIK

Whispers slithered through the streets, thick with manipulation. The voice conjured by someone spewing lies. Each word seeped into the minds of the Siddhe citizens who heard them, poisoning their thoughts and twisting their fears into weapons. I could almost see the ripple of voice's effect—civilians who have never trained for combat, squared off with an army that easily slashed them down. Their eyes burned with a mix of terror and resolve, a lethal combination. The Siddhe King clearly hoped to overwhelm us by the sheer number of those opposing us.

"Lysians and Bavadrins are attacking our capitol," the voice hissed, reverberating through the streets. "They wish to erase our great city from the map. All citizens are encouraged to take arms and protect your homes, protect your loved ones, protect yourselves. These foes will stop at nothing to see you fall. They do not care whether you are weak, whether you surrender, whether you run, whether you are a child. Protect your homes. Protect your loved ones. Protect yourselves."

The lies wove themselves deep, driving desperation into the hearts of their people. They weren't soldiers. As puppets on strings of conjured deceit, fear and manipulation consumed them.

"Iver!" My brother's sudden presence snapped me out of my grim observation.

He ran towards me, his expression tight with urgency. "I found Ariana."

Relief collided with the pressure of the situation. "Take her and run," I ordered, my voice rough. "We need to retreat." He gave a single nod before vanishing into the fray.

For a moment, I stood frozen, the echoes of the conjured voice still slithered through the streets. I turned, my gaze sweeping over the destruction I had caused—the charred bodies, the crumbled structures, and the blood staining the cobblestones. Innocent souls, exploited into standing against us, lay among the wreckage.

This was not how this should have been.

But we had placed too much trust in the Seer, as if she would have cared for the loss of necessary lives enough to warn us against this outcome. But Edda said nothing, and thus never considered facing anything other than soldiers. We should have questioned everything. Should have assumed Clause would use his own people as shields and weapons without care.

My jaw clenched, a bitter taste rising in my throat. "Retreat!" I bellowed, the command like a thunderclap through the ranks of our forces.

I refused to let this become a massacre, refused to let the conjured lies become truth. We had not come to slaughter the innocent. Whatever Clause had planned, he would not use me or my army as tools for his narrative.

Once the retreat began, a ripple of relief swept through the citizens. They stalled at the edges of the streets, and in the alleyways that funneled into the road took to withdraw towards the tunnel. It was as if the tension binding the Siddhe loosened, fear reclaiming its rightful place in their hearts. They didn't pursue, afraid enough to not press their luck, hopeful enough to believe their lives might be spared.

A ripple of energy shifted in the atmosphere. The few citizens who kept eyes on us, as if to ensure we were leaving, suddenly made themselves scarce. We did not make it very far before Siddhe soldiers poured in, their movements more precise and coordinated. Unlike the civilians, these were warriors, trained to wield both swords and conjuring with deadly efficiency. Half wore shiny armor, like the polished steel in their hands. They approached from the city center, and the alleys nearest us.

My army stopped their retreat.

I pivoted, taking stock of the situation. These were not scared citizens with shaking hands—they were confident in their gate, moving like a crushing tide. Magic flared, elemental forces playing between their fingers, reminding me of the fact that they all could conjure.

For a single breath, nothing happened. A moment, before the chaos.

"Hold the line!" I barked at the surrounding soldiers.

And then, everyone was moving.

A Siddhe warrior surged forward, a blade of ice forming in his hand as he lunged at me. I sidestepped, my sword meeting his with a sharp clang. Flares sparked as steel clashed against enchanted ice. With a twist of my wrist, I deflected his strike and drove my blade under his armpit, where there was a gap in his armor. He gasped, his conjured weapon dissolving into shards before he crumpled to the ground.

Around me, the streets turned into a battleground. Flames erupted from one of my men, slamming against a Siddhe conjurer's whirlwind. The elements collided, the air thick with smoke, heat, ice, earth. I deflected a flanking attack from a Siddhe soldier, my blade catching him in the chest as I spun.

"They're closing in!" One of mine shouted, his sword slicing through a Siddhe before turning to face another.

"Keep moving!" I ordered. "We retreat together!"

For every inch of ground we gave, they pressed harder, apparently determined to turn our retreat into a slaughter. But we would not give them the satisfaction.

As another wave of soldiers charged, I summoned a wall of flames, forcing them to fall back or risk being consumed. The fire roared, a barrier between us. For a brief moment, it gave us the breathing room we needed to regroup.

The Siddhe navigated around my wall of flame, taking paths between buildings or under them, as we retreated further from the heart of their capitol.

A Siddhe warrior rushed at me, his blade glowing faintly with enchanted light. He was slender and tall, though knew how to use his limbs with a dangerous grace. His movements were sharp, calculated. I raised my sword, parrying his initial strike as sparks flew from our meeting blades.

Ruthless, he pushed forward, forcing me back a step. I twisted my wrist and drove my blade low toward his gut. He lept back, narrowly avoiding the blow, but not before my conjured fire seared the edge of his tunic.

The smell of scorched fabric and flesh filled the air as I closed the gap between us. He swung again, faster this time, aiming for my neck. I ducked under his blade, the breeze of his strike brushing against my skin. With a roar, I thrust my sword upward, catching him in flesh between his shoulder and neck. He cried out as blood spilled down his side.

Before I could finish him, another Siddhe charged from my right, a spear aimed at my ribs. I wrenched my blade free and sidestepped the attack, slashing upward in a single fluid motion. My sword caught the spearman across the chest, splitting his armor like parchment. He crumpled to the ground with a strangled gasp.

I didn't have the time to celebrate the fact that it seemed he had defective armor.

The first warrior, still clutching his wounded shoulder, summoned a whip of blue energy, like lightning but not, that lashed out toward me. The thorns from the pulsing energy bit into my arm, tearing through fabric and flesh. It burned through my nerves. My muscles constricted with tension. I yelled through clenched teeth at the shock of it. With a flick of my hand, fire erupted along the energy, burning down the path to the man who held the strange conjuring form.

He yelped, releasing his control before my flames made their way to him. But I never needed for the fire to travel to him down his power. All I wanted was to distract him.

My blade drove through his heart with a swift, decisive thrust. His eyes widened, a gasp escaping his lips as he collapsed.

I turned, barely catching sight of another attacker before a dagger gleamed in the torchlight, aimed for my throat. I ducked and caught his wrist, twisting hard until the blade clattered to the ground. With my other hand, I conjured a burst of fire that engulfed his chest. His scream was cut short as he fell, lifeless, to the blood-soaked ground.

My breaths came hard and fast, but I didn't stop. I couldn't.

With every swing of my sword and every blast of fire, I carved through the fight, a force of destruction driven by a need to keep moving.

As another wave of warriors rushed in, I braced myself, flames curling around my hands.

32

ARIANA

The wind was brutal. As if made of icy blades thrown at my face, nearly freezing my nose and lips as it whipped around me, violently pulling my unbound hair. The perch Clause chose for Soren to take me to was high in the castle, a balcony providing a wonderful view of the city below. High enough for a good visual yet low enough to see the individual people and hear their screams.

Soren's grip lingered under my arm, keeping me steady while my eyes remained peeled open, staring at the distance as forces began coming into view, heading towards the heart of the castle.

"Where is the rest of your Dunes clan?" I asked when I could not spot a single one of them anywhere.

He did not reply. Instead, observing the forces heading our way.

"Tell me, when your nephew or someone else in your clan is injured in this war, will you expect me to save them?" My heart tried to race, yet unnaturally remained slow. Sickening moisture coated my skin, almost as though I were ill. It was even an effort to speak.

Soren's jaw clenched, yet he still did not respond.

Movement off to the side of where we stood caught my eye. A few balconies over, one without a railing, stood Malavika. She looked fierce, blond hair whipping all around her. A sword lay in her open palms, held before her. Her lips moved with no sound that I could hear, and her eyes were closed. It was as if she was saying a prayer.

"Why are you still on his side?" I turned to Soren, whose attention remained on the distant forces. "Answer me!" I tried to push him. The attempt was pathetic, barely more than a tap to his chest.

My head spun. I lost my footing.

Soren's hand under my arm kept me from falling. Brown eyes finally met with mine, acknowledging me, lips set into a firm line. "I am on the side of survival. I must think of my people."

"And you would serve a monster rather than try to stand against him?" Breath became harder to find. "I never realized you were such a coward."

Off to the side, Malavika began moving. Her icy blue gaze focused on the world below, on the people rushing in our direction from down the roads. She primed her blade. A shimmering disfigurement stirred in the air before her, and she plunged her blade into it. The sword briefly disappeared. When she pulled back, buckets of blood came with the blade, nearly drenching her feet.

My heart sank.

In the distance, I saw people drop.

"No." The word was a whisper lost in the wind.

I felt weak and helpless. Unable to do anything that mattered. I could only watch as the nightmare unfolded.

Malavika poised to strike again.

I tried to move, to get out of Soren's hold, but could do little more than sway. Clause's influence limited me physically too much to fight. Malavika plunged her blade into oblivion again. Pulling it back with more blood, dousing her and the balcony before it began dripping off from the side in red streams.

A strip of fabric clung to her blade. With a face of annoyed disgust, she angled the sword down, the fabric slipping off before she primed herself to go again.

Below, I did not see a single Dunes Clan warrior. Their conjuring primed them to fight in the front lines. So where were they?

"Soren, please, help me." His withdrawn gaze turned to me once more. "You are a Bavadrin, so stand with us. If you are afraid to make the wrong choice for your people, then free them to decide for themselves."

Behind him, Malavika plunged her weapon and pulled back again. That time, more than just blood covered her blade.

Yellow ribbons encased the blade, long streaks blowing violently in the wind. Surprise painted Malavika's face, and she looked thrown at the sight. After a moment of observing the fabric, she grabbed the textile and began working on cutting her sword free.

Scanning the world below, I saw nothing that gave away what was going on, what the ribbon meant, or even where it came from.

Malavika finished ridding her blade of it and readied herself to strike again. Yet, the distortion before her grew, and when she went to plunge her blade into it, a hand came out of it first, grabbing her wrist. An arm followed that of the hand, accompanied by an entire body as Iver stepped through. He gripped Malavika's sword arm, forcing it to the side. In his other hand, he held a blade of his own, one that he sent cleanly through her.

Her eyes widened in shock, a gasp leaving her as she met Iver's gaze. The sword slipped from her hand and Iver leaned in, whispering something in her ear before stepping back through the shimmering distortion, forcing her to go with him, and the two of them disappeared.

A pulse of hope ran through me. Erik was right. They had a plan; they prepared for everything. With taking Malavika out of the picture so quickly, a new confidence spread through me. Though my heart rate remained restrained, my mind ran wild.

Below, smoke rose in various areas and it drew my eye, searching for Erik. Controlled flames burned through the city. Unnatural wind storms blew through the area. Birds behaved unnaturally, flying towards the chaos instead of away. Some of Clause's guards ran through the streets, meeting with the fight of those heading in our direction. Sounds of grunts and blades rang through the air.

A movement to the side caught my attention as Iver reappeared. And he was not alone.

Kiora's fierce hazel eyes met with mine, before they slid to Soren and she pulled her bow tight, aiming for him.

Iver winked in my direction and vanished once more.

"If you wish to live for a few more heartbeats, then I suggest you let her go." The wind carried Kiora's voice to us.

"The Sparrow Archers have returned?" Soren's voice was a whisper of disbelief.

Kiora took a few steps on her balcony towards us, the arrow remaining tight and ready to fly at her command. "We never left. Now, release my friend."

"Kiora, it's okay. He won't hurt me," I said before eyeing the Dunes Clan leader.

"Friend?" Soren stated the word as though it confused him.

"Are you stupid or something?" She snapped at him and glanced at me for clarification.

"Kiora is a Sparrow, and she is my friend. I do not rule the way the Siddhe King does, nor the way my father did," I answered Soren for he likely could never have imagined a Superior being friendly with those who serve.

Iver reappeared beside Kiora with two others.

Kole and Eisyn stepped onto the balcony, swords drawn, with Iver at their side.

My heart swelled at seeing them.

"How's it going over there, little Bavadrin?" Iver's gaze locked with mine.

I offered him a small smile. "I'm okay."

"You sure? Because it looks like you are swaying where you stand," Kole stated, his attention then pressed in to Soren. "And who is this termite?"

Iver's gray eyes moved over me from head to toe before sliding to Soren. "I suggest you release her." Flames coated the fingers on his hand, simmering there as if in wait. Kole and Eislyn whispered something before disappearing within the room attached to their balcony. Kiora remained, arrow still pointed in our direction.

"Soren, you need to let me go." I turned to look at him. "I would rather you not get hurt."

Brown eyes focused on me, yet his hand remained firmly under my arm. He looked to the ground, as though weighing his options, and when he looked up again, there was determination in his eye. "If I release her, she very well may fall off this balcony."

Instead, he moved me forward, bringing me closer to Kole an Eislyn who re-appeared on our balcony.

A shimmering distortion later, Iver stepped through it and towards me, eyeing Soren for a moment before slipping a hand around my waist and pulling me to him. Soren let go of me, and I leaned into the Lysian prince.

Kole continued to watch Soren with a tense gaze.

"What's going on with you?" Iver asked, eyeing me.

"Clause forcefully slowed my heart. I can't conjure, can hardly stand upright." My gaze drifted to Kole and Eislyn, who remained poised and focused on the threat before them.

Soren took a step towards us and Kiora hissed, stilling him. "You take another step and my arrow will find its way between your conjured markings, Dune."

"You got an eye on him?" Iver asked.

"Does it seem otherwise?" Kiora snapped.

He grunted yet finally took his eye from the Dunes Clan leader and turned his full attention to me.

"Can you fix it?" Kole asked.

Iver's lips pulled into a thin line, but he shrugged. "Let's find out."

33

ARIANA

I ver slipped a hand around mine and closed his eyes. Seconds passed, leaving the rest of us standing in tense silence. Nothing happened, and then my vision went splotchy, energy leaving me.

Kole came around to my side, keeping me upright. "You're making it worse, Iver." His words were a growl in my ear.

Suddenly, my vision returned, and my legs stabilized beneath me.

"That's it," Iver whispered, and my eyes widened as I watched him standing there with my hand in his. Somehow, he manipulated the thread of Clause's influence, figuring it out in mere seconds.

With every beat of my heart, I felt stronger. "You are remarkable," I murmured in awe of him.

Iver's lip twitched before his eyes opened. "You hear that, little Sparrow? Your leader finds me remarkable!" He called out to her while keeping his sights on me.

Kiora snorted. "She has clearly spent too much time in the Siddhe lands or has hit her head."

Ivers smile widened at her reply before he addressed me. "I cannot undo what Clause did, but I altered it, allowing ample room for you to feel well enough to move on your own and conjure."

"Thank you." I smiled at him before turning my attention to Kole, who gently released me so I could test out my ability to stand without support.

The world felt firm beneath my feet. Every pulse of my heart sent strength through me, no longer limited by the Siddhe King's conjuring.

Surprise touched nearly everyone except for Iver, who shrugged a carefree shoulder, not the least bit astonished by what he accomplished.

"Well, you certainly look better," Kole observed.

"What of him?" Eislyn nodded towards Soren, monitoring him. Suddenly, the awe of Iver's gift evaporated, leaving behind a tension that had always been.

I turned to the Dunes Clan leader. "Well? What is it you would like to do at this point?"

Brown eyes settled on me. "The choice you give me is to side with you or be killed here and now?" He asked, his voice calm, as though not at all troubled by what he said.

I shook my head. "That is the choice the Siddhe King gave you. I am asking you to stand with us. It is a request, but not your only option."

His head tilted while he viewed me. "What other options are there?"

"You can leave if you prefer. There is no need to involve yourself in a war you do not wish to take part in." I ensured that the next words spoken were clear. "However, you must know that if you try to stop us or harm us, then I cannot ensure your safety. We will fight for what we believe is right."

Soren looked out over the world, beyond the balcony. When he turned back, there was an edge to his eyes. "I am Soren, leader of the Dunes Clan. I bow to no one."

Iver tensed. "Then I imagine your neck is sore from the strain of bending to Clause's rule."

"Indeed, it is." Soren's gaze cut to me. "If I stand with you, then I stand at your side, not beneath you."

Kole chuckled, the sound void of humor. "You have some gall, talking as if you are not standing at the edge of a balcony with an awfully far drop to the ground and are not extraordinarily outnumbered."

"It's okay Kole. The Dunes Clan has always been free. I think it is time that they return home." I took a step towards Soren. "I will uphold our old ways. You and your people will remain free, and in good faith, we will help one another whenever we can."

Soren nodded. "I accept your terms."

"Lovely," Kiora muttered from the other balcony. Her bow and arrow relaxed in her hands. "I'm going to head over to you." She then vanished within the castle.

"You certain we can trust him?" Eislyn asked, her voice low as she glanced at the Dunes Clan leader.

"Yes."

"And if we learn we can't, then we kill him," Kole stated.

Soren peered at him. "You can try, but I need only to land one good blow with a blade to end your life. You, on the other hand, would likely need several before you can even hope of cutting my skin."

New tension coiled around us.

"Our Ariana can simply steal your breath away," Iver smirked.

"We are on the same side and wasting time," I said, all eyes turning to me.

"What's next?" Eislyn asked.

"We need to find Clause and end this," I stated, already moving towards the balcony door and into the room.

Iver's hand reached for my wrist, stilling me. "Things are... a bit messy out there. Erik asked that I find you and bring you back."

"We may not get another chance like this," I said, knowing full well he could just move me if he wished. That I could not stand against him, especially while he touched me.

Iver released me, nodding in thought. "I will help you, but if it seems futile, then I am removing you from this situation."

"Okay," I agreed and we began moving again.

"You wish to kill the King?" Soren followed us through the space and into the hall, where we met with Kiora.

No. I did not wish for Clause's death. And I hated myself for it. For wanting for a different outcome. Despite everything he did, what he forced me to do... maybe my soul was tied to his after all. And some part of it felt sorrow for the man who surrounded his tiny black heart with ice.

"If he does not back down, then I doubt there will be much of a choice," I replied, turning to my friend in time to welcome her arms as she hugged me.

"You are never leaving like this again." Kiora nearly crushed me in her embrace. I felt her heart hammering against my chest.

"Never again." I agreed, and she released me. We shared a brief smile, and that was all we had time for.

"Where to now?" Iver scanned the halls, turning from one side to the other before focusing on me. His body remained strained with tension. It clung to him - to all of us. Though I don't think I ever saw him as anything but casually calm before this.

I glanced at Soren. "Any idea where Clause is?"

"No. But his castle guards may, and I know of one stationed nearby who would likely help us."

I nodded. "Lead the way."

Soren took us down the hall, and then down several more. We followed him, making no sound other than that of soft footsteps rushing down thankfully empty corridors. The atmosphere shifted, colder when surrounded by stone, and warmer when surrounded by that of wood and candlelight. All of it, however, cold or warm, remained grand.

"This place is incredible," Kiora whispered, taking in the sheer size of the castle we rushed down to no end.

Soren slowed, speaking over his shoulder to us. "The guard's post is just around this corner. Do not threaten him and all should go well." He briefly hesitated before adding, "Also, do not lie to him." He did not wait for a reply before continuing.

When we turned the corner, there was a man standing at a post in the hallway.

"Gregory!" Soren called out a name as though they were friends.

The guard's eyes were already trained, watching us as we rushed toward him. He was tall, broad-shouldered, with a stern set to his face. His hand drifted to the hilt of his sword, fingers wrapping around it, yet he did not pull the blade free. At least not yet.

"I do not recognize most of your friends here, Soren." The man stated and held up his palm. "That is close enough."

Soren came to a stop, and we followed suit just a step behind him. "We are looking for Clause," he said.

"He is busy," Gregory replied curtly. There was a strange clarity and sharpness to his eyes as they passed over me before moving toward our entire party. A feeling of judgment embraced the stranger, directing a cold harsh sensation towards the rest of us. No one ever gave me such a sensation before.

"I am sure he will want to see Ariana," Soren said. "Just show us the way, and we will leave you be."

Silence spilled through the halls. It was as if we stood on a ledge and the guard had the power of lowering a draw bridge needed for crossing. Yet he had not decided yet whether to let us cross. And we needed him to help us or we faced a cliff with no way back.

Why did one guard seem to harbor such power? What was so special about him?

Do not lie to him, Soren had said.

"What is your conjuring gift?" I asked, earning those sharp eyes to pin me. He did not move to respond and so I tried to give him an answer to a question he never asked. "I can control mist." I lifted my hand and showed him my fingers as they turned to mist.

"And everyone else?" He inquired.

"Kiora, is a Sparrow Archer and controls airflow. Iver, well, we are still figuring him out." Not exactly a lie, but I certainly was skirting the truth there. "Kole and Eislyn do not conjure, and you already know Soren."

Gregory's brows pulled together, and he looked at Kole and Eislyn. "You are not conjurors?"

"Doesn't mean we aren't dangerous," Kole grumbled, not enjoying being singled out in a way that made him seem less than the rest of us.

Iver snorted. "Alright, *dangerous*."

"Shut up, Iver." Kiora sent an elbow into his side, which he caught, wrapping a hand around her arm and pulling her into him.

"Now, now, little Sparrow. No need to pretend to not like me in an attempt to get closer. You should know, when the condition we find ourselves in is more amicable, I'll let you get as close as you like." He was completely unbothered by the entire situation we found ourselves in. That alertness and calculated gaze from before seemed to have vanished. However, I did not miss how that move placed him between her and Gregory. Was he actually trying to shield her?

"Now is not the time," Kole snapped, anger rolling off him in waves directed at Iver, though his eyes remained trained on Gregory, searching for any sign of threat from the guard.

"Ugh. I hate you." Kiora shoved herself away and out of Iver's hold.

"Lie," Gregory stated simply, though his attention pinned Kiora, who looked at a loss for words with a face turning more into a tomato by the second.

"You can tell when someone tells a lie?" Iver viewed him with interest.

Gregory turned to him. Seconds ticked by until he finally nodded.

Iver chuckled, though said nothing more. Instead, his gaze wandered to Kiora, who seemed to wish to disappear. Clenching her jaw she refused to meet his eye.

I took a step forward, moving to Soren's side. "There is a war that has broken out, and we hope to end it before more lives are lost. If you can decipher lies, then you know I speak the truth when I say I do not wish to control the people here. But, I do wish for my freedom and the freedom of the people who live here. Non-conjurors do not deserve to be kept separated from the rest. Life does not have to be as dark as it has been in the Siddhe lands."

Gregory viewed me, yet did not reply.

"Well, does she speak the truth?" Soren asked. And I wondered whether he truly wished for the guard to tell him. After everything, did the Dunes Clan leader harbor doubts my words were not true?

"She does," Gregory answered, and pulled his sword from its sheath.

34

ERIK

The city smoldered, smoke licking at the edges of the Siddhe stronghold as my army continued in their slow retreat. I pulled back on the flames, not wanting to harm or destroy the homes of the citizens. That was not why we entered the city. The shouts of soldiers filled the air, a mix of barked orders and panicked cries. But what stopped me in my tracks wasn't the clash of swords or the roar of battle. It was the people.

"Not this again," I muttered under my breath.

Dozens of them swarmed from the narrow streets and alleys, a tide of untrained citizens. Their trembling hands gripped kitchen knives, farming tools, anything sharp enough to draw blood. Ash and tears stained their pale faces; trembling lips and wide eyes betrayed their terror. And yet, they advanced.

Fear permeated the air, a sickeningly sweet stench. I could see it in their darting eyes, hear it in the way their breaths hitched as they stepped forward. Terror lived in them, clawing at their insides, and yet something pushed them onward.

I raised my hand, summoning flames that danced along my fingertips. "Stop," I commanded, my voice a growl that carried across the square.

They didn't falter, as if I hadn't spoken.

With a snap of my wrist, I sent a wave of fire spiraling toward them. It wasn't meant to harm, only to scare. The heat singed their brows and forced them back a few steps. But even as they recoiled, they did not flee, and they moved forward again, their feet dragging as if against their will. Reeking of terror.

Something was wrong. My soldiers picked up on it as well, muttering amongst themselves while preparing to defend and fight.

I scanned the group of civilians, my attention catching on one who did not fit in with the rest.

At the back of the crowd, standing tall and unnervingly still, was a man cloaked in dark armor like a general. His immaculate attire seemed untouched by the surrounding chaos, and his expression was a chilling mask of indifference. He stared not at me or my soldiers, but at the trembling citizens, his unwavering gaze unrelenting.

Why wasn't he focused on us, the supposed threat? Why would a warrior direct such intensity toward his own people?

Then it clicked.

Conjuring. He was controlling them.

The boldness in their trembling steps, the defiance in their terror-stricken faces wasn't their own. It was *him*. His will coursed through them like invisible strings, forcing their fear-wracked bodies to advance. They weren't fighting for survival or freedom. They were being *used as puppets*.

"Begin to back away, slowly." I instructed my warriors closest to me. As long as this did not break into a full on battle where we were forced to slaughter innocents, then I could end it before it even began. I just needed a moment of focus.

The conjured flames coiling around my hand flared brighter, licking the air with dangerous intent. I pressed my thumb and pointer finger together, feeling the pulse of raw power surge through me, alive and waiting to be unleashed.

Power pooled within me, reaching past me, down a thread of energy to my target. My flames remained close, preparing to jump to the end of that thread. I would annihilate him.

The Siddhe's eyes darted toward me, a flicker of realization breaking his concentration. Just for a moment, the strings he'd been pulling faltered.

Good. I wanted him to see me. The male who would end him.

With a snap of my fingers, my power tore free, crossing the distance between us like a bolt of pure wrath. The air crackled as it struck him dead center, a blinding surge of energy consumed him in an instant.

His scream barely formed, the sound ripped away before it could fully leave his throat. I squinted against the brightness of the blaze, there one heartbeat and gone the next. His body crumbled into ash, disintegrating into the wind, leaving nothing behind. No evidence he'd ever stood there, only the faint whisper of smoke carried off by the breeze.

The crowd froze, their weapons clattering to the ground. Their gazes lifted to me, fear raw and unmasked. This time, they did not advance.

I let the flames dissipate from my hand and tried to keep my voice neutral as I said, "You are welcome to leave with us, if you wish."

They scattered, disappearing into the narrow streets they had come from.

Some of my forces chuckled in response. They felt powerful, seeing the reflection of fear in the eyes of those who looked upon them. Yet I had never felt so weak. We had come to find my sister, to free Ariana, to free the people trapped here. Instead, we made the people fear us.

"Retreat." The remnants of my army fell in line behind me.

As the last tendrils of ash dispersed in the wind, I caught a movement in the shadows just beyond the square. My gaze snapped to it, but before I could summon more flame, a figure stepped forward.

Iona.

Her blond hair was veiled by her cloak, her face half-hidden by the shadows, but I could see the faint curve of her lips. "Impressive," she murmured. Despite the distance, I caught the amusement which laced her low voice. "You were always the most skilled out of the two of us."

"Keep moving," I instructed those around me, while keeping my eyes on the woman before me.

The last three years were evidently not as horrific to her as any of us imagined. She stood, bold and appearing as healthy as ever. It both relieved me to find her whole and disturbed me. That she would bend her head for a different King, willingly following the man who had taken her from us, and do so by choice. That was not something my mind had the time to wrap itself around yet.

My flames flickered at my fingertips as I watched her approach, though she cautiously clung to the shadows of the street. "Are there more like him? Controlling the citizens?" I asked, choosing to focus on what was easier.

She leaned casually against a broken column, as if we

weren't standing in the aftermath of death. "There are," she said, her tone matter-of-fact. "Two of them, nearby. I could show you." She peered to where the general had stood. "You can easily incinerate them."

"Why the sudden desire to help?" I asked, narrowing my eyes at her. We were retreating, yet I could not ignore the value of ridding the Siddhe of conjurors with the power of manipulative control. Standing against the Siddhe was going to be difficult enough without having those who wished to stay out of the fight being thrown at us.

She didn't answer immediately. Instead, she tilted her head, her gaze slipping past me as though she were measuring something unseen. Then her attention returned to mine. "Do you want to kill them or not?"

I held her gaze, searching for some hidden motive. "I do." Maybe if the citizens were not so scared of being controlled, they would actually take a stand and leave this place.

"Then advance," she said, stepping closer, her voice dropping to a conspiratorial whisper. "And make it look convincing. Capture me. Drag me along if you have to. If anyone sees me with you, it needs to seem as though I'm here against my will."

She truly intended to stay here, even though I could offer her an escape. I hesitated only for a moment before I reached for her arm. She didn't flinch as my grip tightened around her wrist. This was the closest I had been to my sister in years, and yet it was as if she had never been farther away.

"If this is some ploy," I warned, my voice a low growl.

"It's not," she said, a faint smirk tugging at her lips. "Believe what you will of me, the freedom of choice is not something I think should be taken from people."

I yanked her forward, pulling her closer until she was firmly under my control. "Then what of the woman you had chained in your whorehouse?"

She shrugged a shoulder. "I always left her with something sharp, in case she wished to slit her throat. The girl had a choice. And chose to remain chained to a bed instead." Her cloak shifted as she stumbled, the effect perfectly false.

"Keep up," I ordered, loud enough for any lurking eyes to hear, as I turned and began marching in the direction she indicated. I lowered my voice as I hissed, "You disgust me."

"My heart breaks," she muttered dryly.

We made our way through the darkened streets. The tension between us was substantial, though mostly on my behalf. She did not seem at all bothered by me or my presence. Iona kept pace beside me, her steps light and deliberate, as if she had already mapped out the path ahead.

"Is he truly dead?" she asked suddenly, her voice barely above a whisper.

I knew she meant of our father. "Yes."

I should have left her wondering. Forced her to ask for every detail that she might have wanted, been curious about. She said nothing more, but I could feel her waiting, silently urging me to fill the void. And so, I did.

"After you disappeared," I began, "Father sought the Oracle. He never shared with anyone exactly what he was told, only that you had been taken by the Siddhe King." I glanced at her, trying to gauge her reaction, but her expression remained veiled. "He said he wouldn't pursue you. That it was for the best —for all people. We couldn't go against him without challenging for the throne. As soon as he passed, we planned to get you out of here."

Her silence stretched. I wanted to ask her what she thought

of that—what she felt—but the words lodged in my throat, stubborn and unwilling. Iona had always been the wild one, a storm with no intention of calming. She shared a streak of recklessness with Iver, but there was something darker in her, something more precarious. Unlike him, her unruliness came with a sharp edge, a sense of calculation that could turn perilous and cruel.

Still, we loved her. Even when her choices cut, even when she twisted away from us and toward her own shadows. We never turned our backs on her. Not Iver, not Jorn or Edmond, not me.

And yet... here we were. With her back turned to us.

I hated this—this divide, this hollow chasm of uncertainty and betrayal. What had become of us? What had become of my family?

"How did he die?" Her question broke my train of thought.

"He became sick with the Blithe. The healers did what they could but you know they can not heal something like that. They prolonged his life, but only for several months before he passed."

She nodded.

My steps slowed at the sounds of rushing movement and voices ahead.

The tight streets we took had been eerily silent, until they emptied onto a larger road. Iona stopped abruptly, pointing toward a narrow alleyway. "There," she said. "Two more of them." She pressed herself against a wall, remaining out of sight.

I peered past her. People moved down the road, eyes more vacant than those I had seen under influence of conjuring just minutes ago. They were carrying barrels of something. Two men Iona had directed my attention towards remained focused on the people around them.

Iona said, "One of them has the power to compel a person, the other has the power to magnify conjuring. Together, they can do this." She waved a hand out before us as if to show off the mindless people under their control.

"Why are we not affected?" I clung to the shadow's peering out only to get another glimpse at the two men.

"He cannot expand the effect once it is in place. The spell needs to be cut to be re-spun."

"What are they doing?"

"Explosives. This is a contingency plan. If an army somehow breaks through and gets to this point, they will be torn apart or buried under rubble."

"How did you know they would be here? That this is their plan?" I viewed my sister.

"Does it matter?"

I grunted at her coldness. As if she had not just been asking of our father.

No. I suppose not. Nor did we have the time to discuss. "Stay back."

She tilted her head, a faint, infuriating smirk curving her lips. "I wouldn't dream of interfering."

Ignoring her, I focused on the two men. Flames coiled around my hand, responding to my call with a familiar, exhilarating rush. Careful to keep my fire shielded from their sight, I angled my body. I brought my pointer and thumb together, the energy building, thrumming, eager to be unleashed.

With a snap, the force tore across the space between us, a deadly, precise surge of raw energy. The instant it struck, the figures barely had time to register their end. No screams, no resistance—just a flash of heat and light before they disinte-grated into ash. The wind caught the remnants, scattering them like dust, erasing any trace of their existence.

The citizens paused, snapping free of the compulsion. They looked around in confusion.

I lowered my hand, the lingering heat fading from my fingertips as I turned back to Iona. Her expression hadn't changed, though her eyes glimmered.

"Efficient," she murmured, as if I'd merely swatted away a nuisance.

The people in the streets began scattering.

As we stepped back into the empty alleyway we had come from, I asked, "Do you want to come with us?"

She shook her head. "No."

"Why not?"

"I am needed here."

"Needed?"

She crossed her arms, her gaze shifting toward the looming silhouette of the mountain walls in the distance. "The people within the capital walls fear Clause. But they aren't desperate enough to flee or overthrow him. Not yet." She changed the subject from herself onto the issue of the citizens, and the reason for our retreat.

"And outside the walls?" I pressed.

"Different story," she said, her voice soft but firm. "The citi-zens beyond the mountains, those who aren't gifted, they have nothing to lose. They'd gladly join your forces if you reached them. They hate him for what he's done."

"And you?"

She smiled faintly, but it didn't reach her eyes. "I have my own path to follow."

As Iona began to turn away, she hesitated, glancing back over her shoulder.

"One last piece of advice, brother," she said, her tone deceptively light. "Stay away from the girl. Ariana. She's Clause's. Not meant for you. Never will be."

Her words hit like a blow to the gut, and my anger flared before I could stop it. "Ariana is owned by no one," I snapped, heat burning through my restraint. "Not by Clause. Not by anyone."

Iona tilted her head, studying me with a smirk that made my skin crawl. "You seem awfully certain of that. Certain enough to march into a Siddhe city to reclaim her."

"This isn't about laying claim," I growled. "She's not a possession."

"Isn't it?" Iona countered, her smile widening. "Tell me, Erik, if she were anyone else, if she weren't *her*, would you have done the same?"

"I would have still come here. For you. For our stolen people."

She snorted. "But would you have risked this much? Risked your life with such recklessness? King of the Lysians entering the Siddhe stronghold, a land teeming with conjurors, all on his own."

Her words hung in the air between us, and though I wanted to deny them, the truth in her implication was impossible to ignore. Iona's smile softened into something more unreadable, almost pitying.

"Be careful, brother," she said quietly, her voice losing its edge. "You may not believe she's owned, but Clause does. And beasts like him don't let go of what they believe is theirs."

Before I could respond, she slipped into the shadows, her presence vanishing as quickly as it had come.

I stood there for a moment, my fists clenched at my sides, her words echoing in my mind. My blood boiled with a mix of anger and something else. I shook it off, turning back to rejoin my retreating forces.

Whatever claim Clause thought he had on Ariana, I would burn it to ash.

35

ARIANA

Fire ignited, dancing over Iver's fingertips. It was the only movement within the hall's stillness. Flame light flickered along the blade of Gregory's sword as it remained poised.

Pressure surrounded the entire group. Kiora looked to me for direction. With a brief tilt of my chin, she angled a deadly arrow at the sudden threat before us.

My power drummed to life, pumping through me with every heartbeat, pooling at my feet and palms, invisible to all but very much ready to be commanded.

Soren's face gave nothing away, remaining unreadable.

Kole, Eislyn, and Iver kept their original stances, waiting to see how things would unfold before making a move. Variations of concern and amusement shone in each of their eyes.

Gregory's attention shifted between the show of Iver's conjuring, to me, before ultimately returning to the Lysian. "You intend to bring me harm with the fire you wield?"

Despite the tension, Iver's jaw moved easily. "It depends on what you intend to do with that blade."

The guard nodded, as if that answer was enough of one. "I will take you all to Clause. The chances of us running into other guards will be low, but we should all remain ready." His gaze drifted over all of us as he spoke. "At least a handful of conjurors will surround the Siddhe King. He will probably have one that can whisper long distances, giving commands to Clause's troops in the field, and one that can foretell the future a few seconds ahead of it actually happening."

"So he will see us coming?" Iver asked.

The guard nodded, his lips firmly turning down. "Yes, but barely."

"Still, it is an advantage." Iver's hand lowered to his side, the fire disappearing.

Kole asked, "Could you learn something like that?"

Iver's eyes grew wide. "Not in the span of minutes, unless you intend for us to remain in that room with them for days. Even then, it is doubtful. It seems what Clause told Ariana about some powers coming from a spirit of light and some from the dark is true. I do not feel the gifts that Edda has the same as I can all of yours. It is as though it is an unfamiliar language of conjuring, and I have not figured out how to interpret it."

Gregory took the conversation back. "There will probably be one other with Clause. She is not a warrior, but incredibly valuable in this situation because of her ability to manipulate emotion. She can influence any enemy within their proximity."

"Olive?" I asked, surprised that she would be involved, yet it made sense. She was powerful, even influencing my emotional response one night. It happened so effortlessly.

"Yes." The guard confirmed.

"She can be dangerous," I said to myself, though Gregory did not miss it.

"She will be. Yet, no one is to harm her. This is my one condition. Subdue her, but once it is all over, she must walk away from all of this with her life." Firm lips pressed together, eyes hardening, leaving no room for discussion.

"I would never want to bring her any harm," I said. Olive was always kind to me, and spirited. This war was not her doing, and I did not want someone like her to pay a price with her life.

Gregory's gaze rested on me, observing. "I believe you." He then looked at the rest of the group. "But can the rest of you promise the same?"

"Who is she to you?" Iver asked, head tilting to the side.

The guard stiffened with the question. "My heart," he finally answered.

"And you can stand against your heart today?" Iver pressed.

"Olive has always known where I would stand if something like this came to pass."

Iver squinted at him a moment before nodding. "I believe him."

Kole released a deep sigh. "You think you know everything."

A smile split Iver's face. "That is because I do, my friend. Why, just look at you and Eislyn now."

Eislyn snorted. "You dare to make such claims? As though we are a product of your involvement."

Iver glanced at me and winked. "Not only my involvement."

Kiora shoved Iver to the side. "Can you get it together? This is not the time for this."

Iver's smile faltered. "The next breath is not promised to any of us, little Sparrow. The Spirits may take us at any moment. So, I choose to enjoy as many of these opportunities as I can."

The scowl fell from Kiora's face and she looked at Iver as though his words actually touched her.

"We need to stop wasting time." Eislyn turned to Gregory, the moment shifting back to what was at stake.

"How far is Clause?" I asked.

"Just a few halls, not far at all." Gregory shrugged a massive shoulder. He glanced to Kole. "Non-conjurors will be a great weapon against the Siddhe King. Yet they will also be the weakest against everyone else. They will need to be protected until the right moment."

Kole's chest seemed to puff up. "I do not need to be protected."

"You will stand against conjurors and fall." Iver arched a brow.

"I stood against you plenty," he growled.

The prince rolled his eyes. "I never tried to kill you. Neither did Ariana, yet she had you on your knees gasping for air in hardly more time than it took for you to take a single step."

Kole's jaw twitched, yet stilled before he could work it enough to respond.

Eislyn's hand grabbed Kole's forearm. "They are right. We live in a world where conjurors are rare. Our Lysian and even Bavadrin land is nothing like where we now stand. In the Siddhe land, it is different. Do not let your pride be our downfall."

Our downfall. As in the two of theirs, because if he was to fall, then so would she. Her words brought a warmth to my soul.

Kole gritted his teeth, though did not oppose, and that was perhaps the best anyone would ever get from him in such a situation.

Soren took several steps to close the distance between

himself and Gregory. The Dunes Clan Leader placed a hand on the guard's shoulder. "Thank you for your help."

Gregory released a breath. "As if you feared that this would have gone any other way."

A smile pulled at Soren's lips, hardly a flicker before disappearing. "We better get going." His hand fell to his side before reaching for his own blade, pulling it free.

We readied ourselves, bracing for something that no one could truly prepare for.

Gregory spoke once more before we began moving. "Once we enter the room, I will tell you the conjuring powers of those surrounding the Siddhe King, moving from left to right."

Everyone nodded in acknowledgement.

A second later, we followed Gregory through the halls with nearly soundless steps. One corridor turned into another and another until we ultimately started slowing. Though our movements quieted, the tension surrounding us surged. As though it were a web that we stepped deeper into with every stride. It clung to me. A weaving of unease, tightening till it became difficult to know where my skin ended and the dread began. But the fear was not only on the surface of my skin, it was within my body, in my blood. It moved through me, trapped inside my bones. The unease threatened to trap me within my mind.

"Here we go," Gregory grumbled as he came to a brief stop before a large wooden door. He did not wait for a reply before shoving the weathered wood. The door opened without a sound except for when it slammed into the wall behind it.

We followed Gregory blindly. Turning the corner, funneling into the room before falling into stillness.

The pressure was sharper than any blade. It sliced through all thoughts, all feelings, everything. Everyone around me seemed to vanish until all that was left was me standing before *him* with my soul feeling bare and horribly vulnerable.

Others surrounded the Siddhe King, yet he alone snared my attention, leaving me unable to take anything else in but the imposing figure with the dangerous eyes focused on me. The sensation was all-consuming, nearly knocking me off my feet.

He, too, looked nowhere else. As if it were just the two of us. A glimmer of surprise shone in those cold eyes, flickering briefly before going out, turning icy.

An overwhelming power flooded the space. Familiar stale air pressed against me before encasing me in his presence. My stomach turned at the feel.

Clause's lips parted and the only thing he said was my name. "Ariana."

Gregory spoke low and quick, letting us know left to right the powers of those in the room. "Air, sight, vines like whips, whisperer..." There was a moment of hesitation before he finished with, "emotions."

Clause not once looked away from me, as if waiting for some sort of response.

I took a deep breath, forcing my lungs to expand, to dare to take up space as I centered myself. The pressure, though uncomfortable, was not truly all-consuming. I could exist in it, push it aside, force my way through it.

Following another deep breath, I spoke. "You know I hate it when you make the surrounding air stale," I said to him and sent the force of my conjuring out of my body. As though trying to use it to push away the sensations brought on by the Siddhe King, attempting to force his presence back and create my own space.

But the feeling remained as the room erupted into chaos.

36

ARIANA

A wall of my mist encased me before expanding out. It circled Kole, keeping him from the others before stretching forward, pushing everyone around Clause aside, except for him. The three of us were walled off from the rest in the room.

Though separated, I felt their attacks and sensed their steps through the thin film of mist I left in the room, surrounding their feet.

Gregory's movements rushed towards Olive, who stood deathly still.

A sensation of whips slammed against the side of my wall. There was something odd about those blows, the depth of them, but they did not last. An intense heat followed the several blows as Iver's flames pushed him back, keeping the conjuror away.

Eislyn seemed to engage with the whisperer, and Kiora kept her distance while preoccupying the air conjuror.

Soren danced with blades, keeping the sight conjuror busy.

I forced my attention to pull inward. Those outside my barrier were a distraction. They were all skilled, and I needed to trust in that, to let them go, so I could focus on the obstacle standing before me.

Clause glanced at the wall of moisture before centering those cold eyes on me. He could walk through my mist if he wanted to, but he wouldn't. Because he wanted this, the two of us with limited distractions.

Kole said nothing, and asked nothing as he approached to stand at my side, briefly drawing Clause's eye.

"And why are you here?" The Siddhe King asked, displeased at having anyone else sharing this space with us.

"I am her blade," Kole answered easily, standing at the ready, sword drawn and poised. He knew his purpose, for he truly was the blade, the only one of us who could get close to the Siddhe King without fear of death from a simple touch.

Clause grunted and turned to me. "You continue to push me, Ariana. To wear thin my patience."

My jaw clenched. "You pushed me first."

He shook his head as though he did not agree. "You stand on the edge of a decision. Do not make the wrong one."

"I have already decided. The only one here with a decision is you. To surrender or force our hand."

"Fire away." A smile curled his lips as he opened his hands, as if inviting us to try. He spoke again when neither of us moved. "Tell me, when all that I have done was to strengthen you, to help you survive this cruel world, why is it that you try to turn on me?" His thoughts remained misguided.

"It is not the world that is cruel, but you. The darkness, the pain, the torment that surrounds me is your making. *You* have tried to destroy me, to break me, not this world."

He took a single step, his lips pressing into a thin line. Darkness oozed from the surrounding atmosphere, stemming from him. "I have opened your eyes to some of the lies spoon-fed to you so others could more easily control you. If the things you learned were cruel, that is only because I have only ever been honest with you. I have shown you this world for what it is. Do not hate me for only bringing you the truth."

If only that was the only thing he brought. "You forced me to take the life of an innocent man. Where is the kindness in that?" That one act tainted my soul. Never would I be the same.

The tension between us pulsated with every steady beat of his heart. It drummed through the air, brushing up against me. Keeping me surrounded by his ominous presence. "That was a lesson you needed to learn."

I snorted. "You sound like Edda. *A lesson I needed to learn.*" I shook my head in disbelief, for he appeared so delusional that he may have actually believed what he was saying. "You did lie, for I thought I saw glimmers of kindness and hope in you over my time here, but that was all a facade. Wasn't it? A trick to have me lower my guard so that when you cut it would be that much deeper."

His brows furrowed. "It was not. I have nothing but love for you, Ariana. You are the most important thing in the world to me."

Kole's jaw clenched, though he remained silent, with his eyes trained on the threat before us.

Even if Clause believed he loved me, I doubted it would be enough, but I still tried to reason with the unreasonable. "Then stand down. End this suffering. Show me you can at least attempt a compromise."

He broke our stare, glancing to the floor as though in

thought. My heart nearly stopped, hoping he was considering my words.

"Clause, please." The soft desperation in my voice troubled me. After everything, why did I continue to carry hope for him?

Gray eyes pinned mine, and within them there was turmoil.

"I don't want us to hurt one another any more than we already have," I said, having to stop myself from approaching him, propelled by the possibility that he may actually hear me.

There was a flicker of sadness in his gaze, and I knew he would not budge from his stance. "Those attacking my castle are not just Lysian and Bavadrins, but some are Siddhe. They need to be punished and reminded of their place. I am their King, and I will not give them mercy for their actions. I will not give up my crown. But I can offer you this, to be the Queen of the Siddhe territory. Stand with me."

We found ourselves in the same position we started in, both unwilling to budge. "A Queen without a voice. Only given the space to stand in your shadow."

"You will have a voice, but it will match mine. For after you see the world as I do, I know we would stand together as a force others could not dream of opposing."

My head remained high, my tone hardening. "My voice will never match yours."

"We shall see." He glanced at his foot. That was when I noticed the thin vine wrapped around it, disappearing beyond the mist wall. A lifeline to someone outside my barrier.

When I encircled Clause, that vine already must have connected him to one of his conjurors, making my power inert against them if Clause wished it so. I did not have time to consider the possibilities before the Siddhe King moved his leg, pulling on the vine.

From the left, a form stepped through the mist as if it were just moisture he moved through and not a true wall. The male was Siddhe, with pointed ears. His limbs were long, willowy, making him appear incredibly tall and thin. Half his face looked freshly burned. *Iver*.

My power pushed past me, down the stranger's lungs, but he did not react.

Clause didn't utter a word before vines erupted from the man's fingertips, lashing out at Kole and me with a speed that made them seem alive with intent. On instinct, my blades were in my hands before I'd even thought to reach for them, I slashed at the vines, but his movements were incredibly quick and unpredictable, easily evading me.

A whip of green shot toward me from the left, and I barely managed to lunge right, falling and rolling across the floor before springing back to my feet. The vines were relentless, darting and curling, striking from every direction. Each swing of my blade bought me mere seconds of reprieve before more lashed out, as though he could summon an endless supply.

They came from behind, thick, unyielding vines wrapped around my waist. I twisted, hacking at them, and they loosened briefly under my blade's edge. Only to grow back stronger, winding tighter with each cut I made. They spread, as if a second skin, circling around my legs, my chest, my arms, encasing my hands with the blades still in them until rendering me completely immobile.

Only my head and neck remained free enough to move. Kole was in no better of a position. They too easily took control.

"That's enough," Clause said, stilling the vine conjuror from crushing us. Though by the looks of it, neither Kole nor I could draw a full breath any longer, our lungs constricted by the pressure.

"You care for this Lysian?" Clause asked, taking a step towards Kole. Darkness shrouded him, his intent menacing.

Panic shot through me. I shoved a wall of mist towards him in a futile attempt to keep him back, but he simply moved through it.

Gray eyes met with mine. "I will take that as a yes." He turned back to Kole, shaking his head at him. "Look at this conjure-less fool, so weak." He took another step. "Unable to protect himself, let alone someone like you."

Danger emanated from Clause as his lip curled in disgust. Hatred condensed into the sharpest of blades directed fully at Kole. With me unable to do anything as time slipped away.

"You need to kill me," I said, earning the Siddhe King's full attention. "I will never stop fighting you. I could never love you." Provoking him so that his focus remained on me was the only thing I could think of until one of us came up with a better plan.

Kole looked at me with wide eyes as though I had gone mad, and perhaps I had, but we needed time. He drew breath only because Clause allowed it at this point, and I was going to do everything in my power to keep him breathing.

Beyond the wall, the fighting continued. Not a single body hit the floor from either side, though Olive and Gregory seemed to have left the room.

My mind scrambled, grasping at flickers of ideas. If I lowered the mist wall, we would be emersed into chaos. Perhaps that would help or perhaps make things worse. I would release Clause without the barrier, freeing him amongst the conjurors with a deadly touch. Keeping the mist up at least kept his focus contained.

"I will never take your life," Clause stated flatly, as his cold unyielding gaze bore into me.

"I will never stop until I take yours, then." I stood on a dangerous edge, and instead of fear, I felt emboldened to push him farther. To show him that he did not harbor the love he believed himself to.

His eyes narrowed. "You do not mean this."

My body shifted, attempting to move, but it was impossible with the bindings. "I doubt you would enjoy finding out which of us is correct."

His jaw twitched as he stared at me. The space between us turned frigid enough that if I were to breathe out, I wondered if ice crystals would remain suspended in the air. Cold little shards never to dissipate, for there was no warmth left between us to melt them.

"How about you go one on one with me?" Kole said through clenched teeth to the Siddhe King. "Then we will see who is weak." He brought the attention back to himself, which was what I was trying to avoid. We needed time to figure out a plan, not for *him* to push Clause, the King with no qualms regarding taking lives. My only protection was the fact that Clause believed he loved me.

Clause turned back to Kole and took another step in his direction. "I am a King. That means I do not have to bloody my hands with filth."

Kole snorted, his eyes burning with a challenge. "Perhaps I too do not wish to bloody my hands with filth? Someone too weak to fight his own battles, afraid of a little blood, afraid to get his sleeves stained. What a prim and proper little princess."

"Kole, stop," I pleaded as Clause took another step.

"Don't worry, Ariana, we will silence him soon enough." Clause paused, looking down before picking up the blade from the ground. It was Kole's sword. He must have dropped it when the vines took him.

"Clause!" I called his name, but he only took another step in Kole's direction. The space between them was closing too quickly, just two or three more paces and the Siddhe King could send the blade through him.

Panic shot through my body, taking over every fiber, shaking me from within. I struggled to move, but could not.

"This, *Lysian*, is just another one of the many people holding you back, Ariana, keeping you from rising to your full potential." He took another step. His movements were so horribly casual. So effortless. So terrifying.

The dread within my chest was overwhelming.

"Wait!" I called out in a final frantic attempt to pull the attention back to me.

Clause's head began to turn, but Kole's words stopped him from glancing at me. "Don't you dare look at her!" He growled. "You do not deserve to even breathe the same air as her, for your eyes to view her, to touch her. She deserves so much more than to be forced to go another day under the same roof as you." Kole turned to me then and simply said, "I trust you."

I could not comprehend what was happening. My mind stopped working. He trusted me to do what? Watch him die before my eyes?

My heart constricted, reverberating in my chest to the point it no longer effectively moved blood through my body. A cold numbing sensation spread through me, beginning at the soles of my feet. My muscles trembled against the hold of the vines.

"Say goodbye," Clause said, and I was not sure if he was talking to me or Kole as he took his last step.

Ice shot through my body, panic melded with my conjuring, spreading but finding no escape.

Time slowed, yet ran out at the same time.

Thoughts turned into a blank void in my mind. I stopped breathing, my eyes widening.

Clause pulled back, moving the blade into position to strike.

My power pooled within, as if attempting to protect me from what I was about to witness. But it was not enough. I needed more.

When Clause plunged his arm forward, a tortured scream ripped out of me, burning through my throat. It shook the mist walls until they fell, disintegrating around us. The world instantly expanded, and the noise of other battles blended with the moment. But the sound was muffled against that of my heart beating against my ribs.

Power surged within, filling me, cutting my scream. Strength did not encase me, but became me. My body no longer held me, not when it belonged to the mist. The vines could not keep me, because I flowed like a river of air around them.

I vanished into the mist.

I became nothing, and yet I saw and felt everything. The way Clause's back rippled as his arm thrust forward. Kole's eyes widening yet still fearless as he watched the blade aiming for his abdomen quickly approaching.

It all was happening so incredibly fast, but I was faster.

In a flash, flesh covered me once more, the mist materializing into a body that tethered my soul to our world. And in my hand, a sword vibrated from the impact that rang through the air as it met with the one Clause wielded, keeping it from striking Kole. Had I picked up the blade in my movement? I had not even realized.

A look of surprise passed over the King's features.

Placing pressure on the sword, I forced Clause back a step.

The shock of what had just happened must have shaken the ground beneath him. For the first time, he appeared as though he stood on unbalanced ground. His eyes wide, in pure surprise as he took in the sight of me.

"I will not watch you take another life from me," I vowed through clenched teeth.

A hand grabbed my shoulder, yanking me back through a shimmering distortion, taking me away from the Siddhe King.

37

ERIK

Eislyn and Kiora appeared just outside the Siddhe capital with Iver, where our forces were quickly retreating into the forest. Both females were panting, wide-eyed, and startled, as if they were not expecting to be moved. Kiora lowered her bow and arrow, twisting around and studying her new environment.

I changed my direction, running towards them while the retreating troops tried to avoid getting in my way. Our combined forces flooded through the forest, like fluid shifting around the terrain, heading towards the horses and the Bavadrin lands.

Iver vanished before I reached them.

Blood coated Eislyn, though I could tell by the scent it wasn't hers. Both of the females appeared relatively unharmed.

"Ariana?" I asked when I reached them. Fear threatened to close around my throat at the fact she was not with them.

Eislyn and Kiora swiveled towards me.

"She was shrouded in mist. I assume she is okay as long as the mist was around," the Sparrow answered, though the way her lips turned down it was clear she was nervous. "Kole was in there with her."

"The Siddhe King?" Pain stabbed at my chest for the fact that she had to endure being near him.

"Also shrouded in that mist," Eislyn said.

Ariana was with *him*. I was spared from imagining the worst when she appeared at my side with Kole and Iver. The relief was followed by a shock that stopped my heart in my chest at the sight of her. She stood before me, before all of us, completely bare of clothing.

"Our princess here turned herself into mist during that encounter," Iver said before my shock could meld into something uncontrollable as he slipped off his wool cloak.

Soldiers around us tripped over themselves, running into each other, as they caught sight of her.

Fire erupted around us, as finally my mind worked enough to form a barrier between us and the rest of the warriors, to shelter her and warm the space.

Ariana's eyes were wide as as she looked down, face instantly turning red as she realized the state she was in. Her nipples pebbled against the cold before she wrapped a hand across her chest as Iver draped his cloak around her.

"Thank the Spirit that whole thing is over," Kole muttered, looking a little green from the travel methods. He awkwardly looked everywhere but at Ariana.

Ariana scanned the group at once, taking a quick inventory of all present while tugging the cloak securely around herself.

Kiora gave her belt to Ariana to singe the wool around her waist. "Once we get to the horses, I'll give you some real clothing to wear."

Ariana nodded, her face still flushed, her gaze lingered on me a fraction longer than the rest. "Soren?" She turned to Iver.

He shook his head. "He warned me that we had about thirty seconds to get out of there before the room flooded with backup. Said to leave him, that he would find a way to work the event to his advantage with Clause. That." He stopped himself, eyes flickering to me like he was considering whether to say the rest in front of me.

"Finish that sentence," I instructed my brother.

Iver frowned, turning to Ariana once more. "He said that he would like to remain so that you would have an ally when you returned."

She stiffened.

"Ariana is not going back there." My voice dropped, gaining a lethal edge. The thought of her returning there made my whole body turn to stone with horror.

The back of Ariana's hand briefly brushed mine, as if in reassurance. "We are retreating?"

I let the fire recede so she could see. Ariana glanced at those moving around us, away from the Siddhe stronghold. Though she tried to refocus, I caught sight of the dimming shadows in her gaze at Iver's words. The threat he spoke into existence. That there was an expectation that she would find herself at the monster's mercy once again.

Her fear pathetically crippled me. My pledge to destroy the darkness threatening her did nothing to help her. For even though I controlled flame, Clause's darkness was too profound. It would engulf the light. I needed to find a way to change that, to spare her from him.

I nodded, forcing my jaw to relax enough to answer. "I'll explain, but we need to keep moving and get as far away from here as possible. Our horses are close by." I needed to place distance between the Siddhe King and Ariana.

"Let's go then."

We took off, running till we reached our horses. The Sparrow gave Ariana real clothing to change into, though Iver insisted she still keep his cloak. Once she was dressed, I guided her to my stallion, and she did not protest when I told her she would ride with me. Once mounted, we continued the sprint through the Siddhe land.

It did not appear as though the Siddhe's chased, still we set a grueling pace. Not slowing till we crossed into the Bavadrin territory. Ariana relaxed then, her muscles loosening, her body leaning into mine a bit. I shifted my hold of the reins so that my arms better settled around her.

The fearful fist that held my heart began releasing its hold with the feel of her in front of me. Leaving an aching in my chest. Everything she had seen, been forced to do. Icy bitterness clamped down on my heart at the thoughts. This astonishing, compassionate, clever woman did not deserve any of this. The pain she now undoubtedly carried in her soul should never have been there.

She had a monster chasing her, nipping at her heels. Relentless. But I was the monster she chose, and I would not stop til I ended the Siddhe King. I would become her champion.

"Are you okay?" I asked after a while. Neither of us had spoken since getting on horseback.

"We accomplished nothing," she said with a sigh. Her shoulders even seemed to droop.

"I got you back," I offered. To me, that was a victory.

"At the cost of how many lives?" Her voice seemed distant.

"We will learn from our mistakes, and next time will do

better." I thought we were better prepared, but we were not. Conjurors we wished to free stood against us. For some reason, we had not planned for that. All of us assumed that in the chaos they would simply fall back, and then run once they saw the barrier opened to them.

She was silent a moment before saying, "Your sister." Something sharp stabbed me in the gut at the mention of her. Last thing I ever expected was for Iona to choose the Siddhe over the Lysians.

"She made her choice," I finally said. There was nothing more to do. I wouldn't drag Iona from the place she claimed to want to remain.

Ariana and I fell into silence again until she asked, "Why did you retreat?"

I tensed at the memory that had snapped me out of my fury-filled rage. When I did not reply right away, she twisted to view me, green eyes appraising.

"I nearly killed a child who stood up to me. Protecting his home, and his family. Nothing but fear and determination in his eyes." I shook my head as if that could shake some of the guilt that seemed to cling to me like a thick oil. My hands were stained with a lot of blood already, not that I particularly minded that. But not the blood of *children*. That was a line I would never be comfortable crossing.

"The citizens will need warning if we are to try to take the city again," she murmured, turning back around. "We should have thought of that. Considered that they would be afraid, not everyone will run from the danger. I was so certain they would want to be freed that we would be seen as liberators from a monster's rule. But some of them prefer to remain under his command."

"We will do things differently next time."

"What we need is to force Clause to give up his control, or kill him by involving as few people as possible." I could nearly hear her frown, as if troubled by not knowing how to accomplish this.

"I won't give up until we find a way," I promised.

We started further slowing. "Are we making camp here?" Ariana asked.

"No. We are going to rest for a few hours, but then keep moving. Best to put as much distance as possible between us and the Siddhe."

She turned, so that I saw the profile of her face. "I need to talk to you. Alone."

"There is nowhere we can go right now that won't be overheard." We couldn't have privacy while out in the open and surrounded by Lysians.

She nodded. "When we get back home, then."

We dismounted. Ariana left me to find Willis, the two speaking for some time before she returned. Most were already dozing, trying to regain whatever energy they could before continuing on in a few hours. Ariana lay down beside me on the ground, and I wrapped an arm around her, pulling her close. The touch made her shudder, and I couldn't help but tighten my hold on her. As if there were a chance she could somehow slip away if I did not anchor her to myself.

After several heartbeats, she ran her hand along my arm, then intertwined her fingers with mine. Her hand seemed so small compared to mine.

Despite all we had done and been through, she still smelled of wildflowers. That perfume was one of the first things I ever noticed about her. Nuzzling her neck, I breathed in the scent of her. Her pulse spiked, and she shifted gently against me. I had no idea how, after everything we had just gone through, she could maintain such a pull on me. It was as if thoughts of her demanded so much space in my mind that little room was left for anything else.

"I missed the feel of you," she whispered into the darkness.

Ashes. Her voice was the most seductive of songs. If we weren't surrounded by others, lying outside on cold, hard ground. I would have ensured that the memories of the events we just escaped tormented neither of us. Both of our minds would have been thoroughly preoccupied. I would have shown her precisely how thrilled I was to have her back.

She shifted in my arms again. The movement exposed her neck to me. I couldn't resist the temptation of the soft skin there. I ran my teeth along the edge of her throat. Her breath hitched.

"Ay." Iver's voice sliced through the otherwise stillness of the night. "If you wish for an audience, I am sure there won't be a shortage of volunteers once we get back. Some around here need some beauty rest."

"If they want to screw to release tension, then who are you to stand in your King's way," Kiora answered. Interesting choice of words.

"Mhh, you sound tense, little Sparrow. Perhaps you need some tension released?" The smile in Iver's voice was clear in his tone.

The only thing that kept me from telling my brother to shut his mouth was the small chuckle that came from Ariana.

"In your dreams," Kiora shot back.

"I'll see you there," Iver promised, no doubt winking in her direction despite the fact she couldn't see him in the darkness.

"For the love of the Spirit. Will you shut your mouth? Some of us really are trying to have our beauty sleep, as you put it." Kole grumbled.

Iver chuckled. "Alright, beautiful."

Silence fell over the group once again, though the heaviness that had been with us this entire trip seemed somehow less. And for the first time in days, with Ariana in my arms, I briefly drifted off to sleep.

38

ARIANA

"We need to tighten things up around here," Iver stated. We were all clean and rested compared to the last few days of travel, sitting in the Bavadrin council room which was becoming more familiar than I liked.

"Are you either the King or the Leader Superior? Because I don't think you can make such commands," Kiora offered him a tight-lipped smile. It had been more of a suggestion than a command, but Kiora didn't hear it that way.

I looked across the table, meeting the sapphire eyes that always seemed to watch me. Erik's lip lifted just a touch. If allowing them to volley back and forth with their words allowed me to stare into those eyes longer, then so be it. I had missed him. The presence of him. The sight of him. The way he made me feel safe and seen and whole.

"Just a suggestion, little Sparrow." Iver smiled, his attention easily resting on her.

"Stop calling me *little*." Her eyes narrowed.

He raised a brow. "You have seen yourself? Stood next to a Lysian? Yeah?"

"Must you enjoy aggravating those around you?" Eislyn commented with a resigned sigh and a knowing stare.

Iver turned to her. "Awwh. Miss my attention on you and Kole?"

"Feel free to keep the Sparrow," Kole muttered, leaning back in his chair, and folding his thick arms over his chest.

"I belong to no one," Kiora snapped at him.

"Do you wish to change that?" Iver's smile grew in invitation.

Willis sighed but said nothing, as if waiting for me to put an end to this.

Kiora bristled. "I am going to cut out that tongue."

"Oh, but I am certain it would be so much more enjoyable for you if you let me keep it, *little* Sparrow." His gray eyes sparkled.

"Before this conversation went off course, what did you mean by 'tightening things up'?" Erik focused on his brother, finally bringing the crossfire to an end.

Iver ended Kiora's torment by returning to the point of this gathering, figuring out how to strengthen our homes and forces, before ultimately figuring out how to dethrone the Siddhe King. "I mean our exiled cousin in the mountains, Hedrek. He is a problem, one that we cannot continue to entertain." He did not mention the other thing we still needed to figure out. Mal. The assassin recovering from her wounds in my dungeon.

"If we told him of what we know, is there a chance they might stand with us?" I asked, looking at Erik for his thoughts.

"I would need to let him and his followers off of that mountain." It was not a flat no, nor was it a yes, nor really an answer at all.

"We won't know unless we try, and he is a strong conjurer. It would be useful to have more of those to stand with us, just in case." I offered.

Erik tapped his thumb rhythmically against the armrest of his chair as he contemplated.

"Can these Lysians be trusted?" Willis leaned his forearms on the table.

Kole snorted. "No way."

Erik's thumb stilled. "You all need to understand that my hands are stained with the blood of Hedrek's direct family and followers, a lot of it." The heavy stare of a King settled on me, and I was well aware of it. I had seen him single-handedly eliminate a handful of those Lysians. A chill ran through me, not out of fear, but awe of the lethal power of him. "Perhaps we could come to terms for a time being, but as soon as the Siddhe King is handled, I doubt we would live amicably."

"What are the choices, then? Just kill them all?" Kiora's brows were drawn, not liking the idea. "Can we at least try to talk to them before deciding? Test the waters."

I nodded. "I agree. Perhaps they have even more conjurors. It might be helpful in what is coming." I looked at Erik. Ultimately, these were Lysians on his lands, the final decision was his.

"We will talk to them and see where that takes us," he said and I offered him a small smile.

Iver leaned back with a grin. "Edmond is going to just love this idea."

"Edmond is not King," Kole grumbled.

"He has been playing King back home while Erik has been staying in the Bavadrin lands," Iver replied.

"Playing at King and being King are not the same." Kole leveled his stare at Iver.

"Right." I took the attention of the small gathering. "If there is nothing else, I need to speak to Erik alone, please."

"Lovely, I am famished." Iver stood, setting his sights on the one he didn't seem capable of looking away from for very long. "Sparrow, you want to come grab a bite?"

Kiora gave him a side eye as she moved towards the exit. "Not with you," she said cooly.

"What about a bite of me, then?" He grinned, following her out as she groaned in reply.

The others filed out behind them without nearly as much flourish till it was just the Lysian King and me left.

Erik remained seated across from me, his posture exuding a quiet but undeniable authority that made my muscles tense involuntarily. The room seemed to buzz with his presence, the air thickening as if charged with electricity. With everyone else gone, the intensity of his presence seemed to amplify.

His stare bore into me, holding a weight that felt almost physical, heavy enough to make my knees tremble. I could feel the force of his gaze like a touch, sending shivers skittering down my spine. It was as if he could see straight through me, unraveling my thoughts and desires with just a look.

In a feeble attempt to regain my composure, I rubbed my lips together, feeling the dryness there. His sapphire eyes flickered down to my mouth, and I was acutely aware of his gaze tracing the movement. A rush of heat flooded my cheeks as his eyes lingered, my heart pounding erratically in my chest. When his gaze returned to mine, I found myself captured by those piercing eyes once more. A small, knowing smile curved on his lips. He knew the effect he had.

I needed to get this out before just sitting across from him turned my mind to mush. Before I could do nothing other than crawl across the table to him. "There is something I need to tell you, and I have no idea how you will take it. My guess would be not well."

The delicious curl of his lips vanished. "Does anyone else know whatever this is?"

"I don't think anyone on this side of the border knows yet."

He nodded.

Spirit, how was I supposed to say this? My stomach twisted with nausea. "I need to try and get this out, so please just listen."

He waved his hand across the room. "The floor is yours, Ariana."

I drew in a breath, steadying myself before I began. "Around the time when you all breached the Siddhe city, I saw a painting. It was hundreds of years old, one of Clause and his mate. She looks exactly like I do, apart from my ears. He said that I was the reincarnation of his mate. That he and I were destined for one another, that our blood sings for each other. This is why I have this unexplained pull towards him." As I spoke, Erik was completely still. His face portrayed nothing. "When I saw the Spirit at my ascension, they told me I was *the* curse. I think I was reincarnated to be his downfall because he doesn't let anyone close, except for me." I paused there, not knowing what more to say.

"Why does he not also assume you are the curse to be his downfall?" Even Erik's tone portrayed nothing of what he was thinking or feeling. It was a bit terrifying.

"He says the wording of the original treaty cannot be confirmed, that it was just passed down by word of mouth. What's to say that it was not a curse, but a gift, that the breaker of it would receive from the Spirit? But I saw and *spoke* to the Spirit. They told me I was a curse."

The Lysian King held my stare as he considered my words. "What do you feel for him?" The question sent an uncomfortable chill through me.

If I were a Lysian, I might have barred my teeth at him. "You know what he made me do." The temperature of the room plummeted.

The hard look in Erik's eyes softened. "I just need to hear it."

"It would be a lie if I did not say that it saddens me that he has turned into the person he now is. He is lonely. He says he loves me but I do not think he knows what love is any longer. He wants to break me, to change me. There is nothing in my heart but aversion for him. I reject him. He is not my mate, even if I am some reincarnation of her. I do not want him."

He swallowed, tension barely leaving his shoulders. "But you are still drawn to him?"

I forced another deep breath, keeping the fear away. Whether Erik rejected me for what I was about to say, would not sway my response. I would be honest with him. He deserved to know everything. "My body seems to easily react to him. Like there's some messed up control he has over my blood."

"But your heart wants nothing to do with him?" Erik remained rigid, sitting before me.

My eyes slid shut. "No." Then I whispered my fears, "You probably want nothing to do with me."

"I didn't say that." My eyes opened, finding him watching me. That gaze was unnerving. "I still very much want you."

I felt those words all the way down to the spot between my legs. "I- I thought you would be mad," I said in surprise.

"Oh, I am enraged." His head tilted, the movement fully predatory. Sapphire eyes seemed to burn with blue flame beneath the surface. "My desire to incinerate him out of existence is second only to my desire for you."

My throat tightened. "You are certain?" I was afraid that he might have walked away after I shared this with him. For how could we fight a pull created by something neither of us fully understood?

"From what you say, I have your heart. He does not. You may crave him, but you crave me, too. I am ready to do whatever it takes to sever that connection you say you do not want. Burn it out of existence. Have you crumbling apart in my hands till that tether has absolutely nothing it can hold on to." His words *stroked* me.

My heart all but stopped in my chest. "What did you have in mind?"

His eyes darkened, the tension in the room thickening. "You should rest first. We have been back for two days, and you have hardly slept."

"I don't intend on resting much till this is all over. My mind cannot risk me stopping for very long." Pause for long enough and everything I had done, the people whose deaths I was responsible for came crashing in. I did not have time to fall apart. To heal. So instead, everything was pushed aside for me to deal with later.

Erik seemed to understand, for he stood, and came around the table. He pulled me from my seat and moved me until I sat on the table in front of him. The skirt of my dress rode up on my thigh when he stepped between my parted legs. His hand brushed my hair back before his fingers dug into it, holding the back of my neck. "Is this what you want, Ariana?"

I *burned* for him. "Yes."

His lips crashed hungrily against mine. I ran my hands along his muscular arms and broad shoulders. Clinging to him, I threaded my fingers through his hair, consumed by desire. The kiss deepened. He was all I wanted. This was exactly what I needed. And he was extraordinarily giving.

I cursed our clothing, separating our skin. Fisting his shirt, I pulled in frustration, eliciting a small chuckle as he continued to claim my mouth before leaving a trail of kisses over my jaw. His lips traveled down my throat, across my chest. My skin ignited wherever he touched. I needed to get out of this dress. My hips rocked against him, feeling the hard length of him beneath his pants. Just the thought of his cock made my head fall back with a moan.

"So eager," Erik crooned.

"You set me on fire," I admitted.

With a smirk on his lips, he fixed his dark gaze on me. "Good. Do you want to know what I plan to do after that fire deliciously wrecks you?" Lips pressed into my throat once more and I was slowly dying with need.

There would be nothing left to do anything with. But I asked, "What?" as my back arched.

Erik's hands moved over my shoulders, down my breasts, to my hips. His lips stopped their torment at my neck as he rose to his full height. Dark blue eyes drifted over my lips, neck, chest, waist, legs, before rising to meet my eyes once more. Holding my stare, he took a knee, one hand on my hip, the other pushing my dress higher up. I tensed, only for it to melt away with the heat of his attention. Erik kissed my inner thigh, licking it, grazing it with his teeth. "I will lick this realm's ashes from your skin." His hand found lace, and he tugged. I shifted, lifting my hips enough so that he easily pulled it down past my ankles. His mouth moved up higher. "I will rebuild your soul with my tongue." And that tongue did remarkable things between my legs before it plunged into me, devouring me.

My body was no longer mine to control. I withered, gasping for air. He was dragging me down into a fiery pit with the things that mouth did. My skin burned with the blood in my veins. My toes curled. I was completely vulnerable, and he seized everything he desired. He continued relentlessly, even as I climaxed. Pressing my hand to my mouth, I tried to stifle my screams of pleasure.

Finally, he relented. Allowing me to catch my breath as he rose to his feet before lowering his pants and releasing the length of him.

He gripped my legs, and I fell back onto the table. "You will become the fire that I wield," he said as he worked himself into me.

But I was already exactly that. Burning for him. Unable to think clearly. Completely at his mercy, under his command. At his touch, I simmered or raged. Whatever he desired of me.

As he took me, I felt full with him, tight. Each movement left me gasping for air. In and out. My soul felt each thrust, reaching all the way to my toes.

He placed a possessive hand on my hip, then moved it between my breasts and up to my throat. The touch pushed me over the edge again. "You are mine, Ariana." The growl in his voice had me falling into an abyss. The feel of the release was life-consuming. Leaving me a mere shadow of my former self.

39

ERIK

Ariana lay in my arms, beautifully asleep. Her naked body pressed to mine, so warm and inviting. My eyes drifted over her, taking in the soft glow of her hair in the moonlight seeping in through the window. Her hair was re-woven with the stones of her Bavadrin culture. Her face looked so serene, and peaceful. Full lips that could cast spells with her whispers and those lovely, breathy sounds she made when I took her in the right way. My thumb brushed against her jaw, unable to stop myself from touching her with more than my gaze. I wanted to feel her, all of her. My fingers lightly traced the length of her neck. Following the slope of her shoulder, down her arm.

She shifted, and I stilled, cursing myself for not having more self-control. Rest was not something that was easily found these days, especially for her. So when she finally settled in my arms, I should let her sleep.

During the days, she seemed so strong and certain in all she did. It was almost as if her time at the Siddhe kingdom did not affect her at all. *Almost.* In those moments when the day hit a lull, or something triggered a memory, shadows would dance across her vision. She shook them from her thoughts, doing her best to pay them no mind and move on, but they lingered.

Darkness followed her, creeping into her consciousness, and I wished I could rid it from her mind completely. But there was no way to permanently erase the nightmare she lived through.

Instead, we found a sanctuary in one another. A temporary place we could reach, together, where our worries and thoughts were wiped clean enough to allow for some rest before darkness returned.

She did not talk about the boy whom Clause killed with hardly a touch or the old man whose life she was forced to take to spare the rest. If ever she wished to, I would listen. I would be whatever she needed, shelter her however she allowed.

Ariana shifted, her brows briefly drawing before relaxing again. I pulled her closer, tightening my hold. Nuzzling her neck, I breathed her in. She had no idea how absolutely intoxicating she was. She twitched, and I nearly hoped that she was waking. It was a selfish hope for Spirit knows she needed rest, but my craving for her was intensifying with every minute that passed.

I drew in another deep breath. Noting the familiar wildflower scent that was her signature, as if fields of them bloomed under her skin, and something else. I stilled, breath caught in my throat. She emitted the scent of something distinct. Mildly sweet, and easily recognizable, *fear.*

Pulling back, I gently shook her shoulder, scanning her face. "Ariana?"

Despite her neutral expression, she exuded the unmistakable smell that came from her all too rarely. I tightened my grip

on her, trying to wake her. "Hey, Ariana. Ariana. Wake up."
There was no response, as if unreachable. "Ariana?"

Something was wrong.

I jumped out of bed, scooping her up with the sheets
surrounding her. In a few steps, I opened the door into the
hall.

Two Bavadrin guards stationed in the hall stared at me with
wide eyes. They glanced at Ariana in my arms. The sight of her
shocked them senseless enough that they reached for weapons.
"Inch those hands closer to your swords and I will incinerate
you," I warned. Both froze and went a shade paler. "Where is
the nearest healer?"

The guard to the left replied, "The closest would be Royden.
I can go retrieve him."

"He isn't in the building?" Anger tinged my words at the
rediculousness of not keeping a healer closer to their Leader
Superior.

The guard shook his head. "The healers are still working on
the troops after the return from the Siddhe."

"Get the one you speak of, then." He took off at once,
sprinting down the hall, and I turned to the other guard. "You,
go get Willis."

He hesitated. "But-" His gaze fell to Ariana.

"I have her. No one is going to get anywhere near her unless
I wish them to. Now go alert her second in command and bring
him to my brothers room."

"Right." The guard took off.

I prowled down the hall, stopping in front of Iver's door, and
gave it a few good kicks.

He flung the door open, quickly taking inventory of me
standing in the hall with Ariana in my arms. The alarm in his
eyes faded when he realized it was just us, and he turned to me.

"You couldn't have put on some clothing first?" He stepped aside.

"I will snap your neck, Iver," I growled, entering his room. "What is wrong with her?" She seemed somehow smaller as I held her, defenseless against whatever had her. Ariana was the cause of my fear, filling me with irritation and anger that I knew not what to do with. A feeling of pure helplessness slithered into my stomach, coiling there. Even though she lay in my arms, she may as well have been worlds away, for I was powerless to help her.

Iver raised a brow. "You expect me to know? She is alive and breathing." He looked over her. "I guess you cannot wake her?"

"No."

"Put her on the bed," Iver moved deeper into the room, and I followed. Gently, I laid her down.

My brother handed me a robe and examined Ariana. He reached for her. His fingertips disappeared beneath the blanket and I could not contain the growl that ripped out of me. A warning for him not to get too close.

"Easy, Erik." He tugged her arm, moving it out into the open before pressing his fingers to her wrist.

"Her heart is racing." I snapped. He did not need to touch her to know that.

Gray eyes pinned me. "*Clearly* I can hear that. I am trying to gauge the force of her heart, feel the pressure within the veins beneath my fingertips." He looked back at her with a frown. "She is uncomfortable, whatever this is." Useless information. Obviously, she was uncomfortable.

"Can you fix it?"

"I am thrilled that you find me so impressive. But I have no idea what this is. It could be conjuring of some kind or a poison."

"We have eaten and drank all the same things."

"From the same glasses? using the same utensils and plates?"

"This isn't poison."

"How do you know?"

Footsteps raced down the hall as one of the guards returned with the healer. The old man was nearly dragged and thrown into the room. He looked antique. His gaze found Ariana and he approached at once while the guard stood by the door, nervously shifting on his feet.

"Can you fix this?" I asked.

He held a hand over her, moving it as if feeling her energy. A frown pulled down on his dry lips. "No healer can help her. You are right, this is not poison. There is nothing to be done but wait for her to wake. I don't think this should last very long, at least not past the morning."

"What is it?"

He scratched absentmindedly behind his ears, though maintained his focus on her. "I believe it is a Dreamer. They used to be more common amongst our kind, but have vanished."

I looked at Ariana with dread, knowing full well where these conjurors likely had gone, and who was responsible for this.

40

ARIANA

D rifting off to sleep in Erik's arms had to have been my favorite way to fall asleep. Especially after a thorough exploration of each other's bodies. Ending in our souls intertwined, bodies trembling, and our thoughts void of anything but the moment we shared.

With my mind thoroughly emptied, I fell asleep quickly. The dreamless nights were my favorite. This, however, was not that.

I slipped into a dream that was not mine, pulled into a room I did not recognize. It was as if I closed my eyes at home, and opened them standing somewhere else. The walls were stone. Torches hung on each of them. There were no windows. A single bed, desk, and two chairs were within the space. None of it was remarkable in any way. There was a wooden door, otherwise there did not seem to have been any other way in or out.

Deep inside, I reached for my internal river of strength, harnessing it to rise and flow through my veins. Nothing happened. I couldn't sense a thing, as if the door to my conjuring was shut.

I was defenseless. Taking another inventory of the room, I searched for anything that could have been used as a weapon. Settling on the chairs, I turned towards them, fingers curling around the back of one before every muscle in my body tensed at the familiar sensation flooding the room. *Stagnant air.*

I whirled around and froze when my eyes locked with Clause's crisp stormy gaze. My heart jolted into my throat.

"Hello, love," he said. Power rippled through him, out of him, surrounding me.

I could hardly breathe, my muscles locked in place at the sight of him. This was not possible. I had escaped him, left him in the Siddhe lands.

He viewed me with a cold, cunning stare, rendering me speechless. I needed to get out, to run as far away as possible. But there was no escape. I was surrounded by walls and he stood between me and the only door in this place. Not that I even knew whether it could be opened or what was on the other side.

Panic shot through my veins. My body grew more and more desperate for oxygen, yet I could not draw a full breath. My head spun.

Clause took a step in my direction and I took one back, away from him, forgetting all about the chair I was going to grab, not that it would have done me much good. He stopped mid-step, gaze never leaving mine. "I have told you before that I will not hurt you." As if that was the only reason I would want to keep my distance.

"Doesn't mean I want to be anywhere near you." I managed to reply despite the tightness in my chest.

His lips curved upwards, though the look in his eyes

remained ice. "Don't tell me you prefer the Lysian whose arms you sleep in." His voice was uncomfortably hollow.

My heart fully stopped as panic surged through me. Once it restarted, it took everything in me to try and not react to his words.

I needed to get out of this place.

He continued moving towards me at a leisurely, slow pace. "I have to admit, I hate that you continue to give your body to him." I retreated until my back hit a wall and I had nowhere else to go. Clause remained just hardly out of reach. "That you allow him to touch you." He took another step, crowding me now. "Allow him to bury himself inside of you."

His audacity to insinuate he had a say in what I did awoke the rage within. I grabbed on to that feeling, preferring it to the panic.

As if intending to caress my cheek, Clause's hand lifted. I moved my arm, hitting his arm and blocking the hand.

"Do not touch me." I seethed.

His jaw ticked with... was that *irritation*? The hatred inside of me was so bitter that I could taste it on my tongue.

"Do not tell me you are angry, after the mess you made in my city."

"I thought it was *our* city," I snapped.

"You are not standing at my side, are you?" Gray eyes narrowed before he turned from me, walked across the room, and dragged one of the chairs around so that it faced me. He took a seat. The relief of the distance he put between us was extraordinary.

"What do you want now?" I dared to ask. There was a reason he pulled me into this place, whatever this was. Some sort of dream that was not one.

"For you to return home," he answered, as if it was simple.

"Your home will never be mine." I forced the words out despite my clenched teeth.

He sighed. "My patience has its limits, Ariana."

"You are delusional if you think I will ever stand by your side after what you made me do."

He looked genuinely surprised. "I am going to explain a few things, as it appears you do not listen, nor pay attention." I bristled, though didn't respond, and he continued. "After you took that sad soul from the whorehouse, you crossed one of my men. Punishment had to be served. Perhaps I could have chosen something different for it, but once I spoke it to existence, it was final. You may think me immoral. But trust is important, even if I do not have it for others. *My* word is final. This keeps things in line. My people know where I stand when I speak. They believe me. I would not take back or amend your punishment once it was spoken."

My entire body stiffened. "So, you took a child's life and forced me to kill my friend. Just so you wouldn't lose face?"

Clause leaned back in the chair, a cruel smirk on his handsome face. "I let you choose which life to take. I did not force you to pick a friend. And do you know how many innocent lives your little stunt took in efforts of your escape?"

A glacial hand snaked around my heart and squeezed at his words.

"I am not going back with you," I said, changing the subject.

He allowed for the switch, saying, "Maybe not today, but you will." His gaze briefly traveled over me and I was thankful to have a shirt and pants on, things I was not wearing when I fell asleep. When his eyes met with mine once more, there seemed to be a sadness melding with determination in them. "Until next time, Ariana." He vanished.

Startled, I remained pressed to the wall. The heaviness of

his presence left with him, the air becoming lighter and more fluid without his control. Yet I did not exactly feel alone.

"Hello? Is anyone here?" I said into the room. No one responded. "Who are you? Where are you?"

Suddenly, it was as if I was thrown from that space, the dream abruptly ending. My eyes flew open, finding myself naked though covered by a blanket in Iver's room with several people staring at me.

Those last words rang like echoes through my mind, *until next time, Ariana.*

TO BE CONTINUED...

ACKNOWLEDGMENTS

I'd first like to thank my husband, whose love and support follow me through every dream I chase.

To Stephanie and Mylene, your sharp eyes and thoughtful beta reading has helped in ways I will always be grateful for. To Sarah, for your polishing prowess.

To Danielle and Chelsea, thank you for lifting me up, encouraging me, and reminding me what magic looks like when I needed it most.

To the Enchanted Shadow Society Book Club, you are extraordinary, and your enthusiasm has meant more than words can hold.

And lastly, to you, my reader. Thank you for giving this story your time and a space in your heart. I hope the journey moved you. I hope it lingered. And I hope you'll walk beside me again, when we return for the end of the trilogy.

To everyone who helped bring this book into the world, thank you. Truly.

THE BREATH OF MIST TRILOGY:

Breath of Mist
Heart of Torment
Soul of Carnage